PRAISE FOR *A DISGUISE TO DIE FOR*

"Meet Margo Tamblyn, the newest, savviest, smartest heroine to join the cozy mystery world . . . Weave in a quirky cast of characters, a fascinating setting, a fast-paced plot, and yummy recipes, and you have a thoroughly appealing whodunit that will keep you guessing all-night long."

—Kate Carlisle, *New York Times* bestselling author of the Fixer-Upper Mysteries and the Bibliophile Mysteries

"Margo Tamblyn is in the business of creating new identities in costume—the perfect concept for a mystery series. Both madcap and moving, *A Disguise to Die For* has the right amount of humor, poignancy, and danger for a most irresistible whodunit. Highly recommended!"

—Naomi Hirahara, Edgar® Award–winning author of the Officer Ellie Rush Mysteries

"A fresh, funny voice, irresistible characters—and oh, the costumes! No disguising the fact that Diane Vallere's new cozy is a winner."

—Lucy Burdette, national bestselling author of the Key West Food Critic Mysteries

D1020950

Berkley Prime Crime titles by Diane Vallere

Material Witness Mysteries

SUEDE TO REST
CRUSHED VELVET
SILK STALKINGS

Costume Shop Mysteries

A DISGUISE TO DIE FOR
MASKING FOR TROUBLE

Masking for Trouble

DIANE VALLERE

BERKLEY PRIME CRIME
New York

BERKLEY PRIME CRIME
Published by Berkley
An imprint of Penguin Random House LLC
375 Hudson Street, New York, New York 10014

Copyright © 2016 by Diane Vallere
Excerpt from *Silk Stalkings* copyright © 2016 by Diane Vallere
Penguin Random House supports copyright. Copyright fuels creativity, encourages
diverse voices, promotes free speech, and creates a vibrant culture. Thank you for buying
an authorized edition of this book and for complying with copyright laws by not
reproducing, scanning, or distributing any part of it in any form without permission.
You are supporting writers and allowing Penguin Random House to continue to
publish books for every reader.

BERKLEY is a registered trademark and BERKLEY PRIME CRIME and the B colophon
are trademarks of Penguin Random House LLC.

The Edgar® name is a registered service mark of the Mystery Writers of America, Inc

First Edition: October 2016

Printed in the United States of America
1 3 5 7 9 10 8 6 4 2

Cover art by Mick McGinty
Cover design by Sarah Oberrender
Book design by Kelly Lipovich

This is a work of fiction. Names, characters, places, and incidents either are the product
of the author's imagination or are used fictitiously, and any resemblance to actual persons,
living or dead, business establishments, events, or locales is entirely coincidental.

PUBLISHER'S NOTE: The recipes contained in this book are to be followed exactly as
written. The publisher is not responsible for your specific health or allergy needs that may
require medical supervision. The publisher is not responsible for any adverse reactions to
the recipes contained in this book.

If you purchased this book without a cover, you should be aware that this book is stolen
property. It was reported as "unsold and destroyed" to the publisher, and neither the author
nor the publisher has received any payment for this "stripped book."

To the lovers of Halloween, be you young or old.

Acknowledgments

As a lifelong fan of Halloween, it stood to reason that one of the three Costume Shop Mysteries would take place over the holiday. What better excuse to indulge my costume-living self? This book captures some of my all-time favorite costumes, either those I've worn myself or have been told about by others. It seems there's a whole group of us out there just itching to take on a different persona every now and then.

Thank you to: Gigi Pandian for your valuable feedback. You keep me on the right track! Kendel Lynn, for your ongoing friendship and encouragement. Katherine Pelz and the team at Berkley Prime Crime who gave Margo Tamblyn a home. Jessica Faust, for recognizing the germ of a series idea in the midst of chatter about teddy bear costumes. Thank you to my parents, Mary and Don Vallere, for the costumes I had while growing up, and to Josh Hickman, for sharing my love of Halloween and costumes to this day.

Thank you to John, Carlos, and the staff at Ozzie Dots Vintage Clothing, Costume, and Accessories, for being so supportive. Your store is the best, and I encourage anybody in the Los Angeles area to shop there.

Thank you to the Los Angeles Courts for calling me for Jury Duty. The environment proved to be creatively stimulating, and much of this book was written during that week. (Who knew!)

And lastly, to the readers of cozy mysteries. Our books come alive when you read and enjoy them. I love hearing from each and every one of you.

Chapter 1

Monday

THE LAST TIME I was this close to an angry lab rat had been high school. That time, I'd understood the rat's anger. He'd been forced to live in close quarters with four others, and having once shared an apartment with four girls myself, I recognized the universal crankiness that comes from the invasion of personal space.

Today, the angry lab rat in front of me had a different reason to be upset. I'd just accidentally jabbed him in the head with a fistful of pipe cleaners.

"Hold still," I said. "If I don't get these pipe cleaners in at the right angle, the ears will never stand up." The lab rat mumbled something unintelligible. "You have to stop talking! I can't understand you."

The rat reached his arms—two furry white appendages that ended in pink oven mitts—up and lifted the carefully crafted mask from his head. "You're going to have to put more ventilation in there," Kirby said. "I could barely breathe."

Kirby Grizwitz was a part-time employee of Disguise

DeLimit, my family's costume shop. After my dad's heart attack six months ago, Kirby's hours had become more regular, filling in his spare time between swim team practices. Usually his job responsibilities included keeping the racks straight, handling rentals, and cataloging new inventory, but October was to our costume shop what April was to tax accountants, and our individual job responsibilities flexed to fit the needs of the business. Our whole town of Proper City went a little crazy around Halloween, and somewhere in the eighties the Proper City High School had adjusted their curriculum to include a weeklong break. Aside from Kirby's committment to the swim team, his days were available and he picked up extra hours at the store to help out.

Today's need was to put the finishing touches on a giant lab rat costume for Kirby's chemistry teacher. He'd allowed—the teacher, not Kirby—his honors class to choose his costume for this year's Halloween, and they'd decided to go ironic. Enter Disguise DeLimit.

"More ventilation. I can do that. But look, the ears are perfect." I took the head from Kirby and turned it around so it faced him. He seemed unimpressed. The chimes over the front door rang, and Ebony Welles walked in. I quickly pulled the rat head over my jet-black hair and stepped behind the register.

Ebony was a strong, black sixty-year-old woman in a 1970s wardrobe. She had a brushed-out afro, a collection of bell-bottoms to rival J. J. Walker, and a white bichon frise named Ivory. I'd never known my own mother because she died in childbirth, but Ebony was like a mom to me—having stepped into the surrogate role sometime around when I was five. She and my dad had never been more than friends, though they often acted like an old married couple, especially when it came to raising me. Somewhere along the last five years, her concerns had shifted from convincing my dad to raise my allowance to helping me find a nice single man and settle down.

Ebony had enough superstitions to challenge the most powerful rabbit's foot, and this time of year, she preferred not to venture far from Shindig, her party planning business. When she did, she added what we called her October Accessories: garlic necklace, silver bullet earrings, and a rubber mallet that no one could explain except that it might help her destroy zombie brains.

I watched her scan the interior of the store. When her eyes alighted on me, I stood straight up. She pointed a shiny black talon at me. "See, that right there is what's wrong with this holiday. There ain't no good reason for a giant lab rat to be running around our city."

I dropped down behind the counter, knocking a tray of vampire teeth into a plastic tub filled with foam clown noses. The tub spilled and round foam balls rolled across the floor. The mask shifted so I could no longer see, and, even more than before, I had trouble breathing.

As it turned out, Kirby was right. The mask needed more ventilation.

Muffled sounds from the costume shop blended in with indiscernible noises around me. I put my hands on the head and lined up the mesh that I'd inserted for vision and watched a group of teenage boys flip through a rack of motorcycle jackets.

"She's coming this way," Kirby warned.

I put my hands on the back of the counter and pulled myself up enough to peek over the top. Sure enough, Ebony was steps away from where I crouched.

"It's no use, Margo. I know it's you."

Slowly I stood and pulled the rat head off. From the corner of my eyes I could see my hair defy gravity thanks to static electricity. I set the head on the counter and smoothed the ends of my flip with my fingers.

"It doesn't matter. I was just trying it on to show Kirby that the ears were straight. That's not my costume for tonight."

"I certainly hope not. No way you're going to meet a man dressed as a giant rat."

"What about you? What are you wearing tonight?"

"Ebony doesn't need a costume. You know why? Ebony is going to be safely locked away inside of her house." When she was worked up, she liked to refer to herself in the third person. The idea of spending time at an old, rundown hotel that she not-so-secretly believed was haunted definitely got her worked up.

"Best costume has come from Disguise DeLimit for the past twelve years. You don't want to help our odds? We're not about to let it fall into the hands of an amateur," I said.

"You'll win. You always do." She looked down at the rat head and tugged on the pointy, blood-tipped teeth that jutted out from under the nose. "He is kinda cute," she said. She adjusted his blood-tipped fangs, smiled, and left.

Kirby pulled the pink mitts off of his hands and threw them down on the floor next to me. "I thought she'd never leave. That garlic was making me hungry for pizza." He reached around behind him until he found the ties that kept the rat suit closed in the back, undid them, and shrugged out of the body of the costume. It fell to the floor in a mound of shaggy white fur, and Kirby was left wearing his Proper City Prawns swim team T-shirt and jeans. He kicked the costume to the side by the plastic tub of colorful clown noses and stormed away.

Halloween was a week away, but tonight was the big kickoff costume party at the long-vacant Alexandria Hotel. The tall brick building had been abandoned decades ago and was sorely in need of some TLC. A wealthy developer purchased it but had agreed to allow the residents of

Proper City to hold our annual party inside. Ebony had turned down the job of converting the interior into a suitably haunted but not dangerous reception hall. Something about not wanting to stir up the ghosts and goblins who had taken to the hotel after it had been boarded up. Candy Girls, the tacky ready-made costume/theme party supplier—who, much to our chagrin, occasionally gave both Ebony and Disguise DeLimit a run for our money—had ended up with the job.

The annual kickoff party was a special, private celebration for those of us involved in the planning of the Proper City Halloween festivities. It started at six so even the youngsters of the participating familes could go and was the first chance people had to show off their costumes for the Halloween season. Ebony might have planned to stay away, but not me. In a couple of hours, I'd be in my own costume, meeting up with a friend in the parking lot, ready to see how everything turned out.

The cowbell over the door chimed and I looked up. A fiftyish man in a black business suit walked in. His shirt and tie were impeccable, and his briefcase was practically brand new. His white hair was parted on the side and smoothed into place, and contrasted sharply with the black frames on his glasses. I came out from behind the counter and met him halfway in the store.

"Nice costume," I said. "Government agent? We carry clip-on IDs if you'd like to accessorize."

He looked down at his suit and then up at me, confused. "I'm looking for Jerry Tamblyn, owner of Disguise DeLimit. Is he here?"

"No, he's not. I'm Margo Tamblyn, his daughter. I run the store these days. Can I help you with something?"

The man's expression told me he wasn't here to rent a costume. He reached down to a bookcase filled with brightly colored clown feet and pushed the feet to the side, knocking a few pair onto the floor. I scooped to pick them up. He set his briefcase on the top, popped open the locks, and pulled out a white envelope.

I glanced around the store. Kirby was busy with the teenagers by the rack of black leather jackets. One of the girls held a pink satin jacket with PINK LADIES embroidered on the back. Two teenage girls held up shapeless red and white striped all-in-one jumpsuits that we rented with blue wigs. Thing One and Thing Two from *The Cat in the Hat*. Always a good choice.

"If you're selling something, I'm not interested," I said. "We're pretty busy right now, so I can't spare any more time."

"I'll only take a moment of your time. I've tried at length to contact you by mail. I can only assume from your lack of response and your continued focus on renting costumes that you've chosen to ignore the issue."

"What issue?"

"The issue of Halloween. As you know, this year's festivities are scheduled to take place at the Alexandria Hotel in West Proper."

"I know all that. What's the problem?"

"The problem is that I now own the Alexandria Hotel, and I've restricted access to the party to those in my employ." His mouth pulled into a line that must be what passed for his smile. "Read the letter inside. The situation is self-explanatory." He checked his watch again, and then closed up his briefcase and lifted it from the now empty shelf. "Good day, Ms. Tamblyn," he said. He turned and left without waiting for me to look inside the envelope.

Kirby joined me. "What was that all about? Government agent needs Jerry's testimony about some aliens?"

"No. That man said he bought the Alexandria Hotel. He said now that it's under private ownership, we're being banned from entering a costume in the contest!"

Chapter 2

"BANNED?" KIRBY SAID. "Who can do that? And why tell you now? Jerry's going to have a fit when he hears this. Halloween is a big deal to happen to a costume shop." He shook his head.

Kirby was right about two things: Halloween was our busiest time, and Jerry—my dad and owner of the costume shop since the '70s—was going to have a fit when he heard. I'd recently moved back to Proper City to take over the day-to-day running of the shop so he could pursue his lifelong dream of traveling the country in search of unique items for our inventory. I'd been the boss for all of six months and already we were in trouble.

I scanned the papers. Legal jargon was like another language to me, but it became clear enough what we were being told. The city council had taken a vote, and because the Alexandria Hotel was under private ownership, any benefits normally allowed to the businesses of Proper were being restricted to those businesses also owned by the same firm: Haverford Venture Capital.

The party, historically funded by donations from the neighborhood, was being underwritten by a private investor. As such, no businesses outside of their own could benefit from financial gain. If the winning costume was found to be from Disguise DeLimit, we would be sued for breach of contract—a contract we had nothing to do with writing and had never been given an opportunity to sign.

"How is this even possible?" I said.

"There was an impromptu city council meeting last night. That's probably what they were talking about," Kirby said.

"How do you know that?"

Kirby was a senior in high school. Until recently his biggest concerns had been wining the district championship and making enough money to buy a dune buggy. He'd never impressed me as the type to follow politics.

"I have government fourth period. One of our projects is to sit in on a city council meeting and write up what happened." He scratched the side of his newly shaved head. "Our teacher said nothing good comes from impromptu city council meetings. I guess he was right."

"But the timing seems awfully suspicious, doesn't it? To deliver this notice today?"

"I'm telling you, Jerry's going to freak." Kirby said.

"I'm not going to tell him. Not yet. He doesn't need the extra stress, and maybe I can fix this."

A heart attack six months ago had caused a shift in my dad's priorities. While some people might slow down and take things easy, Dad wanted to sell Disguise DeLimit and see more of the country. The problem was with me. My own priorities had shifted, and I'd decided to move back home and take over running the store. We hadn't worked out a price as of yet, so technically the store was still in his name. I suspected that he wanted to make sure I was in it to win it and not merely doing it as an act of generosity.

We were lucky; the town of Proper City, Nevada—a mere forty miles from Las Vegas—had long ago experienced an identity crisis. City planners had mapped out restaurants, public transportation, a post office, and a library, but their failure to give residents an identity had led to a unique twist: our city loved costume parties. Not only for Halloween, but for birthdays, poker games, engagement parties, wedding showers. The Super Bowl. The Academy Awards. And at least one Mad Hatter's tea party, just because.

I'd grown up in Disguise DeLimit, wearing costumes to school instead of clothes from the mall. I'd taken a detour—moving to Las Vegas to work temporarily as a magician's assistant—but ultimately, I knew, this was where I was meant to be. Besides, now I got my kooky outfits at wholesale.

The true test of running a costume shop comes in late September and runs through October. The Halloween season. We had five thousand costumes available for rental, in addition to the various ones we sold. Kirby wanted us to broaden our scope by building a website and shipping costumes around the country, but for now, I was content to learn the ropes and do the best I could.

For the first Halloween in forever, my dad wasn't at the store to ensure business as usual. He trusted me to do that. He'd never been able to get away from the store in the past, but the opportunity to buy some inventory had come up, and we'd agreed that I could handle things for a few days while he made the trip. A few days had turned into a week thanks to a blizzard on the East Coast, and business as usual was about to blow up in my face.

"It's okay, Margo. People still know that we have the best costumes. Think about how many rentals we've had over the past month with people getting ready for Halloween. We just about blew up the sewing machine, it's been so busy. This is a minor setback," Kirby said.

"I hope you're right," I said.

Kirby filled a rolling rack with garment bags that were bursting with completed costumes. He rolled the rack out back to the delivery van. I considered stopping him, telling him there was no point making any more of the store's deliveries, but I couldn't bring myself to face that possibility.

To Kirby, the matter was settled. I hadn't mentioned my deepest fear to him. That once people heard the costumes they'd rented weren't eligible for the prizes in the annual contest, they weren't going to be happy. It wasn't just bragging rights that they'd win. The grand prize was a thousand-dollars. They might think that we knew all along and that we kept it from them so we could get their money.

I glanced back at the sheet of paper and flipped to the last page. *Approved Businesses* headed the sheet. Underneath was a list of stores that had been purchased by Haverford Venture Capital and were allowed to benefit from the privately funded party. And on the top of the list was Candy Girls.

I should have known.

Candy Girls, our shop's main competitor, was a bigger, newer, all-around impersonal party supply store. It was the main employer of the eighteen-to-thirty-five-year-old female population of Proper City. They'd mounted more than one smear campaign against us, most of which resulted in a backfire that doubled our business.

But this was bigger than a smear campaign. Not only would Disguise DeLimit not have the winning costume at tonight's party, but chances were, the winner would come from our biggest competitor. It would be the end of an era.

Kirby looked at me from across the store. His ginger-colored brows pulled together, and his freckles stood out against pale skin. I shook my head—a response that neither clued him in nor comforted him—and shoved the papers into the back pocket of my hobo pants. The store was scheduled to close in twenty minutes. We'd adjusted our hours so we'd have time to make deliveries tonight before the party. Now that extra time would be spent making phone calls to everybody who had rented from us. The girls by the Dr. Seuss costumes waved at me, and I pushed our troubles aside and went back to business.

Normally our costumes rented for three days, but the week prior to Halloween was different. Proper City had first been founded by a prospector named Pete, who swore off booze, gambling, and women if he'd only strike gold. He did, and Proper City was born. After his death in the '30s, the town fell onto hard times, and the only new citizens were scofflaws looking for asylum from California. The state line was only a few miles from our border, which made Proper City popular for a whole other set of reasons.

In the '50s, a group of city planners who felt that Nevada needed a family-oriented town to counter Las Vegas got together and designed their version of fantasy-land. Streets were named after fairy tales, and zoning had approved one library, one post office, one movie theater, and one grocery store. Other businesses came and went, but a few stuck around. Mom-and-pop stores like Disguise DeLimit—even though ours was a pop-and-daughter shop—were fewer and farther between.

When you're a town that was born on paper, you have to find your own identity, and Proper City's love of costumes became ours. We became the costume capital of the world. Just about anything that was cause for a party became a cause for costumes. There was a page of photos on our city's website that showed off everything from Laila Mishkin's teddy bear party—yes, teddy bears got costumes too!—to Sol Girard's Wild West Poker Game. But even a community who wears costumes for any occasion can recognize that Halloween is the time to pull out all the stops.

We extended the three-day rental window to a week during October so people could have the confidence that whatever they selected would be theirs for the full seven days of festivities. And now . . .

When the last of the customers had finished with their rentals, I locked the front door and moved the money and charge slips from the register to the safe. Soot, my cranky smoke-gray cat, swarmed around my ankles and meowed at me. Perhaps a dog would have been willing to wear a costume around the shop, but the most I'd been able to get Soot to wear was a tiny necktie that hung from his collar.

"What am I going to do, Soot?" I asked. Soot licked his paw and rubbed it over his face. "Proper City is a community, and people have come to trust us. This"—I waved the paper—"is the kind of thing that can break that trust. Should I call everybody who rented a costume and notify them?" I shoved the papers into the back pocket of my hobo pants, scooped up Soot, and carried him to the office, where I started making phone calls.

At four, Kirby returned to the store and joined me in the office. "The deliveries are all made and the store's locked up. How's it going in here?"

I stared at a stack of rental papers. "So far, four cancellations."

"That's not so bad. How many people have you called?"

"Five."

"Oh. Well, one didn't cancel. Maybe all of the duds were at the top of the stack."

"That was Don Digby. He knows he can't get a proper alien costume anywhere but here, but I could hear the disappointment in his voice."

Don Digby was my dad's best friend. The two of them had bonded over conspiracy theories and blues music. Don didn't expect to win the contest. He considered Halloween an opportunity to bring the truth about a hidden government secret to the public and, because of that, suspected he was under surveillance and, therefore, would never win the contest.

I couldn't even begin to think about telling my dad that I'd screwed up so badly my first Halloween running the store. This was his favorite time of year. Before he'd left, he'd spent a week putting together the windows, a diorama of Nosferatu seated at his table with Jonathan Harker. Silver candelabras and serving bowls were filled with grapes, bread, and even a turkey. They were on loan from the local antique mall. The silver serving dishes, not the food.

"There has to be a way to fight this," I said. "That guy can't just barge in here and give me papers a couple of hours before the party. That's not fair."

Kirby reached for the shelf above the desk and picked up a metal box with hinges on the back and a handle on top. He set it in front of me, opened the lid, and pulled out a stack of unopened white envelopes. "I thought these were bills, so I put them in the bill box. Jerry always paid the bills at the beginning of November."

I picked up the stack of envelopes. *Haverford Venture Capital* was printed above the return address. I tore the envelope open and slid the paper out. It was a notice to appear at the city council meeting. The date was yesterday.

"How long have these been coming?"

He shrugged. "It's October in Proper City. Jerry always arranges for the utilities to bill us for two months in November so he doesn't have to remember to pay them."

"He must have started doing that after I moved away."

"He started it last year. It was my idea." Kirby gestured toward a stack of mail in the inbox. "Just about the only other stuff we get is junk mail. We'll shred it when we have time, but who has time?"

"Everybody knows this is our busy time. If somebody

needed to get in touch with us, they'd come to the store and talk to us." Which was exactly what the man with the legal papers had done.

I ran my fingers over the return address. "I'm going to go see Paul Haverford." I stood up and pulled a ratty overcoat over my turtleneck and patched trousers. I grabbed the keys to my Vespa scooter, picked my helmet up from inside the back door, and left.

When the city planners had designed our town, they'd created one major road that connected our two disparate ends. Creative people that they were, they named the main line that connected the two ends Main Line Road. I turned left on it and drove to the far corner, then turned slightly right at a five-point intersection. An aerial view of Proper looked much like a crop circle, and the road that led to the return address on the envelope was at the end of one of the radials that extended from the end of Main Line. The sun was dropping, and the air had turned chilly, snapping at my hands. Shoulda worn gloves.

I didn't spend much time at this end of Main Line Road. It was mostly populated with business offices and hotels. A couple of rundown apartment buildings. I'd heard rumors about the people who rented in West Proper. They weren't the type to put down roots and start a family.

The parking lot to Haverford Venture Capital held a handful of cars. I parked my scooter in a visitor space next to a maroon sedan and locked my helmet to the seat. My hands were red and raw. I rubbed them together quickly and approached the front door. Through the glass doors, I saw the white-haired man who had been at Disguise DeLimit. He was arguing with another man, who wore a camel topcoat over his suit. White Hair looked my way when I entered.

"Can I help you?" he asked.

"I'm here to speak to Mr. Paul Haverford about these papers," I said. I reached into the pocket of my overcoat and pulled out the envelope.

"I'm Paul Haverford. Wait for me in my office." he said. He held his hand out toward an open door to my right.

I looked back and forth between him and Camel Coat and then went inside. A few seconds of silence passed, and then Camel Coat spoke. "If you don't tell your lawyers to back off, the deal is over."

"There's no need for threats," Haverford said.

I turned around and looked at them. Haverford saw me and closed the door in my face.

The office was immaculately maintained. A large mahogany desk sat in the middle, in front of heavy book-cases filled with leather-bound books. Framed diplomas from an impressive assortment of schools hung from the wall. On the desk was a name block that read PAUL HAVER-FORD. I sat in a soft burgundy leather chair opposite the large wooden desk and waited.

The longer I sat in the office, crossing and recrossing my legs, the more nervous I became. Having grown up in the costume shop, my confidence level was directly linked to how I dressed. Costumes gave me confidence, which was why I dressed up as different characters most days of the year, not just for one day in late October. But today, I was dressed in a red turtleneck sweater and a pair of hobo pants that had been patched with mismatched squares of plaid. Not the best outfit for a business meeting.

I pulled out my cell and called my friend Bobbie. We'd both been keeping our costumes a secret and planned to meet up in the hotel parking lot, but today wasn't exactly going according to plan. When she didn't answer, I left a message.

"Bobbie, it's Margo. Something came up this afternoon and I'm going to be late to the party. I might as well tell

you my costume. Look for a"—the door opened and Paul
Haverford entered—"giant spider. See you tonight." I hung
up and powered it off, and then stuffed it into the pocket
of my hobo topcoat.

"Ms. Tamblyn, from the costume shop," Paul Haverford
said. He held out his hand and I shook it. "You are here to
discuss the paperwork that I dropped off."

"Yes. Today is a little late to notify us about this change.
We're the most popular costume shop in Proper, and we've
rented hundreds of costumes already. A lot of people are
going to wear theirs to the opening reception tonight.
There's no way for us to notify everybody and tell them
that they aren't eligible for the grand prize."

"We've been trying to notify your dad about this for
several weeks now."

"My dad is out of town. I run the store now. He made
arrangements to have the bills turned off in October so we
can concentrate on making costumes. Proper City is such
a small town that everybody understands. I didn't open
your other letters—"

"So you received them prior to today?"

"Yes, but—"

"That's the confirmation I needed." Haverford smiled
an evil smile. "Ms. Tamblyn, when I decided to put my
money into Proper City, I did so knowing that I would not
be a popular man, but with the right decisions, I would be
a rich man. A richer man," he said with a chuckle. "The
way to grow a city isn't to turn off utilities for a month,
ignore your bills, and allow citizens to play dress-up. It's
to infuse the city with cash, evacuate the undesirable residents, bring in the kind of chain restaurants and retailers
that people desire."

"The people here don't desire that sort of thing. We like
our restaurants and shopping just the way they are."

"I'm not concerned with what the current residents of Proper want. It's the new residents that I'm thinking about. The tourists that will come when I have the zoning laws changed and bring in gambling, and the families that will move here because they're looking for employment in one of the factories I build."

"But that's not what Proper City is all about," I said. "This town was founded by Pete Proper and he outlawed all that stuff. We don't want a bunch of factories and casinos. That's why we live here and not Las Vegas."

"Your loyalty to your family business is charming," he said. The evil smile was back in place. His emphasis on the word "charming" made it sound like he really meant to say "repulsive."

My cheeks flushed hot. Despite the fact that I was dressed like a homeless person, that I was half this man's age, and that I wasn't a business professional, I was angered to the point of action. I picked up the legal notice that he'd dropped off at the store, stood up, and tore the papers into tiny little pieces.

"This is what I think of your plans to change Proper City," I said. I threw the small squares at his desk. They fluttered apart and scattered to the front and the back of his name block, one small piece covering the end of his name so it now read HAVERFO.

"Violate the agreement and your store will be penalized with a large citation. The law is on my side, Ms. Tamblyn. It won't take much for me to drive Disguise DeLimit out of town." He picked up a couple of squares of torn paper and let them fall through his fingertips. "I wasn't planning on focusing on the small businesses in town until I had my new infrastructure in place, but maybe I'll make an example out of you."

I stormed out of his office and drove home.

*   *   *

IT was closing in on six when I parked my scooter behind
Disguise DeLimit. The delivery van was in its usual space,
which meant that Kirby had finished early. Either that, or
enough people had canceled their costume reservations
that his workload had been cut in half.

I let myself in and dropped my keys into the bowl we
kept by the back door. I found Kirby in the office. One pile
of paper in front of him had gotten bigger. The other had
remained much the same.

"How did it go with the rest of the calls?" I asked.

"I don't know. There's a good chance that a lot of people
are getting ready and won't get my message until too late.
How about you? Any luck talking to that guy who was here?"

I took the topcoat off and hung it on a hook on the back
of the door, and then leaned against the desk. "That guy
was Paul Haverford. Of Haverford Venture Capital. I went
to the address on the envelope."

Kirby whistled. "Dude came here himself? I thought
when you were that rich you paid people do to your dirty
work."

"He's not making any friends, that's for sure. There was
another guy there when I arrived. They were arguing when
I showed up, and then the other guy left."

"Don't worry too much about it. Jerry'll fix it when he
gets back. Go on, get ready for the welcome reception
tonight. There's nothing else you can do. Disguise DeLimit
might not be eligible for the costume contest, but that
doesn't mean you can't represent." He held his fist up. I
made my own fist and bopped it against his. He left me
alone in the office.

Kirby might be right, but this wasn't my dad's problem
anymore. It was mine. And I didn't think ignoring it was
going to make it go away.

My hands were still cold from the drive back, so I pulled my red sleeves down over my hands and gripped the fabric into a fist. Soot jumped onto the desk and stood on top of the pile of envelopes.

"What am I going to do?" I asked my cat. "That guy made me mad. I tried to tell him that today was too late to notify us, but he didn't want to listen. I got so angry I tore up his paperwork and threw it on his desk. I've never done anything like that before."

Soot meowed.

"He said he was going to make an example out of us." I felt tears well up behind my eyes and I tried to blink them back. One big fat one escaped and ran down my chin. I shook my head and it fell onto my sweater. "I wanted to make things better but I made them worse."

Most of my life, I'd preferred to watch others than to take action myself. I'd been through a long string of therapists and counselors to try to get to the root of my issues but none had helped. It all came back to one thing: my mother died in childbirth, and I had a version of survivor guilt. Despite what my dad had told me my whole life, I felt like maybe my mom should have lived and I shouldn't. I'd grown up shy and tentative, always afraid to upset the apple cart.

I'd moved to Las Vegas at my dad's encouragement. He'd all but pushed me out of the nest so I could develop my own life, an act that triggered my feelings of abandonment. Not wanting to feel completely alone, I'd adopted a little gray kitten from the candy store next to my apartment. Over the past several years, Soot and I had had a lot of conversations about my personal growth. I paid him back in gourmet cat food and the occasional catnip mouse.

We were seven days away from Halloween. Because the holiday was such a production in our town, it took more than a day to set up the party. This year, a pre-party party was taking place at the Alexandria, a chance for those involved in the heavy lifting to don costumes, mingle, and not worry about performing or maintaining special effects. Photos from the pre-party often ended up in the last-minute mailings that went out to everybody on the city's mailing list, teasers of what they could expect if they joined in.

I changed from my hobo clothes into a pair of black leggings and a black hooded sweatshirt, and then stepped into a black, zip-front jumpsuit. It had come into the store in a lot of uniforms, and I'd done a couple of adjustments to make it fit closer to the body. I'd also painted a red diamond on the belly of the suit, lest anybody not know that my spider outfit was indeed a black widow. I pulled my hair back into a low ponytail and then pulled the hood of the sweatshirt over my head and knotted the cord below my chin. For the moment, I looked less like a spider and more like a cat burglar.

I pulled on a pair of pointy-toed black booties that had belonged to my mom in high school. My dad had never parted with her belongings, and I'd discovered them one day while organizing our back stock. Once I learned what they were, I transferred them to my own closet. In a way, I felt like I knew her through her clothes.

The most important part of my spider costume was the large black cotton cocoon that would fit over my shoulders like a backpack. In fact, after constructing it out of a heavily starched black denim, I had taken apart a backpack and attached the padded straps and waist cord to the cocoon to keep it in place. Legs, constructed from foam pool noodles fed into long black knit tubes of fabric, had been sewn to the cocoon. They were attached to one another with invisible thread, and the top legs had a small loop on the end. I slipped my index finger through the loop and held my arms up. My gestures controlled the top legs, and the invisible thread forced the other six legs to follow along whenever I moved. Our giant black widow spider had been a popular costume for as long as I could remember, but I liked to add something special to my personal costumes. My secret weapons for tonight were the cans of Silly String that were strapped to my wrists inside the sweatshirt. A plastic tube ran the length of my palm. When I flexed my hand down, the tube hit the top of the Silly String and my "web" spewed out. There might be other spiders at the Alexandria Hotel, but I doubted they'd be able to spin a web like mine.

I arrived about half an hour later and parked in a corner space of the lot. I locked my helmet to the scooter and zipped my keys into one of the pockets on the jumpsuit. Already a crowd stood outside the building, showing off costumes and laughing among themselves. Costumes were the great equalizer, I thought to myself. When you were in a costume, it didn't matter who you were by day. The two Batmen standing to the left of the entranceway spoke to each other as if it were perfectly normal to hang around outside an abandoned building, talking about football while wearing tights and a cape.

I stood back from the crowd and glanced up at the building. The Alexandria Hotel was one of the few buildings that had been in Proper City during Pete Proper's time. Constructed in the early 1900s, it had the hallmarks of the Victorian era, but after a couple of earthquakes and at least one fire, the bricks were dingy and discolored. After Pete died, it was rumored that the hotel had been used by gun runners who needed a safe haven outside of the California state lines. When the city planners had taken control of Proper City's future, the windows and doors had been boarded up so vagrants couldn't gain access. Word spread that scofflaws would have to find another hideaway.

The building had stood like that, self-contained and falling into disrepair, for the next sixty years. If Pete Proper had left his ghost behind, this would have been the location for him to take up residency.

As angered as I was by the conditions that the new owner, Paul Haverford, had placed on the costume contest tonight, I had to admit, the spooky hotel was the perfect backdrop for our city-wide party. The boards had been removed from the windows, and tattered sheer curtains floated in and out of them. The effect was otherworldly. Six floors up, I thought I saw the shadow of a figure move past one of the windows. *Odd*, I thought. Nobody had mentioned anything about the upstairs being open for tonight. I leaned closer and tried to make out details of the person, but he was gone.

Chapter 3

FAINT SOUNDS OF a pipe organ floated from inside the building. I stood rooted to the ground, searching not just one, but all of the open windows for signs that a person had been there. Must have been my imagination. It was particularly active on nights like this.

I hadn't bothered with theatrical makeup for my costume because I knew there was too much of a chance of it getting smudged while under my helmet. Instead, I'd applied fake lashes on both the top and bottom of my eyes to mimic the spidery theme. A few of the lashes had stuck together at the outer corners of my eyes, and every time I moved my hands to my face, the legs of the spider costume waved about, drawing attention to me. I blinked repeatedly to unstick them—the lashes, not the spider legs—finally opening them as wide as I could. The lashes pulled apart like two sides of Velcro. I looked left and right to make sure they were fine, and then straight ahead.

Into the eyes of a giant voodoo doll.

The figure was dressed in gray fleece, including her

hands, head, and feet. Pins, easily a foot long, jutted out from various parts of her body as if they'd been jabbed in by an angry person out to exact pain. Her body was sectioned off and labeled: heart, brain, stomach, various internal organs. I laughed when I saw that.

"Not bad, Bobbie, not bad."

The voodoo doll reached up and lifted her hood—crafted much like an executioner's hood—up from the hem, exposing the face of my longest-running friend, Bobbie Kay. "How'd you know it was me?" she asked.

"Your walk," I said. "You have to be a real costume expert to know how to change your movements if you don't want people to recognize you."

"How do you think a voodoo doll walks?" she asked.

I smiled. "Very carefully." Before she had a chance to make a comment about my own costume, I flexed my wrists and shot a spray of Silly String at her. She jumped away, startled, and then laughed.

"I see I'm not the only person with an interactive feature to their costume."

"Yours is interactive? How?"

She reached around to her back and plucked an oversized pin from a long narrow receptacle. "Go ahead, stab me. Anywhere you want."

I took the pin and tapped the sharp end against her heart. The tip met with little resistance. I put more pressure on it and it popped into the fabric and took hold.

She looked at it, now directly out in front of her. "The heart? That's so predictable, Margo."

"You should have known. I am a black widow spider, after all."

Slowly we made our way to the entrance. A woman dressed in a cheap plastic witches costume stepped away from the building and blocked my path. Even with her hair hidden under a pointed hat and a widow's peak drawn onto her forehead, I recognized Gina Cassavogli, the manager of Candy Girls.

"Gina," I said. "Nice outfit, but it's Halloween. I'm surprised you didn't want to wear a costume." Beside me, Bobbie snorted a laugh.

"You have a lot of nerve coming here," she said. "You know your costumes aren't eligible to win the grand prize this year."

"That doesn't mean we're not welcome. We are the preeminent costume shop in Proper City. We were here before Candy Girls ever opened and we'll be here after you close."

"We're not closing. Didn't you hear? We've just been purchased by the developer who plans to redo all of Proper City. Our logo will be on every tourist brochure, not yours. We're part of the future." She stepped back and looked at my costume from head to toe. "Spider. How original."

I would have sprayed her with my web, but she wasn't worth the Silly String.

"Let's go inside," I said to Bobbie.

Large plastic cauldrons filled with dry ice had been positioned around the lawn, and several men dressed as grim reapers wandered around, dumping pitchers of water into them. The resulting fog flooded over the top and then snaked around the ground. Here and there, fake tombstones decorated with creepy sayings jutted above the fog. Vines of ivy had been scattered about too, making the act of walking across the ground somewhat akin to navigating a labyrinth.

Inside the hotel, a ghostly blue figure floated a few inches above a piano. The keys moved in time with the music, giving the appearance that the blue phantom was playing the song. I looked above the figure for wires but saw nothing.

"This is incredible," I said to Bobbie. "How'd they do that? It's just floating there."

Bobbie moved closer to the ghost. A man in a black suit, white shirt, and narrow black tie stepped out from the shadows. "Step away from the ghost, ma'am," he said. His hands were clasped together behind his back, and he had dark sunglasses on. A curly white cord ran from the collar of his shirt to his ear. "Displays are not interactive." He reached up and touched his earpiece and looked down. A few seconds later he looked back up. "Refreshments are behind you." He held both hands out to usher us in the other direction.

"Now, he knows how to play a role," Bobbie said. "The earpiece and the monotone voice? Brilliant. I bet he's in community theater." I turned back but the man in black had backed into the shadows again.

"Creepy," I added.

We stood off to the side of the party, pointing out costumes and guessing identities. Despite the last-minute news about our costumes' eligibility, I picked out several that had come from our store. My dad had been particularly proud of the Universal Monsters he'd made for the local Elks Lodge. They stood by the bartender, looking like a *Famous Monsters of Filmland* cover.

Something green caught my attention. I turned away from the Elks and faced the Incredible Hulk.

"Hey, Dig. Nice costume."

"How'd you know it was me?" he asked.

I could see it was going to be an oft-asked question. "I can see your Tweety Bird tattoo underneath the green makeup."

He held one of his arms out and flexed his bicep a few times. "Hard to hide these guns," he said.

Dig Allen was a black hipster trapped in the body of a five-foot-ten, fifty-year-old mechanic. He had an anchor tattooed on the other forearm, and in cooler, non-costume-appropriate situations, favored bowling shirts with the sleeves torn off. He owned a towing company a few miles from the costume shop and carried a torch for Ebony even though she was a decade older than he was.

He held two plastic cups filled with punch. "Are you here with Ebony?"

"Ebony is convinced that Halloween parties are an invitation to the undead to join us. She's probably at home on her sofa with Ivory watching a James Brown concert on Blu-ray."

"Should have figured." He extended a cup toward me and I waved it off.

"Sure you don't want it? It's good. Ghostly Grog," he said.

"No thanks," I said. "There's got to be some water around here somewhere."

Dig took a drink from one of the cups. "You think maybe she wants some company with James Brown?"

"I think she might not want the Incredible Hulk sitting on her white suede sofa. Just a thought. But I admire how you just don't give up."

"Give up on my Ebony? Never. She'll come around."

Dig headed toward the complimentary cheese and crackers, and I went in search of something I trusted more than Ghostly Grog. I'd never been much of a drinker, and whatever inclinations I had toward alcohol had all but vanished after working in Vegas. I saw my share of drunken bachelor and bachelorette parties. Maybe whatever happened in Vegas did stay in Vegas, but I hadn't wanted to test the theory.

The air in the hotel was musty, and my throat felt raw from inhaling dust and dry ice. I interrupted a group of monsters and asked the Wolf Man if he knew where I could get a bottle of water.

"Is that you, Margo? It's me, Sol Girard. Nice costume."

"Sol, that's right, I forgot you're an Elk. You guys look great. Did Kirby call you earlier tonight?"

· Sol grumbled. "Everybody knows the best costumes here came from your store. If somebody wants to make a bogus rule that we're not eligible, that's their problem."

"I'm glad you understand. We had a couple of last-minute cancellations because of it."

"Yeah, that's why there's so many witches and wizards here. That's the only thing Candy Girls had left on their shelves." He took a drink and glanced at my empty hands. I kept them by my side. The rest of the monsters were close enough that every time I moved my arms, a spider leg popped one on the tush. I didn't want to send any mixed signals.

"You want some Ghostly Grog?"

"Actually, I'm looking for a bottle of water. Do you know where they put that?"

"Not sure. I'd help you look but my wife sent me here with a Crock-Pot full of Swedish meatballs. New recipe. If I bring any home, she'll think they weren't any good. You want some?"

"Sure."

Sol handed me a plate of meatballs. Cross-sectioned green olives had been recessed into the meatball, making each look like an eyeball. They were small enough to pop a whole one into my mouth, and I finished the serving in a couple of minutes.

"Want more?"

"Better save some for the rest of the crowd. Tell her she outdid herself."

I coughed a couple of times, the dry ice getting to me. Sol filled a plastic cup with ginger ale to tide me over until I found the water. I complimented the rest of the monsters and went into the next room.

Fewer people were in here: a couple of wizards, a man in a black sweat suit that had been printed with a skeleton that glowed in the dark, and the requisite number of scantily clad witches. I shouldn't have been surprised by the number of them. Candy Girls carried mass-produced, pre-assembled costumes, so the only variety was what color wig they bought to wear under their pointy hats.

If the front section of the hotel was the reception hall; this area included the hotel lobby. In front of the long marble desk was a row of wooden barrels filled with water. Signs had been attached to each. BOBBING FOR APPLES, WHICH WITCH IS WHICH?, and DANGEROUS WATERS. Children in colorful costumes inspired by cartoons and superheroes ran about, taking turns with each of the games.

Cobwebs had been strewn across the front desk, and a couple of skeletons in suits and bellboy costumes were positioned around as if they'd continued to perform their duties from the afterlife. I stopped two people and asked about water and they pointed me farther inside. When I reached the back, another man in a black suit with sunglasses and a white cord by his ear stepped away from the shadows.

"Stay in the party areas, miss," he said in a flat monotone much like the man by the pipe organ. He too had an ID badge clipped onto his suit pocket. It said Agent Smith.

"I just want a bottle of water," I said. "I heard they were back here."

He put his fingers to his earpiece like the first guy had done, looked down for a second, and then looked back up at me. "Food and beverage is being staged on the second floor," he said. He raised his hand toward me as if he were about to grab my throat. I pulled back. His hand stopped a few inches in front of me. "Wait here. I'll get it for you."

He moved a heavy velvet curtain from the wall and pressed an elevator call button. He stepped toward me and put his hand on my bicep. I swung my arm in a backward circle and the spider legs jumped to attention. The room was dark, and he seemed caught by surprise. The elevator doors opened.

"I can get it myself, thanks," I said. I jumped in and jabbed the Close-Door button. The velvet curtain that had kept the elevator door hidden now swung back into place. The last thing I saw was Agent Smith's hand get caught up in the fabric as the doors closed.

My heart was racing. Whoever the men in black were, they definitely weren't breaking character. Were they part of Paul Haverford's team? Through my interactions with most of our customers, I was able to pick out who was who, but these guys were good. Too good. They gave me the creeps.

I pushed the button for the second floor. The elevator had received the same fake-spider-web treatment as the front desk. Considering my costume, I should have felt at home. I sensed that even though this was an old elevator, there was a camera watching me. I looked up at the cracked panes that covered the ceiling and spotted a glowing red light in the corner. Without thinking twice, I aimed one of my Silly String canisters at it and shot. The thin foamy spray sprung out and covered the light. Somehow, the juvenile act made me feel better.

The elevator passed the second floor. I jabbed at the number 2, but it continued to ascend. When it reached the sixth floor, the doors opened. I stepped out and the doors closed behind me.

I looked for signs to indicate which direction to go. There was nothing but a bunch of lumps: furniture that had been covered in white sheets long ago. The cobwebs on this floor had a different appearance, as though they hadn't been applied for the party. Instead of fog, a layer of grit and gravel covered the floor. The leather soles of my black booties were quiet against the dirty residue, but if I wasn't careful, I'd track it back downstairs when I left.

The only light came from the open window, where tattered white curtains blew in and out with the breeze, and a small night-light that had been plugged into a wall socket on the opposite side of the room. I remembered the figure I'd seen walk past the windows when I was outside, and I shivered. I returned to the elevator and pushed the call button.

The floor indicator lit. A series of numbers, one through twelve, showed the floors in a semi circle. A black arrow was pointed toward the six, which was where I was. Like many old elevators, this one must have been programmed to rest at the top or the bottom floors when not in use. The doors did not open. I jabbed the call button again and leaned toward the fixture, listening for indications that the contraption was moving.

The air in the room felt colder than it had when I'd arrived, and even though I had leggings and a hoody on underneath the black jumpsuit of my costume under the spider cocoon and legs, I was downright cold. The sound of the wind whipping by the curtains raised my paranoia. Everything that made this the perfect setting for Halloween made it the worst place to be caught alone. I hopped from foot to foot until the doors opened, and then jumped inside and pressed the button for the first floor. And then, I noticed that I wasn't alone.

In the darkness, on the floor, was the body of a white-haired man in a business suit. Paul Haverford. A trail of blood trickled down from a gash on the top of his head.

Chapter 4

I LEANED DOWN and jostled his arm with my hand. The spider legs swatted against his legs and waist. His arm fell from his lap to the floor. I made a noise between a gasp and a scream. His head rolled to the side.

I pressed my fingers against the clammy flesh on his neck. There was no pulse. I grasped his lapels and shook him. His jacket fell open, exposing a cranberry monogram on his shirt. PWH. His already seated body slumped down the interior wall of the elevator. I jabbed my finger at the first-floor button, but the elevator doors did not close. I tried Close-Door—second floor—anything to make the elevator move. Finally, I hit the Alarm button. The bell cut through the night air, drowning the sound of the pipe organ. I thought again about the party. I had to notify someone about the dead man without alarming the families and children in attendance.

I grabbed the man's ankles and pulled him onto the faded Oriental carpet. As soon as his head cleared the opening, the doors closed. The arrow above the elevator indicated its descent. My already dry throat closed up, resulting in a coughing fit. I stumbled to the window and pushed my head and shoulders through.

"Help," I yelled. "Somebody, help!" I hollered. A few people looked up and pointed at me, nudging others, as if I was part of the entertainment. "Call the police," I cried. "There's been an accident!"

A couple of spectators clapped. One man cupped his hands around his mouth and yelled, "Don't jump!" Another pointed to the right of me, "Spider-Man will save you," he called.

I glanced to my right. A figure dressed in a Spider-Man leotard clung to the rusted-out fire escape by the sixth floor. I was too far away to make out anything but his costume, but with a frightening chill, I realized I might be looking at a murderer.

I backed out of the window and slammed the casing shut. There had to be an emergency exit, but I didn't know the layout of the hotel. Before I could act, several men dressed in black suits appeared from the corner of the room. A flickering Exit sign was partially hidden under a fake cobweb. Stairs. They'd come up the stairs.

They moved quickly to Paul Haverford and felt his neck and wrist for a pulse like I had done. One of them pulled a radio from under his jacket. "We have a deceased male on the sixth floor. Apparent injury to the head."

The men stood up and looked at me. I held my hands up in front of me and stepped backward. "I didn't do it," I said. "I came up here for water. I tried to stop on the second floor but the elevator came up here."

"Ms. Tamblyn, please step away from the body," one of the men said.

"How do you know my name?" I asked, backing away again. I felt cornered and didn't know which way to run. Fear pumped adrenaline through my arms and legs. One of the men reached into his jacket, and I screamed and threw my hands up over my face. The man pulled out a wallet and flipped it open.

Finally, a person who could carry off a costume. As it turns out, the man was really a woman. Detective Nancy Nichols of the Proper City Police Department.

I looked back and forth from her badge to her face to her badge to her face. Her normally long blond hair had been cut short and slicked back. Dark sunglasses hid enough of her face to hide her identity. She tipped her head back and pulled what appeared to be a watch from her throat. "Voice lowering device," she said. "Part of the costume." I started to talk but she cut me off with her hand, palm face-out. "Wait over there, Ms. Tamblyn. I'll need your statement."

I stepped away from the body and sat on the corner of one of the sheet-covered sofas. A puff of dust rose when I sat and now filtered through the air like tiny particles of history. So much of what I'd seen at the hotel looked to have been rigged for the party tonight, but not this. Not a murder.

Detective Nichols had been appointed to the Proper City Police Department about the same time I'd moved back to Proper. She had the build of a pro volleyball player and the just-the-facts manner of a census taker. If I hadn't been firsthand witness to a more human side of her, I might not have liked her very much. It had been the day I learned that my dad had a second heart attack while on a costume scouting trip, and despite the fact that I'd been interfering with her investigation, she'd dropped everything to make sure I was okay. After that, it had been hard to dismiss her simply because she'd also been mistakenly interested in Ebony's role in a homicide. Still, it didn't mean we were destined to be friends either.

She gave instruction to the two men who'd arrived with

her and then joined me by the sofa. When she didn't sit, I stood.

"Ms. Tamblyn, what happened here?"

"Water," I choked out. I cleared my throat a couple of times. "Do you happen to have any water?" I asked. She shook her head. One of the men in black handed me a plastic bottle and I took a long gulp. "I don't know what happened here. I came up here to get some water. One of the men in black—wait, are they all with you?" She nodded once. "Good costumes," I said, temporarily distracted. She didn't react. "Sorry. I heard there was water on the second floor. The elevator didn't stop there even though I pushed the button. It came up here. I was waiting for the elevator to come back, and when it opened, he was in there."

She waited a few seconds. "Do you know who he is?"

"Paul Haverford. He's the developer who owns the hotel. He came to Disguise DeLimit earlier today."

"What was the nature of his business at your store?"

"He was there to deliver some papers to us. Some legal documents."

She made a note on her phone with a plastic stylus. "You said you were waiting for the elevator to come back. What makes you think it wasn't waiting here?"

"You know how these old buildings are. When they're not in service, the elevators float from the bottom floor to the top. I got off and the doors closed. It had to go somewhere. When the elevator came back to the sixth floor, he was inside."

She made a few more notes but didn't reply. I looked at the elevator display. The arrow hadn't moved from the sixth floor. But where had the body come from? He hadn't been inside when I rode up.

I shivered. Detective Nichols glanced up at me. Her eyes dropped from my face to my body. I wrapped my arms around my torso for warmth. The spider legs moved in like fashion, bouncing like an oversized black rib cage around me.

"Is there anything else you'd like to add to your statement?" she asked.

"You should look for Spider-Man," I said. She didn't move. "I yelled for help out the window and people thought it was a stunt, like I was acting. Somebody pointed to the fire escape and said Spider-Man would save me. He was on the fire escape."

"We'll check it out," she said. She slid the wand back into the case of her phone, closed the case over it, and slipped the whole thing into an inside pocket of her black suit jacket. "You're not planning on leaving town, are you?"

"No. Why?"

She stared at me long enough to make me uncomfortable. "Follow-up," she finally said.

"I'll be at the shop if you need to talk to me. But if I think of anything"—I made a gun shape out of my index finger and thumb, and pointed it at her—"I'll call you."

She turned to one of the men in black behind her. "Scott, escort Ms. Tamblyn to her vehicle," she said. The officer nodded. "Stairs," she called behind him.

The officer led me into a dark hallway.

"Are you the one who gave me water?" I asked.

"Yes, ma'am. I knew you were thirsty. You asked about water before you got onto the elevator."

"You didn't want me to get on the elevator. Why?"

"These elevators were programmed to stay on the first floor. Mr. Haverford asked us to keep people from going to the other levels."

"But you said you were going to—"

"Get it for you. I was thirsty too."

We walked past the sheet-covered furniture, past a wall of windows, to a nondescript door in a corner. An Exit sign had been mounted above it, but the light was burned out.

The officer opened the door and we went inside. The air was stale and cold. I forced myself to swallow a few times though my throat was just about shot at this point. We descended the stairs and reentered the hotel on the first floor behind the check-in desk. The skeleton hotel employee sat with his hands positioned on his keyboard, a layer of spider web stretched over top. He grinned freakishly—as if he knew something about the night that nobody else did—all part of the elements that made the past hour so surreal.

In the time that I'd been upstairs, the Alexandria Hotel had emptied. An ambulance sat by the sidewalk, the rear doors open. Clusters of people only now half dressed in costume stood around the perimeter. Uniformed officers who looked like partygoers themselves circulated among the crowd, taking statements. The sun had dropped, but the streetlights hadn't come on yet. We were a week away from daylight savings, and the timer on the city-run lights had already been reprogrammed to accommodate the additional hour of sunlight. It happened this time every year.

My scooter sat alone in the corner. I wrapped my arms around my torso, no longer worried about how silly I looked. The officers nodded at me, as if they knew the role I'd played in the discovery of the body. I checked in with them and they said I could leave. I gave them a tight-lipped smile, pulled my keys out of my pocket, and drove home.

Tuesday

The next morning, I dressed like a gangster. Pinstriped double-breasted suit, white shirt, fat necktie with tie clip. Black-and-white spats. I parted my hair on the side and slicked it back with a thick styling cream, and then secured it into a ponytail at the base of my head, which I tucked into the collar of my shirt—the ponytail, not my head. I slipped a vintage class ring onto my pinky and finished the look with a fedora.

It wasn't abnormal for me to dress in elements of costume on a regular basis. Growing up, my dad hadn't had time to go to the mall and pick out a wardrobe for me like other parents did. My school clothes had largely come from the inventory of the shop. Once I'd gotten old enough to shop for myself, I'd found that my identity was wrapped up in those costumes, and dressing like everybody else made me feel invisible. I'd learned to work the sewing machine in order to produce costumes for the store and had amassed a collection of patterns from yard sales in the neighborhood. My daily ensembles were like characters that I took on and off. They gave me a sort of power, like if I was dressed up as a character, then nothing that happened to me was real. Probably not the healthiest mind set, but it worked for me.

I'd once had an art teacher who said that we were what we wore. He said he could take a picture of every student on the first day of class and compare it to a picture of us on the last day of class and there wouldn't be much variation. Not only had I blown that theory out of the water, but apparently, my ever-changing looks were a cause for concern. The teacher pulled me aside one day and asked if I wanted to talk about my search for an identity. I dropped my portrait class and signed up for pottery instead.

Whether my teacher had been right or not wasn't the issue today. We were in that special week before Halloween, and that meant we brought out the big guns. In a town like Proper City, where costume parties were the norm, everybody had a party to go to, and some people, more than one. We had two types of customers: those who splurged on an expensive costume and wore it everywhere for a week, and those who wanted something different for every one of their social engagements. Dressing in costume this week was simply a business decision.

I tossed a cup of soy milk, a banana, some blueberries, and a couple of leaves of kale into the blender, whipped up a breakfast smoothie, and transferred it into a metal flask. We sold the same one at the store, and it was the perfect prop to add to the gangster costume. Soot reminded me to fill his bowls with fresh food and water before I went downstairs. I gave him an unwanted hug first, cleaned out his litter box, and left him with his head buried in vittles.

The store was a mess. We weren't scheduled to open for a couple of hours, so I had the time to straighten it, but there was something more pressing on my mind. The legal documents that Paul Haverford had delivered.

I'd only managed to fall asleep last night after a long shower and a lot of tossing and turning. Paul Haverford's dead body hadn't been the first that I'd ever encountered, but that didn't make the situation any less disturbing. Coupled with the atmosphere of the Alexandria Hotel, the eerie sounds of the pipe organ, the emotionless men in black who now appeared to have been police—and not all men—and the tendrils of fog from the dry ice, my memories had morphed into nightmares. By the time I'd gotten home, I'd triple locked every door in the house, turned on a night-light, and moved Soot's food and litter box into my room so I wouldn't wake up alone. He probably would have been fine keeping me company if it wasn't for the multiple bathroom breaks I took, thanks to the gallon of water I drank before bed.

I'd torn up and discarded Paul Haverford's most recent legal notice in his office, but I still had a stack of unopened envelopes in mine. I opened one and pulled out the paperwork. The letterhead said PWH, and the rest was the same legal jargon I'd seen on the documents I tore up last night.

I slumped into my swivel chair and read over the text, this time with my full concentration. After twenty minutes and only two paragraphs, I knew I was going to need help understanding the legalese. I didn't know any lawyers, but I knew someone who did. Tak Hoshiyama, former employee of the district attorney's office. Since I was in the privacy of the office in an unattended store, I called instead of e-mailing. He picked up on the third ring.

"It's Margo," I said. Before he could speak, I rushed ahead. "I need help deciphering some legal documents. Do you think you could come over?"

"I might. Where are you?"

"The store." I paused. "I'm alone."

"I'll be right there."

Fifteen minutes later, there was a knock on the front door. I came out of the office and unlocked it, and Tak came inside.

"You're still alone?" he asked.

"Yes."

He closed the small space between us, put his hands on either side of my face, and kissed me.

Chapter 5

AFTER THE KISS, Tak leaned back and slid his hands down from my face to around my waist.

"You kissed me in the middle of the store," I said.

"I didn't want to waste an opportunity." He grinned. "Where is everybody?"

"Kirby has swim team practice this morning, Ebony's superstitions keep her at home this time of year, and my dad's flight out of New York was delayed."

He looked over his shoulder. "I feel like we're going to get caught."

I returned his smile. "So do I. Let's not risk it."

Tak Hoshiyama was the most interesting man I'd met in recent history. His father was Japanese and his mother was American, and he had the exotic looks that came with such a mix. His longish hair was almost as black as mine, though his was probably not courtesy of a box of Clairol. His lips were naturally red, and his strong, angular chin perfectly matched the lines of his straight nose. In addition to his good looks, there was an unmistakable air of confidence about him. Maybe it was because he was good at math.

We'd met six months ago when I'd first returned to Proper City, and got to know each other over a homicide investigation. I'd felt attracted to him almost immediately and couldn't deny the way he seemed to be able to read my mind. But, there were problems with us dating. Namely, his father.

Tak had been raised in Hawaii, schooled at Princeton, and worked at the Clark County DA's planning office, where he put his natural skills of planning and spacial relations to work determining zoning laws and reviewing building permits to use. A situation that tested his moral boundaries had led to his suspension and eventual resignation.

His relationship with his parents, the owners of Hoshi-yama Kobe Steak House in Proper City, had been what brought him to Proper City. Those same relations had been strained ever since he'd returned. His father felt that Tak had disgraced the family by being put on leave. And after he'd quit, his father accused him of throwing away his career for something far less important: me.

We'd decided to keep our relationship a secret—not just from his father, but from everybody. But Ebony—the woman who had practically helped my father raise me—saw Tak's attention toward me as an indication that my love life had a pulse. She dropped not-so-subtle hints whenever he called or stopped in to say hello. It got to the point where we both realized it would be far easier if we both just moved on. Turns out, neither one of us wanted to.

When he and I had started our secret liaison, I'd had the bright idea to program each other's numbers into our phones under "Private Number." That way if we ever missed a call, nobody would be the wiser. Quickly after that, we'd developed a system for spending time together.

We'd text each other with a situation and a destination—*bank ATM, diner parking lot, post office*—and meet up as if it was purely coincidence. As long as nobody pulled the video feed from the ATM, we were probably flying under the radar.

I led Tak to the office. "Does the name Paul Haverford mean anything to you?" I asked.

"Other than the fact that he was found murdered last night?"

"Other than that."

Tak leaned against the desk. "He owns an investment company. They buy old buildings, flatten them, and sell off the land to the highest bidder. His name used to come up in the planning office. I think he was fighting the city council about building on the west side of Proper. Seems there's a loophole in the zoning regulations out this way. There are a couple of miles of desert that haven't been accounted for. If he was right, whoever owns that land could make a tidy profit if they interest the casinos in moving out this way or partner up with an outlet mall. Paul was applying for the permits when I left my job. It wasn't my case, but you hear things. What's your interest in him?"

"Paul Haverford was the new owner of the Alexandria Hotel. That's the old rundown building where all of the Halloween festivities were to take place."

"But that's where his body was found. You're not going to . . ." His voice trailed off, and he looked concerned.

"Tak, I'm the one who found him at the hotel. His body was left in an elevator. I was on the sixth floor and somebody put his body in the elevator when I got out, and a whole bunch of people—children and families!—would have found him."

"Why were you on the sixth floor? I thought the hotel was off-limits except for the ground levels."

"I wanted some water. Whoever set up the food and beverage stations seems to have forgotten that not everybody wants to drink Ghostly Grog. Somebody told me the water was on the second floor, so I went up looking for it."

He leaned back against the desk. Tak had an analytical mind, and I could see that his thoughts had shifted.

"Paul Haverford was here in the shop yesterday. He served us with these papers." I waved the papers in front of him. "He banned the store from participating in the Halloween festivities and said we'll be violating his legal rights as property owner if we pushed the issue." I handed the legal documents to Tak and tapped the paper. "Apparently this says that Disguise DeLimit can have no part in Halloween."

Tak looked at the date stamped on the outside of the envelopes. "These were mailed. You said he brought them here yesterday?"

This was the part I'd been dreading. "These are the documents that have been sitting in my dad's inbox since they arrived. The copy Paul Haverford brought here yesterday is, at this moment, scattered over the surface of his desk, where I threw them after I tore them up."

"Back up."

"After I closed the store yesterday, I went out to his office to talk to him. He was arguing with another man, a really tall guy in a camel coat. The guy left and he came in to talk to me—Haverford, not the stranger. He wasn't a nice man, Tak. He said he was going to make an example out of Disguise DeLimit and run us out of Proper City."

"What did you say?"

"Not much. I tore up the documents, threw them on his desk, and left."

"Why didn't you know about these?" He held up the papers I'd handed him.

I dropped into the chair and ran my fingers over the

stack of unopened envelopes. "Apparently my dad has the utility companies turn off our bills for the month of October so he can concentrate on running the store. Kirby thought these were bills. He filed them in the unpaid bill box." I put my hand on the aluminum box. "I should have known about them, shouldn't I? I should have told Kirby to give me everything that came in to the store. If I had opened them myself, I would have known what was going on. All of this could have been avoided."

Tak picked up the envelope and studied the address. "Not necessarily. This is addressed to Jerry Tamblyn and marked confidential. It even says here 'To be opened by addressee only.' So technically, you did the right thing."

"Except that somebody killed Paul Haverford last night." I unscrewed the cap from my flask and took a drink of smoothie. When I finished, Tak was staring at me like I'd lost my mind. "What?" I asked.

"I know you're upset, but I don't think you should be drinking in the morning."

I tipped the flask at him so he could catch a whiff of blueberries. "It's a prop. I filled it with my breakfast smoothie."

He shook his head at me. "You're an odd bird, Margo Tamblyn."

"That's what you like about me."

"Aye, matey, it is."

"Pirate? I'm a gangster. A wiseguy, see?" I stood up and modeled my outfit. "Get your costumes straight."

We bantered a bit, enjoying the relative privacy of the unopened store.

"Do you want to go through exactly what happened last night?" he finally asked.

"I just did."

"Not the confrontation. The other part. At the Alexandria."

I remembered the way Detective Nichols had thrown me off by already being at the party, and how the atmosphere at the house had heightened my sense of fear. But Detective Nichols wasn't just Proper City's police detective. She was Tak's ex-girlfriend. I didn't want to bring her up to Tak. Soot and I could address that later.

"Not now. I have to get the store ready to open."

Just then the door to Disguise DeLimit rattled. Through the shades that filtered only a minimal amount of light from the already bright sun, I recognized the detective. She was flanked on either side by uniformed police officers. This time they weren't costumes.

"You didn't park your car out front, did you?" I asked Tak.

"No, I took the Zip-Three."

"Leave out the back door. I'll call you later."

Tak looked torn but disappeared into the back before she spotted him. I unlocked the door.

"Good morning, Detective."

"Ms. Tamblyn," she said, glancing only briefly at my gangster outfit. "We need to talk."

"I gave you a pretty thorough statement last night and you said you got everything you needed."

She looked me directly in the eyes. "That was before I learned you might have motive to see Mr. Haverford out of the picture."

Chapter 6

"EXCUSE ME?" I asked. "I might have been angry with Mr. Haverford when I went to his office earlier in the day, but that doesn't mean I wanted to hurt him."

"So you admit that you were in his office," Detective Nichols said.

"I'd be foolish not to. That building must have security cameras, plus I'm probably the only visitor who ever graced that office dressed like a hobo."

One of the officers behind the detective tucked his chin as if he were hiding a chuckle. Nichols glared at him. He drew his mouth into a line and stood up straight, all traces of humor gone from his face.

"I admit that it wasn't my finest hour to tear up his legal notice and throw it on his desk, but that's a far stretch from committing murder."

"Ms. Tamblyn, I think it would be best if we had this conversation someplace else."

"Can I make other arrangements for the store first? This is a big week for us and my dad trusted me to run the place while he was gone. I don't want anybody to think we're not opening."

She looked at her watch. "How long is that going to be?"

"Give me fifteen minutes."

The last thing I wanted to do six days before Halloween was have an unexpected conversation with Detective Nichols about Paul Haverford's murder. But it did seem as though I was one of the last people to have interacted with him, and there was a chance that something I had seen could help her do her job.

I called Ebony and begged her to check on the store, and then left a brief note for Kirby that an emergency pulled me away but that I'd be back. There wasn't really any other way to explain my not being there during our crucial time.

Detective Nichols gave me the option of riding with her or driving myself. Easiest decision of my life. I drove behind her and parked in a visitor spot.

Much of Proper had been built in the '40s and '50s, which lent itself to the storybook charm that matched the streets. The police station was no different. It was a small building with white siding and blue trim. A navy blue awning over the front door shielded anybody who cared to enter from the desert sun. The word POLICE had been stenciled above the door and on the side wall. A dark blue throw rug sat in front of the door. It was faded in the center and showed faint signs of having been used by people with dirty soles.

I followed the detective into the station. An orange candle in a glass jar sat on the raised counter in front of a woman in a bulky sweater with a black cat in the center. Behind her, a wall of beige filing cabinets lined the wall, topped with white metal trays filled with blank forms. A potted ficus tree sat in the corner next to a water dispenser.

The scent of pumpkin filled the air. A bulletin board to

the left of the front lobby held an assortment of colorful notices tacked on with equally colorful thumb tacks. The bright colors gave off a kindergarten vibe, until I spotted a cage of dingy, chipped metal bars to the left. The county jail cell, scented by the Yankee Candle Company.

We passed the cell and the front desk. Detective Nichols offered me a cup of coffee and I declined, mostly because I was suddenly nervous and uncomfortable and unsure what to do with my hands. This was my first time in a police station at the detective's request and I wasn't sure how to act. The detective led me into an empty room. The carpet was the same shade of blue that had been used to paint the exterior of the building. A large round table occupied the center of the room. Wooden and vinyl chairs on castors sat at varying positions around it, as if the last people who had been in here had gotten up suddenly. Detective Nichols extended a hand toward one of the empty chairs. I sat down. She pulled a chair out away from the table and sat next to me.

"Ms. Tamblyn, let's go over your statement from last night again. Tell me what happened, starting with you going to the sixth floor. Don't leave out any details."

I went back over it all—from Sol pouring me a ginger ale at the downstairs bar, to one of the men in black telling me the water was on the second floor, to the elevator not stopping until it reached the sixth. It was the same information I'd given her when it happened, the same info I'd been over a hundred times since last night.

"You claim that you were looking for water. Several of the people we spoke to had water bottles from a station outside."

"I didn't spend much time outside. When I arrived at the hotel, I went inside to look around. I—I wanted to see the costumes," I finished.

"Let's get back to the man who told you the water was on the second floor."

"He was one of your guys. His name was Scott."

"Not him. The first guy."

"The one who wouldn't let us check out the blue blob?"

She raised her eyebrows at me and a series of horizontal wrinkles appeared across her forehead.

"He was dressed as a man in black, like you. Black suit, white shirt, black tie. Hair parted on the side and slicked back. White curly cord running from his ear down to the back of his shirt."

She made a note on her tablet. "What else can you tell me about him?"

I tried to remember details but came up empty. "He was the first man in black. Then there was Scott. Other than the fact that they scared me, I don't remember anything else about either one."

"They scared you, how?"

"The first guy was all business. He got right up in my face and told me to go away. Then I asked the second guy about water and he said it was on the second floor. He said he'd come with me and he grabbed my arm. Right there, he violated rule number one of a Halloween party: don't touch strangers."

"There are rules to Halloween parties?" she asked with notable sarcasm.

"There are rules to running a haunted house," I said with dignity. "By nature, it's a creepy setting. You expect the patrons to suspend their disbelief and enter a building filled with spirits and monsters and people pretending to be undead. The understanding is that even though it's scary, nothing bad is going to happen to you because it's entertainment. Nobody's going to grab you, and you're not going to have to defend yourself. If you think about it, a haunted house is one of the safest places you can go in your life." An unwelcome image of Paul Haverford's last moments popped into my head. "Or it should be."

"Did you have something to do with the planning of that event?"

"No."

"So why were you there? From what I've learned, that was a closed event for the planners and volunteers who put the week's festivities together."

"Disguise DeLimit has always been a big part of Proper City's Halloween. There's a costume contest every year, and for the past twelve years we've provided the winning costumes. That costume gets used in the city's social media campaign leading up to Halloween, and it draws a lot of last-minute customers to our store."

"But you were advised not to attend the party, correct? So technically speaking, you had no official reason for being there."

"Did someone complain?"

"With all due respect, the person who might have complained isn't alive to do so."

I didn't like what she was suggesting. Defensive denials sprung to my lips, but I pressed them together and stayed silent. I couldn't see as how it would do any good.

"Tell me about these annual Halloween parties," she said.

"There's been a designated haunted house every Halloween that I can remember. Volunteers put in time to convert it so the children of the neighborhood get a treat. This year it was the Alexandria Hotel. Last night was the Halloween kickoff party, so the house was open. Everybody knows that some of the people are volunteers who've been positioned around the interior to make the place seem scarier. That's what I thought the men in black were. But now I'm confused," I said. "If you were in a costume, then you must have been off duty."

She leaned back. "Ms. Tamblyn, if you were going to create a costume where you dressed up as me, what would that costume entail?"

I shifted in my seat and cut my eyes to her outfit. When I looked back up, I met her stare directly. "Black pant suit, white shirt. Gold watch on a black band, and a gold identification bracelet, both worn on the left wrist. Long, sandy blond wig. Badge on a black lanyard hanging around my neck. Gun at my left hip."

She nodded once. "Very observant."

"It's my job to know how to make a costume."

"Describe what I was wearing last night."

"Black pant suit, white shirt. Gold watch on a black band—" I stopped. "But you were in a costume. Your hair was styled differently, and you had those sunglasses on. And the white cord that ran behind your ear."

"Before taking this job, I heard about Proper City and the costume parties. I have to say, it intrigued me. A town filled with people who like to dress up. It's like something out of *Grimms' Fairy Tales*."

"The city planners had fairy tales in mind when they named the streets. Even this police station looks like something out of a storybook. We just took it one step further."

She continued as if I hadn't spoken. "The Alexandria House has been a hot topic lately. When I found out it was going to be ground zero for Proper's Halloween celebration, I thought it was a good idea to check it out. We made arrangements with Mr. Haverford to be at the party. He asked us to blend in, so we did."

"But one of your men didn't know the protocol, so when he grabbed me, I knew something was wrong. I got out of there and went to the second floor by myself."

She didn't reply. I'd gotten more comfortable as I sat there—the side effect of getting to talk about costumes— but I became very aware that the only reason I was there was because she thought I was holding something back.

There was a knock on her door frame. One of the

uniformed officers gestured for her to come into the hallway. "I think you should see this," he said.

"Wait here," she said. She followed the man out of the office and left me alone.

Detective Nichols had surprised me by indicating that her costume had been another version of what she wore every day, but it said something that I'd long understood. Costumes could make you stand out or blend in. Costumes could make people treat you differently. Dress in scrubs, and people treat you like you're a doctor. Dress in a white shirt and khakis and carry a clipboard, and people treat you like you're a survey taker. It was one of the reasons I loved dressing in costume so much. Every morning when I woke up, I could be anybody I wanted.

I glanced down at my pinstripes, pinky ring, and spats. They didn't exactly scream "upstanding citizen with nothing to hide."

A few minutes later, Detective Nichols reentered the room. This time she carried a small portable DVD player. She set it on the table between us and pulled her chair up next to mine.

"Ms. Tamblyn, tell me again about what happened at the party."

"I pushed the button for the second floor, but the elevator didn't stop until it reached the sixth. I got off the elevator and looked around anyway. When I didn't see any water, I tried to leave. Truthfully, it was a little creepy up there. As soon as the elevator doors reopened, I jumped inside. I didn't see Paul Haverford's body until after I pushed the buttons. His head was bloody. I felt his throat for a pulse but there wasn't one. The door wouldn't close, so I pulled him out of the elevator and tried to revive him, but it was too late. I called for help out the window. You and your men came up the stairs, and you know the rest."

The detective's face showed no expression.

"It's the truth. I thought I was doing the right thing. I didn't know where the stairs were, and before I had a chance to get help, you arrived."

She watched me for another couple of seconds, and then opened up the DVD player and pressed play. A low whirring noise started, and then the blue screen changed to a view of the elevator from the Alexandria House. I recognized it immediately because there I was in the center of the screen. Me and all eight of my spider legs.

The memory flashed into my mind a moment before it appeared on the screen, and I tensed, knowing exactly what was about to happen. I felt Detective Nichols watching me as I watched myself look up at the security camera in the corner of the elevator, aim my wrist at it, and then obliterate it with Silly String. The screen went black.

Chapter 7

MY ACTIONS REQUIRED an explanation. Unfortunately the truth wasn't going to help me very much. "One of the things we like to do at Disguise DeLimit is to give our costumes something special. Sometimes it's a prop, sometimes it's a trick. Like this," I said, reaching inside my suit jacket for my flask. Detective Nichols dropped her hands to her hips. I set the flask on the table. She moved her eyes to it and back to me. Her hand hovered by her holster. I unscrewed the cap. "It's a blueberry and banana smoothie," I said. "But it goes with my costume." I waved the flask in front of her, hoping the scent would diffuse the situation.

"What does this have to do with you sabotaging security equipment on a piece of private property?"

"I was dressed as a spider. You saw my costume. My secret was that I had cans of Silly String strapped to my wrists. I constructed a system where I could flex my hands and a plastic rod that ran the length of my palm would hit the button on the can and string would shoot out. Like I was making a web. And when I saw the camera, I just— I thought it was funny."

"Funny."

"I don't know what came over me," I said. "But the Alexandria Hotel has been abandoned forever. It's a historical landmark, or at least it will be soon. The Clark County Conservancy has been petitioning for landmark status for the past six months."

"The Alexandria Hotel was purchased by Mr. Haverford last week. Last night's party was funded by his venture capital company."

"Proper City Halloween parties are funded by the city," I said. "They always have been. That's why everybody wants to get involved."

"I'm afraid those times are over, Ms. Tamblyn. Last night was a showcase for Mr. Haverford's recent acquisitions. Every business there was on his payroll."

"Except for me." I tucked my flask back into my pocket, fighting the urge to take a hit first. Even if it was only a blueberry smoothie, it would help. I'd heard that blueberries were the superhero of antioxidants, and I could use a little superhero boost right now. "Do you have any other questions for me?"

"Not right now. Ms. Tamblyn, I want to be very clear about one thing. A man is dead, and your actions appear suspicious. If you are hiding something, I will find out." She looked at the DVD player and then back at me.

Just as well that I hadn't taken a hit from the flask. I'm pretty sure it would have come back up.

I drove back to the shop, the general feeling of nausea sticking with me. I needed a quiet place to sit and think, but there was no time for quiet sitting and thinking. I was late getting back to the store before opening, and I could already see people outside and a crowd inside. And lots of . . . yellow heads?

I parked my scooter in back of the store and raced inside to see what was going on.

Kirby stopped me as soon as I entered the back door. "I'm sorry. I didn't know what else to do. There were so many of them, and they all wanted something different. There was no way I could run the store by myself, not with this mob. I needed help."

I tried to look around him, but he kept shifting from side to side to block my view. "Kirby, who did you call?"

"My swim coach."

That didn't sound so bad. "That's it? You and your coach have been handling the store? Remind me to give him a discount to say thank you."

"No, you don't understand. My coach couldn't leave school. He's also the algebra teacher and the faculty is finalizing next semester's classes. He made arrangements for the team to help out."

"The swim team?"

Kirby nodded. "Before you get upset, I want you to know that they're taking this very seriously. Even with things as crazy as they were, they all showed up in costumes."

I couldn't take it anymore. I pushed past Kirby and went into the shop. Dotting the store were high school guys in yellow swim caps and white sheets draped around their shoulders.

"What are they supposed to be?"

"Eggs. Sunny-side up." His face turned beet red. "It's the best I could come up with on short notice."

"You did a good job. Come on, there's a line forming by the register."

Together we went to the front of the store. Kirby took a yellow swim cap out of his pocket and pulled it on, and then wrapped a white sheet over his shoulders and secured it with a safety pin. The woman in the front of the line handed him an assortment of prepackaged wigs in neon shades and a credit card. He handled the transaction quickly and moved on to the women behind her. I didn't have to worry about the register with Kirby back there. He was a pro.

THE last-minute Halloween customers kept me from thinking about my morning. If news of our disqualification from the costume competition had spread—or if it was even still valid in light of Paul Haverford's murder—sales didn't show it. We rented several alien costumes, the entire cast of *The Wizard of Oz*, and assembled the complete cast of *Gilligan's Island* for the library staff. In addition to the various zombie, ghost, and Dracula costumes, we sold over a dozen fog machines and the juice to go with them. There were only two left on the shelf, which meant it would be a night of restocking from the back room before we opened our doors tomorrow.

After the last customer left, Kirby locked the door and leaned against it. All around the room, members of the swim team sat on chairs, benches, and even the floor. It seemed a day in the store had taken more out of them than they'd expected. I scanned their faces, not sure how to say thank you. Kirby appeared next to me. "Pizza," he said.

"Pizza?" I repeated.

Several of the guys looked up. "Did you say pizza?" one asked.

"I could totally go for some pizza."

"Dude, me too."

"Okay. Pizza." I turned to Kirby. "How many?"

"More than you think."

I went to the register and handed him a hundred-dollar bill. He blinked at me. I handed him another and he tucked both into his pocket. I caught myself before asking for change and a receipt. They'd given me far more than two-hundred-dollars' worth of labor.

I left the guys to hash out their topping choices and stepped into the office to check my phone. Three missed calls: Ebony, Dad, and Private Number.

I called my dad back first. "Where are you?"

"Chicago."

"Chicago! You were supposed to connect in Arizona. What are you doing in Chicago?"

"Freezing." He sneezed twice. "I've seen more snow in the past two days than I've seen in my whole life."

"Are you wearing a hat and gloves?" I asked.

"Yes, Mom," he said.

I couldn't say exactly when the shift happened, but I knew it had something to do with his heart attack last April. Until that moment, dad had been the dad and I'd been the daughter. But then that phone call had come. I'd been in the middle of Magic Maynard's act, the trick where I was supposedly trapped inside of a heavily chained and padlocked trunk. In reality, I'd dropped out of a trap door below the trunk and waited backstage for the final reveal. One of the stage hands took a call and handed me the phone. *"Margo, your dad's had a heart attack. Come home as soon as you can."*

I'd screamed, and then dropped the phone. Considering my scream had come from backstage and not the locked trunk, we'd ended up refunding the audience's money. Maynard hadn't said a word about it, and I took off for Proper City in the morning.

It was touch and go there for a while. I took as much time off as Maynard allowed and spent my days helping around the shop while my dad recovered. And just like that, we'd fallen into a new routine. Him trying to get away with anything he could—from taking off for Area 51 to scope out alien costumes, being among his first unexpected road trips, to sneaking bacon when I wasn't looking. He'd realized how little he'd experienced in life after my mother had died, and I realized how alone I'd be without him. It came down to the fact that I was more afraid of him dying than he was.

We chatted a bit more, moving on from the weather to important things like the costumes he'd purchased in New York. It seems he'd befriended the costume designer of an off-Broadway, unsanctioned spinoff of *Cats* (*Wild Cats*) and persuaded her to give up their early costumes. I wondered if Soot would give them the meow of approval.

Before we said good-bye, Dad's tone turned serious. "Margo, I want you to know that I'm proud of you. Running a store is a challenge, but running a costume shop the week before Halloween is different."

My heart sank into a pit in my stomach. I didn't deserve his praise and almost said so, but then remembered something one of the security guards at Caesars Palace had told me. People will treat you the way you let them treat you. I knew Dad would always treat me like his daughter, but I liked how it felt when he treated me like a businesswoman too.

"Thanks, Dad," I said. "I'm doing the best I can."

I returned Ebony's call next. "It's Margo," I said. "You rang?"

"You are not gonna believe this," she said. "Are you sitting down? You better sit down. I better sit down. I can't sit down. I don't have time to sit down!"

"Ebony? What's wrong? You sound a little, um, crazy."

"I'd have to be crazy, wouldn't I? This is it. This is how they're going to get me. Hold on," she said. She let out a loud scream.

I pulled the phone away from my head until the scream subsided. "Ebony? Ebony!"

"Primal scream therapy. It's the only thing to deal with stress. That and lemon oil in my tea."

"If you don't give me a straight answer about what is

going on by the time I count to five, I'm calling the police
and sending them to your store. One, two, three—"

"They put me in charge of finding a new location for
Halloween."

"—four, what did you say?"

"The planning committee. They called this morning
and said I'd been selected unanimously to find a new location for the Proper City Halloween Festivities this year
now that the Alexandria Hotel is out."

"That's not so bad. You're a party planner. Think of the
publicity you'll get for Shindig."

"No good is going to come from stirring up the spirit
world. They'll never leave! I don't want the undead in my
business. And that's what I got. The undead. In my
business."

"They're coming to get you, Ebony," I said in my creep-
iest *Night of the Living Dead* voice.

"Don't ever do that again."

I laughed. "You'll be fine. I'll ask around and see if I
can help. And if you see anybody from the spirit world
who needs a costume, send them my way."

After hanging up, I plugged my phone in to charge and
left it on the desk. Almost immediately, a text popped up
from Private Number. *Flat tire, 2 blocks east of restaurant,
10–15 min*, it said. It was code.

I went out front to check on the swim team. The yellow
caps and white sheets had come off, and the guys were
scattered around the store talking and laughing. I pulled
Kirby away from his group. "Do you think any of them
will be able to come back tomorrow? I can offer them a
twenty percent discount good through November."

"Sure, but, Margo? We're trying to raise money for new
track suits. Do you think instead of the discount, you could
make a donation to our fund?"

"I can do that. Are you— Can you— Will you arrange for different costumes?"

"I already have an idea." He smiled. "Even better than the eggs."

Kirby rejoined his teammates and I headed out back for my scooter. It had turned chilly when the sun went down, so I ducked back inside for a long black topcoat, and then left a second time and headed to the rendezvous point.

When Tak texted me, he hadn't said which one of us was supposed to have the flat tire. I arrived on the scene first, so I figured that meant it was me. I hopped off and put the Vespa on its kickstand, and then loosened the valve stem cover and held my key against the center until enough air leaked out to make me not look like a liar. Once again, I'd forgotten gloves, and my fingers quickly grew red and raw. I stood up and balled them into fists and plunged them deep into the pockets of my coat. It was after eight and the road was dark except for the streetlamps that lined it. Few cars were on the road. The longer I waited, the more I regretted letting air out of my tire for believability. This might not have been the best time to become a method actor.

An approaching SUV slowed its pace. It was too dark to recognize Tak's RAV4, but I relaxed slightly. The car's blinker went on, and it pulled over behind me. It wasn't Tak. It was a blue Ford Explorer.

The driver's side opened and an attractive man in a brown leather bomber jacket and crisp jeans got out. He had straight brown hair, neatly trimmed, and glasses that, with a piece of tape in the middle, would have worked well with our scientist costume. As it was, they were just regular glasses that had a slightly geeky quality.

"Is everything okay here?" he asked.

"Flat tire," I said, pointing an elbow at the scooter. "Someone's on their way."

He looked behind him at the empty road. "Someone better get here fast or you're going to turn into a popsicle."

I couldn't help laughing. It couldn't have been cooler than sixty degrees.

"Tell you what. I have a can of Fix-A-Flat in the back of my truck. How 'bout I take care of your tire? I haven't done any good deeds yet today."

I pulled my hands out of my pockets and rubbed them together. I looked up and down the street but saw no signs of another car. "Sure, okay," I said.

"Great." He went to the back of his SUV and returned with a small can. "I'm Cooper, by the way. Cooper Price."

"Margo Tamblyn." I held out my hand.

The second he touched me, he dropped the can and sandwiched his own hands around mine, rubbing back and forth. "The tire can wait," he said. "Let's warm you up first."

It was a little weird having a stranger warming my hands on the side of the street, but it felt too nice to stop him.

"Cute little scooter you have," he said. "These roads are pretty well maintained. Do you think you ran over a nail?"

"There's been some construction in front of my costume shop. If it's not a nail, then it might be a slow leak."

"Costume shop? Is that why you're dressed up?"

I looked down at my gangster outfit. "I'm not dressed up. What's wrong with what I'm wearing?"

"It's—nothing. It's unique." Cooper walked around the side of the scooter and squeezed the front and back tires. "Cross your fingers for a slow leak. That's easy to fix." He pulled a pair of leather gloves from his pockets and handed them to me. "Wear these while I take care of this."

I pulled the gloves on and looked up the street. A set of headlights was headed our way. Cooper had the can of Fix-A-Flat attached to the valve stem already, and the scooter visibly lifted as the tire inflated. The headlights—attached to a gray RAV4—pulled over and parked behind Cooper's truck. Tak hopped out.

"What are you doing here?" he asked.

"You said—" I stumbled around, looking for the right thing to say. "Flat tire," I finished. "This is Cooper. He's helping me out."

Tak looked past me. "Coop?"

The man stood up. "Hoshi? What are you doing, following me?"

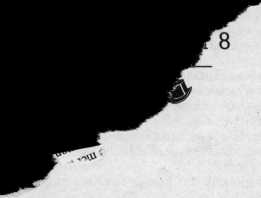

"YOU TWO KNOW each other?" I asked. I looked back and forth between them. They were about the same age, same height, same build. Tak had the strong Asian features he'd inherited from his Japanese father. Cooper was more boy-next-door turned adult. The kind of guy you might not notice in high school who turns out to be a real heart-breaker in his twenties. I had a feeling neither one of them had trouble getting dates.

As I thought the word *date*, I felt Tak's eyes on me. Ever since we'd met, he'd had an uncanny knack for reading my mind. I flushed for a moment.

"This is Tak Hoshiyama. He used to work in the Clark County Planning Office with me," Coop said. "Tak, this is Margo."

A smile toyed at the corners of my mouth, but I didn't say anything. Cooper finished with the tire and stood up. "All fixed, Margo." He capped the can and handed it to me. "Keep this. If it is a slow leak, you might need it."

"Thank you." I took the can. Cooper reached out for

as yo

"We can pac
you a ride home," re

Cooper looked at
other?"

It was the same question
and I looked at each other.

"We've met," we both answ
suspicious at all.

Cooper laughed. "I see. Well, now we've
said to me, and smiled. He looked at Tak. "Hey, ma
want to grab a beer?"

Tak shook his head. "No, I should be getting back to
the restaurant."

"Okay. Nice meeting you, Margo. Keep an eye on that
tire." Cooper climbed into his truck and waved as he drove
away.

Tak pulled a pair of gloves out of the pocket of his coat.
"You left these at the restaurant last week. I meant to give
them to you this morning and I forgot."

"You should have given them to me when your friend
was here. Now he doesn't have any gloves."

"I thought it would blow our cover."

I traded Cooper's gloves for my own. "Do you want to
give these back to him?"

"Not sure how I'd explain things." He looked at me for
a moment, and then stepped closer and kissed me. It was
turning out to be a good day for affection. "Let me take a
look at that tire," he said.

"The tire's fine, Tak. I only let enough air out of it to
make it look good in case anybody actually checked it.
Which turned out to be a good idea."

"You could have told him help was coming."

"I did. He wanted to hel—
"Wha̶t like Coop."
Tak stood ̶o̶r̶ ̶
̶e̶'s st̶

"Doing the same
approving petitions, tha̶

"Mostly. There was sol̶̶̶ ̶lk a̶b̶
positions into utilities, reside̶̶̶t̶, and busi̶̶ ̶ere
was no way to control the workloa̶ that way. We j̶ each
took whatever came in when we had the time to manage it."

"Why did he say you were following him?"

"That's where I was when I texted you."

"The district attorney's office?"

"The planning division. I wanted to find out a little
more about Paul Haverford's plan to take over Proper City."

"You don't really care about that, do you?"

"No, but you do." His expression softened. "Actually, I
do care about it. For years I was on the other side of situations like this. Filling out the paperwork, checking the
reports on the condition of the land and whether or not it
was suitable for the proposed project, approving the building permits, all that kind of stuff. I never thought about
the implications my job had on the community where the
project was to take place. This time I'm on the other side.
I'm a resident, and I can see firsthand what might happen.
So I guess I didn't do it just for you."

"Still, I appreciate the thought."

A pizza delivery van rumbled past us. *Cheesus Crust*
was painted on the side. Kirby swore they made the best
pizza in Proper, which probably wasn't too difficult considering they might be the only one. Soon, Disguise
DeLimit would smell like tomato sauce and cheese. I
hoped Kirby had ordered enough that there would be some
left over for me when I returned.

DIANE VALLERE

"Can we sit in your truck for a little?" I asked.

"No, I really do have to get to the restaurant. The rice supplier didn't make his scheduled delivery and I've got fifty pounds in the back in case of

"Rice Emergency—now there's as much as I liked

We headed our separate ways was no doubt that I ending time with Tak—and —I couldn't deny that was a poor excuse for a relationship. I saw the way other women looked at him, and the insecure part of me, the part that kept track of my personal life in a journal on my nightstand and talked through big, life-changing issues with my cat, wondered if maybe there was another reason he didn't want to tell everybody we were a couple. I shook off those nagging thoughts and arrived home to sixteen empty pizza boxes.

Looked like it would be a dinner of Fruity Pebbles for me.

Wednesday

The next morning, I woke filled with curiosity. I wanted to see the Alexandria Hotel in broad daylight. The air was crisp and dry, but according to the weather report, we were headed for a high in the eighties. Proper City was a desert town, just east of the California border and surrounded by mountains. We didn't have to contend with the sleet, snow, or rain of the states east of us. What we had to worry about were earthquakes. They were infrequent enough that, when a tremor was felt, most of us needed a few seconds to realize what was going on at first. The more likely scenarios were the ones when I came home and found the paintings all hanging at odd angles.

There was no point in drawing unnecessary attention to myself, so I dressed in a khaki forest ranger uniform and tucked a matching baseball hat in my back pocket. Thick CAT boots finished the look.

I blended up a banana, vanilla yogurt, almond milk, and a handful of peanuts and chugged most of the resulting smoothie. Soot meowed and I slid my finger through the mixture and held it out for him to lick. He cleaned it and meowed again. I found an empty bowl and poured an inch of smoothie into it and set it on the floor. The cat food went ignored while he buried his head. When he looked up, traces of smoothie remained on his nose. His pink tongue shot out and swiped at his nose, leaving him clean. I reached down to scratch his fur and then grabbed my keys and left.

When the planners of Proper sketched out the community of their dreams in the '50s, they created a series of small clusters of houses and businesses connected by one long main road. As more families moved here, off-shoots from the main road were created, paved, and named. Sometime in the '80s, the city council had voted for public transportation, and the Zip lines were started. They were repurposed yellow school buses driven by retir-ees around town, and if you understood the routes each of them drove, you could get from any spot in Proper to any other spot in Proper in just under an hour.

I took the Zip-Two for three miles, and then changed to the Zip-Three. It let me off two blocks from the Alex-andria Hotel. I walked the rest of the way. Despite the weather report, it wasn't warm yet, and I welcomed the exercise to get my blood pumping.

The Alexandria looked less scary in the daylight. I'd read a little of its history when the Halloween party was first announced. Built in the Rococo style that had been popular in the early 1900s, it housed twelve floors and a ballroom with a magnificent chandelier. Although Pete Proper, our city's founder, had renounced alcohol when he struck gold, there was an oak bar and restaurant inside, serving the social and political elite. After Pete's death, like much of Proper, the hotel's clientele shifted. Scofflaws and vagabonds, seeking refuge from the laws in California, migrated our way and took up residency. Bootleggers used the hotel as a base of operations, and gambling soon followed. It wasn't until the city planners took over Proper City that the hotel was cleaned up and retrofitted with an elevator. That was in the late '40s.

Today I could see the disrepair more clearly than during the party. The Alexandria was a mere shadow of its once glamorous self. Once-white fire escapes were now covered with rust. Paint peeled away from window casings. The stone façade was dingy with water stains and the general shade of brown that comes with decades of dust imbedding into the brick. Patches of brown grass grew here and there, but mostly the grounds surrounding the hotel were dry brown dirt.

A hybrid hatchback with *NSS* on the side was parked in the lot. A woman was on her hands and knees by the foundation of the building. Her hair was gray from the roots to about halfway down the length, where it turned to blond. It was parted in the center and tucked behind her ears, though long enough that it still dangled down on either side of her head. Small round glasses sat at the end of her nose. Her outfit, camouflage trousers and an olive green T-shirt, could have come from the ROTC section of the costume shop.

She held what looked like a remote control with a small screen in one hand and a large tape measure reel attached to a black handle with the other. Equipment was scattered by her feet. "Hold this," she said. I looked around for another person. She turned her head to me. "You. Come here and hold this."

I approached her and took the end of a large measuring tape. "Don't move." She turned and walked away with the handle of the tape measure reel in her hand. The yellow metal ruler spooled out of the device and bowed in the center. She rounded the corner of the building and, as I guessed from the tension on the measuring tape, kept walking.

The equipment on the ground gave few clues as to what she was doing. An empty blue plastic case like the one my power drill came in sat open. Gray foam filled the interior, with spaces cut out where equipment would nestle. The lid of the case was filled with wavy gray foam shaped like an egg crate. Whatever had been inside must have been fragile. Another similar case, this one black, sat on top of an amplifier. I was leaning closer to raise the lid of the case and peek inside, when the woman returned.

I stood up quickly, expecting her to accuse me of snooping (because I was) or to ask why I was there (because I was thinking the same thing about her). She did neither. She pulled a small notebook out of her pocket, checked the measurement on the tape, and made some notes on it—the notebook, not the tape measure.

"Hand me the level," she said next. I recognized it among the odd assortment of items and held it out. She approached the building and held it up by a horizontal mortar joint. "This is worse than I thought. Come here and tell me if I'm reading this right."

"I think you may have confused me with someone else. I'm not familiar with this type of equipment and I'm not sure what it is you're looking for."

She looked at me over the top of her glasses. "You've read a level before, haven't you?"

"Yes."

"Okay, then. Come here and tell me what you see."

I went to her side and she handed me the yellow plastic level. I lined it up with a horizontal mortar joint. I didn't need to bother looking at the small bubble inside the level to see that it was on an angle. "The building isn't straight," I said. "But that can't be too much of a surprise, can it? Buildings settle."

"I've been monitoring this building for the past forty years. Any settling would have happened a long time ago when the building was inhabited. There's been no change for decades. And now the east corner is two inches lower than the west corner. Do you know what that means?"

"Not exactly," I said.

"Seismic activity!" she proclaimed. "Pete Proper left us a real keg of dynamite when he died."

"What do you mean?"

"There are active fault lines under this entire end of Proper City. If Havetown is built, the construction might trigger an earthquake. If we're not careful, Proper City will implode."

I glanced at the equipment on the ground. "Why here? Why now?"

She stood straight and pushed her glasses farther up the bridge of her nose. She focused on me as if fully noticing me for the first time. "Those are the questions the Clark County Conservancy should have been asking. You're not with them, are you?"

"No, ma'am. I'm just a concerned citizen."

She glanced at my forest ranger uniform. "That's too bad. The conservancy could use a smart woman like you."

"Are you working for them?"

She threw her head back and laughed out loud, as if I'd said something much funnier than I had. "Am I with a nonprofit? Heck no. Those people want to save buildings. I want to save lives." She tucked her remote control thingy (technical term) under her arm and held out her hand. "Francine Wheeler. Seismologist."

"Margo Tamblyn," I said, returning the handshake and leaving off "costumer" as my credentials. "If you don't mind my asking, what is all this?" With a sweeping gesture, I indicated the various items she had scattered in the brown grass.

"My equipment." She looked at the remote control, whacked it against her palm twice, flipped it over, and clicked a small black switch back and forth.

"What's that?"

"Field balancer. It senses vibrations and indicates sub-terranean activity." She checked the small screen, pressed a few buttons, and then tossed it onto the gray foam interior of the blue plastic case. "Batteries must be dead."

Before I could get back to those very good questions I'd been asking, she dropped down to her knees, put a stethoscope on, and pressed it to the ground. She moved the end a few times, and then pushed herself to a squatting position. "Things have quieted down since last night."

"You ran tests here last night?"

"I had to. All those people here for a party in a building that isn't structurally sound. It's one thing for it to become a historical landmark. People respect a historical land-mark. But no, Haverford wanted to get a bunch of people out here so he could take pictures to use in his sales bro-chures for Havetown."

The way she spoke about Paul Haverford made me uncomfortable. Whether or not she knew she was speaking ill of the dead, I didn't know, and thought it best to find out. "Paul Haverford was murdered two nights ago."

"A bit of irony, don't you think? The devil killed in his own lair." She shook her head. "It's almost poetic."

Chapter 9

I WAS STUNNED by Francine's response. She didn't seem to notice. She picked up the blue plastic case, fit the vibration analyzer and accompanying cord into their respective cutout spaces in the gray foam, and then clicked the case shut. "Watch my equipment, will you?"

I nodded. She walked to the other side of the building. As soon as she disappeared, I slipped her business card out of the plastic window on the black plastic case and pushed it deep into the pocket of my khaki trousers. Francine came back seconds later with a cart. She stacked it with the amp, the two plastic cases, and a tote bag filled with miscellaneous tools and cords.

"Have you finished all of your tests?" I asked.

"For now. I've been given a temporary reprieve, but not for long. There's much work to be done." She grabbed the cart and pulled it toward the car in the parking lot. I waited until she drove away before looking at her card. *Francine Wheeler, Lead Seismologist, Nevada Bureau of Mines and Seismic Activity.* Her title was followed by an address, website, e-mail, and phone number. I moved the card to a different pocket that had a flap and a button to keep it secure, and then walked to the front of the building to get a closer look inside.

The party two nights ago had ended before it had gotten started, and it appeared that everything had been left as is. Large aluminum containers sat on either side of the front door, filled with pools of water. The dry ice, I remembered. Someone must have had the task of dropping a piece into the water every fifteen minutes or so to keep the illusion of fog going. I looked inside the bin to the right of the door. Pieces of candy corn floated on top. A scattering of cigarette butts had sunk to the bottom. The water in the bin on the left side of the door was completely clear.

In the light of day, everything that made the Alexandria Hotel the perfect spot for a Halloween party now made it look like a sad, old, forgotten building. If the Clark County Conservancy was successful in their petition to turn it into a historical landmark, would someone come along and return it back to its former glory? Or would it simply be awarded a plaque that mentioned what the building had meant to Proper back in the day?

I was getting distracted. I wasn't here to consider the future of the building; I was here to find clues to the murder the other night. It was after ten, and it would take half an hour to get back to the shop if the Zips were on schedule. As much as I wanted to poke around more, the store came first. I walked the circumference of the building, pausing to look up at the fire escape where I'd seen Spider-Man. The curtains moved by the window. I was startled, until I realized it had been the result of the breeze, just like the other night.

Out of time, I left the hotel and headed toward the Zip-Three stop. Something was bothering me, but I couldn't figure out what it was. I lost myself in thought all the way through my bus transfer and almost missed my stop.

I exited the Zip-Three with a preppy teenager in a black cardigan and pants, white shirt, and thin black necktie. He kept his head down and stopped by the bus station, but as soon as I crossed the street, I heard him follow me. The bill of the hat on my head obstructed my view, but I knew he was there. I turned left at the corner and so did he. Another guy dressed in the same outfit stood inside a recessed doorway, playing with his phone. He didn't look up when I passed, but a few steps later, I stole a glance behind me. The two of them were side by side.

A third guy jogged across the street. I felt like Tippi Hedren in *The Birds*, only instead of birds, I was picking up a tail of teenage boys. It wasn't until I saw Kirby in front of the store in the same outfit that I realized I was being followed by the swim team.

"Hi, Margo," Kirby said. "Don't worry, it's all under control." He held a stack of round patches edged in black with orange words on it. He handed one to each of the boys, who attached it to their cardigans on the left side.

"What is this?" I asked.

Two of the guys looked up at me. "We're the Geek Squad," one said while another adjusted his necktie.

I scanned the group of them and then looked back at Kirby. "Your idea?"

He nodded. "I thought of it last month after my hard drive crashed."

"Yeah," one of the guys said. "I used to think computer lab was for nerds, but those guys are gonna rule the world some day." A chorus of agreement and general praise for the Geek Squad was uttered.

The swim team followed me inside. Kirby gave them assignments for who would work where, and I opened the register and carried a sandwich-board sign out front. Customers started arriving almost immediately, and for the next seven hours all thoughts of Paul Haverford and the Alexandria Hotel were pushed out of my mind.

There was no sneaking away or on-the-side sleuthing to be conducted during store hours. We were so busy that, even with the help of the swim team, we could barely keep up with demand. The mannequins in the widow were changed three times—from Dracula and Jonathan Harker to Little Red Riding Hood and the Big Bad Wolf back to Dr. Frankenstein and his monster. It was a good day for couples costumes. Mr. Smythe, Kirby's chemistry teacher, came in for a fitting for his lab rat costume and arranged to have it delivered the day before Halloween. Cutting it close, but it would be done.

After we closed the store, the guys wandered out front. Neckties were loosened and masking-taped glasses were tucked into pockets. It was like watching the transformation from Clark Kent to Superman (multiplied). Kirby closed the register and moved the money to the safe, and I brought the sandwich board inside and locked the front door. Five days to go.

Once the boys were gone, I called my dad and left a message. "Hi, Dad, it's Margo. Hopefully you caught a flight out of Chicago. The store's doing really well, and I think we need to give Kirby a raise. See you soon."

I opened the door to the apartment and Soot wandered downstairs. I ate a bowl of cereal and thought back over my conversation with the seismologist. Had that really only been this morning? She'd been so indignant, so angry about what Haverford was trying to do with the Alexandria Hotel, but I hadn't gotten a sense of concern for future residents. It had felt more like she'd been doing battle with him and was happy that her opponent had been eliminated from the competition. There had been no remorse.

I'd been surprised by how easily she'd accepted my

presence at the hotel. My outfit most likely was responsible for that, but I hadn't claimed to work for any official organization. Khaki had a language all of its own.

I lowered myself onto the steps. Soot rubbed his back against my shins, and then he wandered into the store and I lost sight of him. It wasn't until now, when the store was silent and I was able to relax, that I realized Francine had avoided my questions. What was it she'd said? *"Those are the questions the Clark County Conservancy should have been asking. You're not with them, are you?"*

I went to the office and looked up the Clark County Conservancy on the web. They had a poorly designed website that must have been maintained by a volunteer. The front page had details about a teddy bear fund-raiser. That could only mean one thing: Bobbie was involved.

Bobbie ran a nonprofit called Money Changes Everything. A one-woman force of nature, she had first started raising money by crafting and selling teddy bears. Bobbie Bears, as they were now called, had become so popular that Bobbie had decided to spread the wealth, partnering with local charities on fund-raisers. Her bears had become known as a symbol of generosity, and if I were the gambling type, I'd place even money on the fact that one of her bears was in every home in Proper.

The rest of the Clark County Conservancy website was outdated, listing events that had happened over the past year on their Upcoming Events page. The Contact page simply had a form—no e-mails, no phone numbers. Instead of bothering with the form, I called Bobbie.

"Who can you introduce me to at the Clark County Conservancy?"

"Well, hello to you too."

"Hi. Sorry. It's been a day and a half at the costume shop and I'm still running at top speed."

"You need to learn to slow down. Relax. You need an outlet for all of this pre-Halloween stress."

"As long as we don't run out of energy drinks, I'll be fine."

"Margo, that's a crutch, that's not a solution."

Bobbie knew of which she spoke. Years ago when she was on the rise as a young entrepreneur in Proper City, gaining notice and job offers from Fortune 500 companies, she'd turned to diet pills and caffeine powder to keep her going. A subsequent addiction led her to check herself into a treatment center. That's when she got the idea to start her own nonprofit. She turned down every job offer that was extended to her, developed an early-morning yoga routine to manage stress, and took up with the bears.

I knew she was right. Running the store had added a new level of anxiety to my life. With my ongoing guilt over my mom dying in childbirth and concern for my dad's health post–heart attack coupled with my secret relationship with Tak and the murder of Paul Haverford, I was about to hit overload. "What do you suggest?"

"Come to my yoga class tomorrow morning. Six a.m. We meet at the PCP."

"Six in the morning?"

"Trust me. You won't believe how pretty Proper City is when the sun comes up. Now, about your other question— are you free for dinner?"

FORTY-FIVE minutes later I arrived at Catch-22, the local seafood restaurant. They served one type of fish every day and offered twenty-two different ways to order it. Considering we were in the middle of the desert, we all knew the catch of the day had been flash frozen and delivered by truck, but nobody seemed to care. It was among the more popular restaurants in town, as witnessed by the line of people waiting for a table. Bobbie waved to me from a booth, where she sat with another woman. I bypassed the hostess station and joined them.

"Margo, what a surprise. Are you meeting someone here?" Bobbie asked exactly as we'd rehearsed. Somehow it sounded more fake than I'd expected.

"No, I'm here all alone."

"Why don't you join us?" She turned to the woman with her. "This is Annette Crowley from the Clark County Conservancy. We were just discussing the Alexandria Hotel."

"No, Bobbie, you were discussing the Alexandria Hotel. I have nothing more to say about it. The Alexandria is no longer an issue for the conservancy." Annette pushed her cup of coffee away from her and crossed her arms.

Annette Crowley was a woman born in the wrong decade. She wore her bangs so short they were about an inch long, leaving plenty of forehead exposed above her arched and penciled eyebrows. She'd pulled the rest of her dark hair back into a tight ponytail that was just a stub. Crayola red lips and pointy cat-eye glasses completed her look.

Bobbie turned to me. "Annette's been petitioning for the hotel to be named a historical property, which would save it from being torn down or renovated too far from its original design."

"That sounds interesting," I said to Annette. "I've seen the interior of the Alexandria Hotel. It's rundown, but it could really be spectacular if it were restored. Is that something the conservancy is trying to accomplish?"

"My job is to get the buildings placed on the historical registry. Once they're recognized, they're legally protected from greedy developers."

"Like Paul Haverford?" I asked.

She tipped her head and eyed me out of the side of her

glasses. "Paul Haverford was the worst of them all. He had deep pockets and bought votes from the city council. Of course, all the money in the world won't help him now." She took a sip of her coffee. "That's why the Alexandria Hotel is no longer an issue."

Chapter 10

ANNETTE CONTINUED. "PAUL Haverford was behind the plans to destroy the Alexandria Hotel in the first place. No more Haverford, no more problems. Our paperwork has already been submitted to the state registry for historical properties. Once the application is green-lighted, the issue will be moot. I expect to have an answer by the end of the month. I never knew it would be so easy to eliminate the competition." She let out a low, throaty laugh.

For a moment, I was stunned silent. Even though I'd had my own less-than-pleasant run-in with the venture capitalist, I knew there was a lot of territory between not liking the man and laughing over his murder.

As I searched for the best way to follow up her pronouncement, Annette changed the subject. "Bobbie, I don't think tonight is the best time to discuss a fund-raiser for the conservancy after all. Call my office tomorrow and have the boy set up a new appointment." She slid herself out of her side of the booth and left.

"Do you believe the nerve of that woman?" Bobbie said.

"If you learn nothing else from me, learn this. Do not set up a meeting with a nonprofit at a restaurant. It's like a game of who can leave first and stick the other person with the bill."

I stood up and switched seats so I was sitting across from Bobbie. "That can't be the only thing bothering you about that meeting, can it? The woman practically admitted that she murdered Paul Haverford."

"No she didn't," Bobbie said, waving her hand in front of me. "She wasn't talking about the murder; she was talking about the lawsuit."

"What lawsuit?"

"I thought you knew. Paul's company was being sued for two-point-five-million dollars. Something about an injunction over a building permit."

I waved the waitress over and ordered clams casino. Bobbie ordered pasta in clam sauce. I waited until she left—the waitress, not Bobbie—before resuming the conversation. "Legal injunction over his building development plan. What does that mean?"

"I'm not clear on the details, but from what I've heard, he planned a development in Proper called Havetown."

"Francine Wheeler mentioned Havetown. What is it?"

"It's a new development. That's why he bought up all of that desert at the far west end of the state, and why he wanted to bulldoze the Alexandria. That's where it was going to be."

"But somebody took legal measures to stop him from proceeding," I said. "And since he already had money in the property, if he didn't find a way to do something with it, he was going to lose a bundle."

"Not only him, but his whole team of investors. It seems that he jumped the gun and bought the land before knowing that his plans would be approved."

"Why would he do that? Seems risky."

"You don't get to be that rich by playing things safe. This probably wasn't the first 'Havetown' he's planned, and he expected everything to go through. You know who could probably tell you more about how this works? Tak Hoshiyama. This is a perfect excuse to call him. You know you want to."

"Come on, don't start with me too," I said.

"What? You two seemed to have some kind of connection when you came back to Proper. What happened?"

"Nothing happened," I said. I felt heat climb my neck and flush my face.

"You're hiding something."

"I don't know what you're talking about."

"Fine. But speaking for myself, I know practically everybody in Proper. So it's exciting, you know, you move back, and I know you from when we grew up, and then Tak moves here, and I know him from when his family opened the Kobe Steak House, but you and Tak don't know each other, so, you know, it's fun to watch."

"I'm glad I can entertain you," I said sourly.

"I'm kidding! Sort of," she added.

I dipped my fingers into my water and flicked them at her. She shielded the spray and flicked her water back at me, and within seconds we were giggling like fourth graders. Our food came and we tried to collect ourselves and act like adults for the rest of the meal. We were only intermittently successful.

I waited until Bobbie was on her way before pulling my phone out and calling Tak. It had been hard not telling her that he and I were secretly seeing each other. And truthfully, I wanted to confide in her. She was my best friend, and it had been a long time since I felt this way. But since returning to Proper, I'd been assaulted with a whole lot of togetherness with every person I knew. Before I got caught up in doing something for everybody else, I wanted to keep this as something just for me. The very thought triggered feelings of guilt. Under normal circumstances, I would have texted Tak, but I had a good cover story, and besides, I wanted to hear his voice.

"Hello?"

"Hi, Tak, it's Margo Tamblyn, from Disguise DeLimit."

He hesitated a moment. "Hi, Margo."

"Did I catch you at a bad time?"

"No, just a second. I'll be right back," he said, presumably not to me. A few moments later, he spoke. "First we have a clandestine meeting at your store, now you're calling me during normal hours. Next thing you know, you're going to ask me to be seen with you in public."

"I trust you can speak freely?" I asked.

"Sometimes I can't tell if we're dating or if we're practicing to be government spies."

"Tak, this is serious."

"Oh, right. You wouldn't have called me otherwise. What's up?"

"Do you know anything about a legal injunction against Havetown, the development Paul Haverford was working on?"

"I heard something about it when I worked at the planning office, but I left before a decision was made. Why?"

"I think it might have something to do with why he was murdered."

He was quiet for a moment. I braced myself for the inevitable "stay out of it," but it didn't come. Instead, he said, "Why don't you come to the restaurant for dinner? It's a slow night and we might be able to talk."

"I just had dinner with Bobbie," I said.

"So, no room for fried rice?"

"There's always room for fried rice," I said, "but I

should probably get back to the costume shop and get things ready for tomorrow. It's T-minus five days until Halloween, and that usually involves a couple of unexpected crises."

"Okay," he said. "I guess we've used up the flat tire excuse, huh?"

"If I complain about any more flat tires, there's going to be a special committee appointed to road maintenance."

He chuckled. "Gotcha. Hey, Margo?"

"Yes?"

"I'm glad you called."

After hanging up, I stood in the parking lot and stared at the phone. I knew what Tak had meant. This was a poor excuse for the getting-to-know-you stage of a relationship. A part of me wondered if there was another reason he was so willing to keep things quiet? He'd been at the restaurant when I called. Had his dad been around? What would he think if he found out the truth? Would he disapprove—and would that matter to Tak?

I drove back to Disguise DeLimit and parked in the small lot behind the store. The back door was open. Kirby would have known better than to leave it unlocked. I went on high alert and crept inside slowly. As I tiptoed through the narrow hallway that ran alongside of the sewing area and led to the store, I made out a figure with long, scraggly hair creeping around the interior. I crouched down behind the large round trash bin that we used to hold bolts of fabric, and watched. The figure had a massive, hulking form. He lifted the cash register and pulled out a piece of paper.

Nobody knew about that piece of paper. It was the combination to the safe.

The man turned around and stooped down in front of the safe. He checked the paper, and then spun the dial. I couldn't allow him to rob the store. Not five days before

Halloween, when we were bursting at the seams with cash to be deposited. I picked up a long pair of silver sheers from the cutting table, pulled the baseball hat down over the top of my head, looked up at the ceiling with a silent prayer to St. Jude, and stepped into the shop.

Chapter 11

"GET AWAY FROM that safe," I said.

The figure dropped the index card. His long gray hair fell in thick locks over his shoulders. He wore a long blue and silver cape, knotted around his neck with a braided silver cord. The man held up his hands slowly, and as they rose from underneath the cape, I saw how badly they were shaking.

Familiar hands. Hands that I had known my whole life. Especially because they wore the simple gold wedding band that my father had never taken off, even after my mother had died.

"Dad?" I asked

"Margo?" he asked back.

I stepped into the store and hit the switch on the wall. The interior was flooded with light. With the light came the recognition that the intruder was one Jerry Tamblyn, dressed as a wizard.

"I thought you were in Chicago?"

"Dallas," he said. "I caught a ride from Chicago with

a FedEx driver. He agreed to order ten uniforms and sell them to us ten dollars over cost. He drove me to Dallas."

"And you flew home from Dallas?"

"We'll talk about that later."

I glanced at the index card that had fallen to the floor. "What are you doing with the combination?"

"I thought you would have changed it by now. Have you forgotten what I taught you? Change the safe combination every thirteen days. That's random enough that no one will figure it out."

"And anybody who knows you keep the combination written on an index card under the cash register doesn't have to figure it out. Why are you dressed like that?"

"I wanted to surprise you." He stood up to his full height—which was suspiciously taller than he usually was—and stretched his arms out to either side. The effect was a bit frightening.

"Why are you so tall?"

He smiled and held one of his feet out in front of him. "Lifts. Nobody thinks about things like that when they're putting together a costume, but I'm telling you, being taller really does make a difference."

Once I got past the fear of being robbed, I ran forward and gave him a hug. The blue and silver cape closed around me, and a piece of synthetic gray hair got caught in my mouth. I spat it out with a *p-tooey*.

"The store looks good," he said. "Almost too good for the week before Halloween. Has it been slow?"

"Not hardly. It's been crazy around here. That's why I was so scared when I thought you were robbing us. I haven't had time to go to the bank and the safe is full."

He stood up and put his hands on his hips. "If I were robbing someone, would I dress like this? Let me ask you a different way: if you were making a costume for a thief, what would it be?"

"Black turtleneck, black pants, black soft-soled shoes, black gloves. Slicked-back hair that was secured in the back. Maybe a baseball hat to block out light. Set of tools in a pouch on the belt. And a half mask."

"Not bad." He relaxed. "What about a light? What about a bag for the stolen goods?"

"Small black backpack marked *Loot*. Flashlight recessed in the bill of the hat. Oh! And a stethoscope. For figuring out the combination to the safe."

"That's my girl," he said with a smile.

Soot wandered up and disappeared under my dad's cloak. The hem fluttered out as he—Soot, not my dad—walked in a circle. It gave the appearance of the cloak moving independently of my dad's body, as if it had magical powers. I watched my dad stare down at it, the wheels of thought in motion. By morning he would have worked out a way to replicate the effect and boost the cost of the wizard costume rental.

Ever polite, my dad waited until Soot had finished his walk around the cloak before moving. Still, the movement of the heavy, shiny fabric scared Soot, who jumped straight up in the air and then scrambled a few steps away when he landed. Our cranky gray cat was a tough guy when it came to mice in the stockroom, but he'd never quite understand the drama of costumes.

"Dad," I said tentatively, "Did you ever meet a man named Paul Haverford?"

He bent down and scooped up Soot, and cradled him in his left arm while scratching his ears with his right hand. The heavy makeup and synthetic hair effectively masked his features. When he spoke, it was in a calm tone.

"Paul Haverford. Local businessman, right? I can't say that I agree with his plans to expand Proper City, but he's a nice enough man. A bit intense when it comes to negotiating, but people in that kind of position of power don't get to be successful without a healthy combination of drive and cojones. Why do you ask?"

"He was murdered two nights ago at the Halloween pre-party," I said. "It's been all over the news here, but you probably missed it because you were on the road."

"I've listened to my fill of country music, that's for sure."

"Country? In Dallas?"

"In Nashville. I stopped off to check out the costumes at the Country Music Hall of Fame. Now, what's this about Paul Haverford being murdered?"

Just this last year, my dad had suffered not one but two heart attacks. During his recovery, I'd learned that he harbored a secret desire to travel the country and scout out costumes—a desire he'd put on the back burner to run the store while giving me the chance to explore the world myself. Once I'd decided to move back to Proper City to run the store and give him the opportunity to sow his oats, I saw how much he loved it. The only thing that would make him give it up was his overprotective tendencies toward me. So I gave him the condensed version.

"It happened at the Alexandria Hotel, sometime during the closed kickoff party. The police were already on hand, so they were able to secure the scene expeditiously. Everybody who was there gave statements and the party was cut short."

He studied me for a few seconds, and I regretted going with "expeditiously" in an attempt to sound more mature. Still, I held his stare because I knew looking away would confirm any suspicions he might have that I wasn't telling him everything.

"Paul Haverford has been buying up lots of businesses around town," he said. "He made an offer on our store, more than once, but I made it clear that I wasn't selling. I probably should have told you about that before I left town, but now it's not just my decision."

"I have no desire to sell the store either. Disguise DeLimit is who we are."

He smiled. "That's what I like to think too."

Soot, who had graciously given my dad a solid five minutes of cat affection, must have decided that five minutes was enough. He wriggled around until he had flipped, and then jumped out of my dad's arms to the ground. He trotted through the store and into the back stockroom. I suspected while the cat was away, the mice had played, but Soot was about to level the playing field.

Thursday

My alarm went off at five thirty. It was still dark. I dressed in a vintage rust-colored sweat suit with YOU'VE COME A LONG WAY, BABY embroidered on a patch on the shoulder. According to our research, it had been a promotional item offered with twenty barcodes from Virginia Slims cigarettes. Interesting marketing: exercise wear from a cigarette company. Maybe that's why the sweats were in mint condition when we acquired them.

I parted my hair in the middle and pulled each side into a low ponytail. It was too early to fuss with makeup, so I smoothed a tinted sunscreen over my face, slicked some lip balm over my lips, hopped on my scooter, and left.

A small group of women were assembled in the Proper City Park, or the PCP as it had come to be known. Various versions of black sports bra and stretchy black yoga pants were the ensemble of choice. Bobbie wore a pink hoodie over black leggings that ended right below her knees. She jogged forward and met up with me.

"You are going to love morning yoga," she said. "The sun starts to rise during warm-up, and by the time we're done at seven, the sky is full-on beautiful."

I looked up at the still-dark sky. "If you say so."

"Come on. We have to get a good spot."

Bobbie was right about two things: the early-morning solitude of Proper while the sun came up, and my need to have a physical outlet. Halfway through the class I let go of everything that had been on my mind. I lost myself in breathing exercises that left me feeling refreshed and stretches that challenged my tight, tense muscles. When the instructor told us we were done, I was shocked that an hour had gone by.

Bobbie and I collected our mats, towels, and water bottles and walked to the parking lot. "Do you feel better? More relaxed?"

"I feel better than I have in days. I think for about five minutes there I actually forgot about Paul Haverford's murder."

"Well, this might be a case of the worst timing in history, but since you brought that up, I have something for you. Follow me."

We walked to her small electric car. She popped the trunk and plunged her hands deep into a cardboard box filled with files. She pulled out a small silver flash drive on a red lanyard and held it toward me.

"About five years ago, Annette asked me if I'd join their board of directors. Their recording secretary received a last-minute grant for field research in Mineral, Nevada, and I ended up taking over as the temporary replacement. This flash drive has their operating budget, their five year plan, and the minutes for their quarterly meetings."

"How long were you on the board?"

"Ever since then."

I reached for the cord and she pulled it slightly out of reach. "I could get into a lot of trouble if they found out I gave this to you."

"Why *are* you giving it to me?"

"Because after you left the restaurant last night, I did a little digging. This isn't the first time one of Annette's opponents had an accident. I believe in their mission and I want to help preserve what's left of Proper City, but if she had something to do with Paul Haverford's murder, then somebody needs to stop her."

Chapter 12

AS BOBBIE HAD predicted, twilight had broken the horizon during our session and the sun had appeared shortly thereafter. Now it climbed through the sky, leaving shades of pink and lavender against a powder blue background. Crisp morning air scented with sagebrush and the faraway notes of brewing coffee comingled. I couldn't remember the last time I watched the sun come up and was happy that I hadn't missed it today.

WHEN I got home, I was met with the scent of waffles. I showered and dressed in one of my favorites: a color-blocked '60s sheath dress, white fishnets, and white patent leather go-go boots. I blow dried my hair into a flip. If it hadn't been the week before Halloween, I might have stopped there, but it was time to pull out all the stops. I pulled on a wide white plastic headband and added large round red earrings that hung in circles that swung on either side of my head. I draped the lanyard with the flash drive around my neck and tucked it into my neckline.

I found my dad and Soot in the kitchen. Dad's wizard costume had been replaced with a pinstriped suit, blue dress shirt, modest necktie. His short hair was combed into place and small glasses were perched on his nose.

"Go-go dancer?"

"Yep. Businessman?"

He picked up a rolled-up *Wall Street Journal* from the counter. "Banker."

My dad speared two waffles, set them on a plate, and handed the plate to me. "You never told me how the store was doing."

"It's been great and we owe it all to Kirby. He arranged for the swim team to come in and help us."

"What did he get you to pay them?" he asked.

"A donation to the swim team for their new uniforms. And all the pizza they can eat."

"Sounds like Kirby's been paying attention in his business class. Last year when the swim team helped out, they did it for a twenty percent discount on costumes."

"You mean this isn't the first time?"

"Don't underestimate him, Margo. The kid's got smarts." He handed me a bowl of softened butter and I spread some over the top of my waffle. I sat at the table, a '50s diner-style with a white top flecked with gold glitter and chrome trim that wrapped around the top. The chairs were chrome with cushions covered in red vinyl. When I was in high school, a local '50s-themed restaurant had gone out of business and sold off their fixtures and uniforms. My dad didn't make a habit of bringing home pieces that couldn't be used in costumes, but he'd made an exception in the case of the table and chairs. We'd spent the weekend painting the walls a cheerful red to coordinate with the cushions, framing album covers from his vast vinyl collection, and re-covering the floor in black and white laminate tiles. It was a costume for the kitchen, and it suited the room perfectly.

"Margo, I took a look in the safe this morning, and we really shouldn't keep that much cash in the store. Do you think you can get to the bank when they open?"

"They open at nine, right? Sure. I can be back before we open at eleven."

"About that, I think you deserve a day off."

"Halloween is in four days."

"I've been running this store for longer than you've been alive. There are two things I've learned." He held up his hand. "One, if you don't give yourself a break, you'll run yourself down and get sick. And two." He paused. "The store can't be your whole life."

I opened my mouth to say something but didn't know what it should be. I'd spent *my* whole life watching the store be my dad's life. He'd never dated; he'd never closed for two weeks and taken a vacation. Was he telling me he'd regretted the way he'd lived his life?

He sat in the chair opposite mine. "Margo, don't misunderstand me. I love this store. When your mother and I took it over, it was a lot of work, but those were happy times." He reached his hand across the table and put it on top of mine. "But life goes on, and we have to find other things that make us happy. You know that's all I want for you, for you to be happy."

I squeezed his fingertips. "And I want you to be happy too, Dad."

"It'll make me happy if you take the day off."

"Fine. Just be warned, I told Kirby the swim team needs to show up in costume."

"All of them?"

"Yep."

"Oh boy."

I finished my waffle and sent a text to Tak. *Bank deposit. Corner of Thumbelina and Main Line Road. Whole day off!* I transferred the money for the bank to a small black pouch, locked the pouch in the small storage space under the seat of my Vespa, and left.

I had a theory that when the city planners were designing what was to become Proper City as I knew it, they were partially distracted by young children. How else to explain the number of streets named after fairy tales or the developments that referenced children's stories?

I turned right on Main Line Road and drove a couple of miles to the bank. They opened at nine, but if Tak got my text, we'd have a couple minutes to ourselves before conducting business. I pulled into the parking lot and glided into a space by the front door. Seconds later, Tak's RAV4 pulled into the lot and parked in a spot in the far corner. I waited for him to get out and join me, but he didn't. An employee unlocked the doors and after one backward glance, I went inside. Marilyn Robinson, a fifty-something redhead who favored leopard print and gold hoop earrings was behind the glass. She'd worked at the bank as long as I could remember. She waved me over.

"Hey, Margo, how's everything at the store? Busy?" she asked.

"You know it. Are you planning on renting a costume from us?"

Marilyn blushed. "I bought a costume from Candy Girls this year," she said. "No offense, but they gave me a coupon, and it's on my way home, and I just thought since they're a start-up business I should support them. You're not going to tell your father, are you?"

A long time ago I'd realized that the longer my dad

remained single, the more ladies around town considered
him a catch. There was something about his devotion to
my late mother that they found charming—or maybe it
was nonthreatening, I wasn't sure which. Either way, he
received his share of invitations to parties and social
engagements, and to the chagrin of the invitees, usually
arrived with his friend Don Digby. By the end of the night,
the two of them would be holding court in a corner trying
out their latest conspiracy theory on whoever would listen.
Marilyn, judging from the blush that crept up her cheeks
when she spoke his name, must be among the women who
thought when he met the right woman, he'd make his move.

The last thing I wanted to do was tell my dad that his
fan club had taken their business to Candy Girls. "Mum's
the word. But what makes you think they're a start-up?"

"Gina Cassavogli said so. She came here on Small Business Saturday and took a seminar, and told everybody how
it was an important year for them. She's right, you know.
Most new businesses don't turn a profit for their first two
years, so the third year is really a make-it-or-break-it time."

"That's what she said?"

"Yes. She said she knew most people in Proper felt a
loyalty to Disguise DeLimit, but she gave us all fifty dollars in Candy Bucks to use toward any costume in their
inventory."

I gritted my teeth. The paperwork that Paul Haverford
had delivered to the store said that Candy Girls was one
of his new acquisitions. Having a millionaire infuse cash
into their business hardly made them qualify as a small
business. If anything, they were Goliath to our David.

"Margo?" Marilyn said.

"What?"

"If you're making a deposit, I need you to give me the
money." She looked at my hand, where my knuckles were

turning white as I gripped the pouch. I unzipped it and fed the mess of checks and cash under the partition. "Wow, your store really is doing well," she said. "No wonder Gina is worried."

My face flushed. The one thing I didn't need was for Marilyn to spread word that we were sitting pretty and putting Candy Girls out of business—not that I didn't think for one second that Candy Girls would do it to us if the tables were turned.

After sorting the cash from the checks, Marilyn fed it through a machine and then punched a couple of buttons on her computer. I stood silently by as she turned to the checks, systematically keying each one in. She paused halfway through the pile and looked up at Tak, who had just walked in.

"It's too bad about his family's restaurant," Marilyn said, her voice dropping lower. "I heard my boss saying the Hoshiyamas applied for a loan. If things don't turn around soon, they'll be part of the revolving door of restaurants in Proper. There aren't a lot of single men your age around here. It would be a shame to lose one over money."

Marilyn keyed the last of the checks into the computer and fed my deposit slip through. After it printed, she fed it under the partition. "Can I do anything else for you? Maybe set you up with a CD or an interest-rich account? Right now you have all that cash just sitting in savings."

I felt myself color again, and I looked over my shoulder. Tak stood by the table of flyers, his back to me. If his family's restaurant really was having trouble, he probably wouldn't appreciate hearing how much money we were making—not that we were, but that was how she was making it sound.

"Maybe I'll take a couple of brochures on your different accounts," I said. I walked to the table of flyers and pretended to peruse the different programs the bank offered. Tak set a piece of paper in front of me and walked away. I looked at the note on the margin. *Sounds like lunch is on you, moneybags.* I looked at his back as he walked away. He stopped when he reached the door and looked over his shoulder, flashing me a secret smile. I smiled involuntarily, and then glanced at Marilyn to see if she'd noticed. She was busy typing on her computer screen. I grabbed the note, stuck it inside the zippered pouch, and left.

Tak was waiting for me by my scooter. "Did you mean it earlier when you said you had the day off?"

"Sure did. My dad surprised me this morning and told me he didn't want to see me all day. Do you have plans?"

"My parents need me at the restaurant this morning. They're training a couple of new chefs."

Hoshiyama Kobe Steak House should have been a success based on the quality of their food. Sesame chicken grilled in garlic butter, scallops that melted in your mouth, shrimp the size of a small fist, not to mention the fried rice. But what made it even more special was the show. The food was cooked on a grill in front of you while you watched. Onion rings were stacked into volcanos and shrimp tails were flipped into the air and caught in the chef's hat or shirt pocket. Whether you came for the food and came back for the show, or you came for the show and came back for the food, you wouldn't be disappointed. Not to mention the stunning embroidered silk kimonos that the hostesses wore. They were the prettiest costumes—I mean uniforms—I'd seen.

I thought about the lanyard hanging around my neck. I wanted to tell Tak about it, but Bobbie had asked me to keep it secret. "I think I'm going to head to the library. See what I can find out about the Alexandria Hotel."

"You're really interested in that?"

"The other night was my first time inside. Now I hear

it's either going to be bulldozed or turned into a historical property. Can't hurt to appreciate it while it's here."

He reached out and put his hand on my arm. "Text me when you finish. Maybe I can get away."

THE Proper City branch of the Clark County Public Library was about half a mile south of the bank. It sat kitty-corner to the elementary school that I'd attended growing up. I parked by the curb and glanced at the playground. The merry-go-round where Bobbie and I had spent hours pushing each other round and round was vacant. New swing sets had replaced the old ones, as had a shiny blue sliding board. A young girl, probably around nine or ten, stared out the window at me. I made a silly face at her and she laughed, and then clamped both hands over her mouth. I went into the library before her teacher could determine the distraction that had caused her outburst.

Being a branch in a small town, the Proper City Public Library didn't have much in terms of resources. If I had weeks, I could request materials to be sent here from the main branch, but I didn't. But today my priorities were clear. Reserve a computer and see what was on the flash drive. Further questions could develop from there.

I was early enough to secure one of the more private computers behind the newspaper racks. Once seated, I signed in and inserted the flash drive into the USB port. The operating system wasn't as current as the computer at Disguise DeLimit, but after a few clicks, I had a snapshot of the file manager. I bypassed the welcome packet, assuming it boiled down to their mission of saving historical properties, and moved on to the folder that held their meeting minutes.

It wasn't the most exiting reading. They seemed to spend a disproportionate amount of time discussing snacks and beverages. The Alexandria Hotel was just one point of interest to them. Going back seven different meetings, I found the same list of buildings they hoped to save. The list included the original movie theater that had been built in the late '40s; a post office in the neighboring town of Jean; the first house built in Moxie, once owned by an early copper miner; and the Alexandria Hotel.

Reports were made about the petitions filed to secure historical status, and fund-raisers were discussed and, occasionally, implemented. I opened and closed files at random, not sure what I was looking for, but hoping I'd know it when I saw it. Worse, each file had been saved as a scanned PDF, so I couldn't search for keywords. It was among the more frustrating ways to spend an hour.

Each report included a list of attendees for the meeting. About eight years back, Annette's name was missing from that list. I checked the minutes before that meeting and it was missing there too. If someone else had been president, it should have been noted. And what had Bobbie said? This wasn't the first time one of Annette's opponents had an accident.

My focus redoubled. I marked the dates of the minutes where Annette had been absent and opened up the files prior to that until I found her name. There was a six month window where she hadn't been present at a meeting. The vice president had stepped up as acting president. What had kept her from fulfilling her position?

I disconnected the flash drive from the computer and approached the librarian. She was a young brunette in a thick blue sweater with a rainbow on the front. Glasses hung on a chain around her neck, and her hair was pulled back into a bun at the nape of her neck. I couldn't have designed a better librarian costume if I'd tried.

"Can I help you?" she asked.

"I hope so. I'm looking for articles from a few years ago. Is there a way to search the library database?"

"Sure. Go to CCPL.org, sign in with your library card, and click the link that says Research and Homework. That'll take you to the different databases that you want to search: government documents, newspapers, photo archives, you name it. Click off the ones you want and you're in."

I thanked her and returned to my cubicle. It took a few attempts to find the screens she mentioned, but once I did, I clicked Newspapers and ran a search for Annette Crowley. The resulting articles mentioned her position as president of the Clark County Conservancy, but nothing seemed to point to her six month absence.

After returning to the search terms screen, I tested "Clark County Conservancy" and "Alexandria Hotel." Aside from an articles about the dark days when the hotel had been ground zero for a drug smuggling ring, I found nothing suspicious. I was about to give up when I got a new idea. I typed in "Historical Landmark Status."

Bingo.

Peppermint House Receives Historical Status

The article was dated eight years ago. It described the petition to grant historical status to a Victorian house on the outskirts of Proper. The building had come to be called Peppermint House in the late '50s because of its red and white color scheme. But it wasn't the novelty of the Peppermint House that caught my attention. It was a mention at the very bottom of the article.

The change in historical status was not a given. Until recently, Haverford Venture Capital, the financial group that held the property title, had plans to demolish the building and use the property for retail space.

Despite the noble efforts of the historical society, the lawsuit with HVC made the battle for preservation too costly to fight. If not for the sudden illness of Paul Haverford, the Peppermint House might not be standing today.

Chapter 13

I REREAD THE last paragraph several times to make sure I was reading it correctly. And every time, I reached the same conclusion. Haverford Venture Capital had been the owners of the last house that Annette Crowley had fought to save. Haverford became ill, his venture capital group stopped fighting the historical society, and Annette won the battle. And then she vanished from the board of directors for the next six months.

I returned to the librarian's desk. "I found the article I needed. Is there a way to print it?"

"Normally, yes, but our printers are broken today. We expect a technician this afternoon but I can't guarantee anything." She checked the clock on her computer. "Oh, and I forgot to tell you, there's an hour limit to the computer usage. I wouldn't enforce it but today we have a line of people waiting."

I couldn't leave without that article. Before logging off, I took a screen shot and e-mailed it to myself. The librarian approached. I yanked the flash drive out of the USB port and hung it around my neck, picked up my keys, and left.

It was close to ten thirty. I texted Tak. *All done at library. You?*

His reply came immediately. *Wait there.*

I spent the next ten minutes debating whether or not to tell him what I'd found out. It was too big a piece of information to ignore, but it would be too hard to explain how I'd happened to be researching that information to begin with. I didn't want to implicate Bobbie in my mess. No, I'd have to keep it to myself until I talked to her. And after I convinced her to see things my way, we'd take what we had to Detective Nichols.

About ten minutes later, Tak's RAV4 turned onto the street. He drove past me, turned the SUV around, and pulled up behind my scooter.

"Want to take a field trip?"

"Where?"

"The district attorney's office. I thought you might like to poke around, see where I used to work."

"Do you think I could see the plans for Havetown? Can you swing that?"

"I think so."

"I'm in."

Tak put my scooter in the back of his SUV and we left. It was a short drive to the Clark County DA's office, and we arrived by eleven. He parked in a visitor's space and led me inside.

It was quickly evident that Tak had been well liked. Every person we encountered stopped to chat with him. We reached a sign-in desk, where he introduced me to a guard and explained that I was curious about some public records in Proper City. The guard asked me to sign in too and handed each of us a visitor sticker. A familiar voice called out behind me.

"You really are following me, aren't you?"

I turned around and saw Tak's friend Cooper. They shook hands in the way male friends do, and then Cooper looked at me. "And you brought me a visitor. Nice to see you again, Margo." He let go of Tak's hand and reached out for mine. When I grasped it, he sandwiched his other hand on the outside and held it gently. "I see you finally warmed up," he said tenderly.

"I would have brought your gloves, only I didn't know we were—"

Tak cut me off. "She didn't know if you'd be here. I should have called ahead to find out if you were working in the office today."

"Now you have an excuse to come back and see me again," Cooper said, still holding my hand. He smiled at me as if I was the only other person in the room. Tak cleared his throat. I pulled my hand out from between Cooper's and adjusted my hair band.

"Margo has taken an interest in the old Alexandria Hotel," Tak said. "The paperwork on that came through when I was still here, didn't it?"

Cooper looked at Tak, surprised. "Sure did. I filed all of it away last week." He looked at me. "Why the interest in that building?"

"It's where Halloween was supposed to take place. I had a chance to see a little of the inside the other night . . ." My voice trailed off.

"The night of the murder," Cooper finished. "Nothing's going to happen with that building now, it seems. Haverford and his team of investors were gung ho on the idea of leveling it and designing a new Proper, but there were enough people fighting him to see that it didn't happen. Construction was supposed to start six months ago but the conservancy filed an injunction. He's been fighting the preservationists ever since."

"Wait. The injunction was filed by the Clark County Conservancy?" I asked.

Both men looked at me. "How do you know about the injunction?"

"I met Annette Crowley last night and she mentioned it."

"It's ironic if you think about it. Haverford bought the property and planned to wipe it out, but because of his murder, he's ensured that it's going to remain exactly as it is. The one thing he didn't want."

"So it's true. He was going to obliterate the entire west end of Proper even though there's a danger in building out that way."

"Where'd you hear that?" Cooper asked.

I thought back over the people I'd talked to in the past few days. "I think it was the seismologist. Francine Wheeler."

Cooper and Tak looked at each other and laughed. "Is she still making trouble?" Tak asked.

"That woman lives to make trouble," Cooper said. He turned back to me. "I don't think she's missed a city council meeting in the past ten years."

"She said there were active fault lines that ran under that whole end of Proper, and if Havetown was built, the construction might trigger an earthquake."

"Margo, how long have you lived in Proper?" Cooper asked.

"Most of my life."

"Have you ever felt an earthquake?"

"No."

"Exactly. There wasn't any risk. I saw the quaternary map myself."

"I don't know what that means," I said.

"It would be easier to show you than try to explain." Cooper put his hand on my elbow and gently guided me toward the elevators. He pushed the Down button. I turned around and saw Tak still standing by the check-in desk.

"Are you coming with us?" I asked.

"Hey, Tak, you should go say hello to everybody in planning. They'd be happy to see you." Cooper pressed the Up button too. The Up arrived first. Cooper held the doors open and waited for Tak to get inside. "You can meet us down in the map room when you're finished." He let go of the doors and they closed over Tak's serious expression.

The Down elevator arrived next and Cooper guided me in. He pressed LL and we headed down. A few moments later, the doors opened on an unoccupied floor. He got out first and waved me forward. "It's okay. This is where we keep the archives."

I followed him into a long hallway filled with large taupe metal filing cabinets. We reached a closed door at the end. Cooper pulled two pairs of white gloves out of a box that sat next to the door and handed one to me. "I seem to be obsessed with giving you gloves. I wonder what that means." He grinned. "There are some old documents in here. We wear gloves to keep the finger oils from tainting the paper."

We took a moment to pull the gloves on and then went into the room. A large wooden table sat in the center. More metal storage cabinets lined the left wall, but the drawers were wider and less deep. Cooper went to the second cabinet and pulled the fifth drawer open. A flat map was inside, covered with a wide sheet of what appeared to be parchment paper.

"Is the table clear?" he asked.

"Just about." I picked up a couple of abandoned pencils and a protractor and set them in a cup that lay on its side. The cup was the type that came with vintage board games and was used to shake the dice. "Now it's ready."

Cooper transferred the flat map to the table by setting it on a large wooden paddle and then setting the paddle on the table. "Same thing they use to pull pizzas out of the oven," he said.

"It is not."

"Okay, it's not." He laughed. "Just testing you."

Once the map was in front of us, I could make out the California/Nevada border and the general location of Proper. Green, orange, and yellow colored the map, and a network of red and purple lines spidered through it. I bent down to get a better look. "What did you call this? A quarter map?"

"Quaternary. It's a map of the active fault lines in Clark County."

"So this shows where there's the potential for an earthquake?"

"Yes. Notice how the lines are all dull purple, whereas the lines in California are all bright red? That's because ours are dormant. There's little risk of construction triggering an earthquake here. California has more to worry about, but even most of their fault lines are deep enough that the activity involved in building construction wouldn't trigger a quake."

Cooper moved closer to me. His head was just to the left of mine. He put his right arm around me and pointed to a network of pale purple lines on the map. "See that?" he asked. His voice was soft in my ear. "That's where Havetown was going to be built. The biggest concern they were going to have was drilling into the hard soil in Proper City."

I tried to pretend that I didn't notice his closeness, but we were alone in the basement of the office of public records, and I couldn't help think of much else. I stepped to my right, putting distance between us. "Does Tak know to meet us down here?" I asked.

"Tak, right." He ran his hand through his brown hair. "Are you and he . . . Oh, man. Did I read things wrong? Are you guys a couple?"

I wanted to say yes, but I didn't know the context of our visit to Tak's old job. So far we'd kept things secret from everybody: his parents, my dad, Ebony, and Bobbie. "We're friends," I said tentatively.

"Friends," Cooper repeated. "Tak and I were pretty good friends once. We still are, only it's never going to be the same."

"What happened?" I asked. As wrong as it felt, I wanted to know something about Tak's past that I didn't already know. Something more than the last six months since I'd met him.

"Tak and I liked the same girl. She went for him. I guess I'm gun-shy now."

"Was that Nancy?" I asked without thinking.

"Nancy? No, it was Lauren." He smiled a lopsided grin. "Who's Nancy?"

"Nancy Nichols. She's the new police detective in Proper. I thought she and Tak had a past."

"That's Tak for you. Half the women he dates, he dates in secret. Makes it hard to keep up with him."

And just like that, my relationship paranoia kicked into overdrive. I felt myself stiffen, and I turned away from Cooper and focused on the map. "What's the significance of the orange and green?"

"Margo, hey, I didn't mean anything by that. Tak's a good guy. If you guys are friends, you probably know that, right?"

"Sure." I smiled. "Seriously, I want to know more about the map."

Cooper dropped the subject of Tak's romantic history and explained what the colors and lines meant. By the time the elevator doors opened and Tak joined us, I felt like I'd gotten a crash course in seismology. I couldn't wait to run into Francine Wheeler again and flex my newly strength- ened muscle.

"Hey, Hoshi. As usual, your timing is crappy," Cooper said. "Another five minutes and I'd have her phone number."

A look that I didn't recognize passed over Tak's face. I

stepped away from Cooper. "Is there any way to get a copy of these maps? Since they're a matter of public record?"

"Sure. I'll have a duplicate made up and have it sent to your store. Disguise DeLimit, right?"

"Did I tell you that?"

"You mentioned that there was construction in front of your store. I admit, I did a little research after your flat tire."

I blushed and snuck another look at Tak. He crossed his arms over his chest and raised his eyebrows. I looked back at Cooper. "Yes, Disguise DeLimit is my store. Thank you."

"Don't mention it."

The three of us headed to the elevator. I forgot about my gloves until I was inside. "What should I do with these?"

"Add them to the Cooper collection," Cooper said. He peeled them off my hands one at a time, starting with the fabric at my wrists, so they were turned inside out by the time they came off my fingertips. "Actually, leave them with me. I'll wash them with mine and add them back to the stash."

Tak and Cooper gave me a tour of the planning offices, but it felt more like their own trip down memory lane. Tak's old desk. The empty cubicle where Cooper hid from his boss when he was late with a report. The secret closet where— They both laughed and didn't tell me what was so special about the secret closet. Truth? I didn't really want to know.

It was after lunchtime when we returned to the main floor. Cooper walked us to the front desk and Tak signed us out. An idea had been playing around at the back of my mind, and the timing seemed right to approach it.

"Cooper, you know how the Alexandria Hotel is off-limits for the Halloween celebration?"

"I heard about that."

"My friend Ebony was put in charge of finding a new

location. Is there any place you can recommend? Any buildings where she could get the permits cleared in a couple of days?"

"I'll think about it, see if I can come up with something. She talked to Sol, right?"

"Sol?" I looked at Cooper. He looked at Tak. Tak looked at me. "Sol who?" I asked again.

"Sol Girard," Tak said. "You're right. I didn't even think about him."

"What does Sol Girard have to do with anything?" I asked, looking back and forth between both of their faces.

Cooper was the one to answer. "Sol owns the other half of the property in West Proper. He had his own plans to develop it into lower income housing before Havetown was announced. If Haverford's plans had gone through, Sol's property wouldn't have been worth more than a handful of dirt."

Chapter 14

I HADN'T BEEN expecting to hear a familiar name in conjunction with the murder. Sol Girard had been at the Alexandria Hotel the night Haverford was murdered. But I'd known Sol for a long time. Along with being an Elk and hosting his monthly poker games, he'd refereed the high school football games when I attended. I would never have suspected that he had a motive for murder. On the other hand, I would never have suspected him of buying up property with plans to develop either.

"How long has Sol been buying property?" I asked.

Cooper shrugged. "I don't know. Longer than I've been in this office. Tak, do you know?"

Tak put his hands in the pockets of his jeans. "I didn't work residential. Sorry."

"It must be in a file somewhere, right?" I asked. "Wouldn't that be a matter of public record too?"

"I'll see what I can dig up," Cooper offered with a smile.

Tak looked at his watch. "We've kept Coop away from

work for long enough. We should be heading back to Proper."

Cooper walked us to the car and he and Tak shook hands again. "Good seeing you, Hoshi. Don't be a stranger." He turned to me, and his voice softened. "You either."

"Thanks for showing me the map," I said. I felt Tak watching us.

"Sure. And hey, if Sol can't help out your friend with a location for the Halloween party, let me know. I'll see what I can come up with on that too."

We climbed into the car and started the drive back to Proper. The first few minutes were uncomfortably silent, and I searched for something to say to break through the awkwardness.

"So Sol Girard owns property in West Proper," I said. "He was at the Alexandria that night, dressed like the Wolf Man. I talked to him."

"Margo, how long have you known Sol?"

"Most of my life."

"And all of a sudden you think he could have killed a man?"

"No, but somebody killed Paul Haverford, somebody who was there at the party. Maybe Sol saw something. Maybe he knows something. Maybe this does have to do with the development of Havetown, and if Sol owns property in that area, he'd probably know about the plans for development."

"I think you should be careful about who you talk to and how you ask questions." He swung the car off the road into the parking lot of a roadside taco stand called Tito's Tacos. "No matter who you talk to, you need to remember that a man was killed. Whoever did it is dangerous."

"I know that," I said. Tak's warning sounded more like a lecture.

He put on the parking brake and reached out for my arm.

"That came out wrong. What I'm trying to say is that I don't want you to be in a dangerous situation again. It wasn't that long ago that you were almost killed in your stockroom because you were asking too many questions."

Tak was referring to a murder six months ago. I'd designed forty detective costumes for a rich guy's mystery-themed birthday party, and someone had killed him at the celebration. Ebony had been about to carve the goose and, in an unfortunate case of really poor timing, had discovered the body while she was holding the knife. Everybody had believed she was guilty—well, not everybody, but the police did and they were the ones who counted—and I'd been the one to expose the real killer. It had been the single scariest night of my life.

"Margo, I care about you." He reached over and intertwined his fingers with mine. "Maybe you should let Nancy do her job."

I felt myself stiffen. Tak didn't know that Nancy—Detective Nichols to me—thought her job was pinning the murder on me, and I didn't want to tell him.

"I'll be careful." I squeezed his hand and he squeezed back.

"Promise?"

"Promise."

"Good. Now, how about some lunch?"

We each ordered a plate of street tacos, loaded them down with onions and cilantro, and found a seat at a vacant picnic table set up around back. Two Chihuahuas romped around the yard, and a man wearing a dirty white apron stood over a small hibachi grill turning chicken. The scent carried through the air, serving as a more effective advertisement than if they'd taken out a billboard on the Las Vegas Strip.

I pretended not to notice the way people looked at me. This time of year, most people assumed I was dressed to go to a party, so the curious glances were less judgmental.

We took our time eating and stayed at the picnic table long after the tacos were gone. For the first time since we'd arrived at the planning office, Tak relaxed. Surrounded by strangers fifteen miles outside of Proper, we seemed to be in our element. Too soon, it was time to head home.

Tak drove to his parents' teppanyaki restaurant. The lot was partially full. He parked in the back next to the Dumpster, hopped out, and pulled my scooter from the back. "Did you tell anybody about the flat tire the other night?"

"No."

"Okay, then if anybody asks, you got a flat tire today. I drove past and saw you and gave you a ride back here."

"Okay." We stood facing each other with the scooter between us. He put his hand on top of mine and gently rubbed his finger back and forth over my thumb. I leaned forward and he pulled away.

"Somebody's probably watching," he said.

"Oh, right." I unlocked my helmet and pulled it on quickly to hide my hurt expression. "See you around," I said, and took off for the store.

IT was two o'clock by the time I parked behind Disguise DeLimit. Cars lined the sidewalk in front and alongside of the shop, and hoards of customers were inside. Upon entering I discovered that half of the customers were Kirby's teammates, all dressed like Elvis with black pompadour wigs and large, '70s-style silver-frame sunglasses. They sat in a row of chairs with Ebony behind them holding a can of hair spray.

Today she was wearing a severe cobalt blue, black, and white blazer over a black turtleneck and tight jeans tucked into black boots with several silver buckles. Her afro had been slicked down to the side of her head on both sides and shaped into a pouf on top. Her full lips were painted a shiny raisiny shade, and her eye shadow and blush had been applied liberally.

"You . . . don't look like yourself," I said.

"Grace Jones," she said. "I look like Grace Jones. You people want me to wear a costume, this is what you're gonna get." She tugged on the bottom of her blazer. "Nineteen eighty-three. Still fits," she said proudly.

"Is everything okay here?" I asked.

"Get over here, girl. We're demonstrating how to use hair spray to keep these wigs from turning from Elvis into Sonny Bono."

I dropped my bag and grabbed a can of hair spray. When I finished spraying, combing, and otherwise styling the jet-black hair of Elvis number four, he turned around and curled his lip.

"Thank you. Thank you very much."

"Kirby? Is that you?"

He laughed and stood with his feet about shoulder width apart, his thumbs tucked into the waistband of his jeans. "Well, I reckon I might go by Kirby some days, but in here it's the King to you." He curled his lip again. Ebony picked up the rat-tail comb and held it up like a weapon.

"Don't you go pushing your luck, you little redheaded punk. If you're gonna dress up as the King, you have to respect what he stood for."

Kirby hung his head and apologized profusely. "I didn't mean no harm, ma'am. I was just, uh, tryin' to, uh—"

"Get on with your bad self. There's customers waiting to pay."

"Thank you. Thank you very much," he said again. The customers waiting by the register broke out in applause, and Kirby's smile grew to the size of Graceland. He left us to join his new fan club and Ebony set the rat-tail comb and the Aqua Net down.

"Fifty shades of Elvis. Not in my wildest dreams did I think I'd see that," she said to me.

"What are you doing here? I thought you didn't like to venture out too close to Halloween?"

Ebony was as superstitious as they came. Her bichon frise, a white puffball, was the polar opposite of a black cat, and don't think that didn't play into her decision to adopt him. On a regular day, she wore a gold medallion around her neck, her good luck charm, and knocked wood, avoided ladders, held her breath over bridges, and scanned every patch of grass in Proper for four leaf clovers. I'd long since gotten used to it.

Shindig, her business, was about party planning, and in our town parties required themes. But Ebony changed when Halloween rolled around. She tucked her medallion into her neckline and added long, silver earrings (to ward off werewolves). She wore a necklace of garlic. And kept wooden skewers—stakes, by her estimation—strapped to her wrist in case she encountered a vampire. The year I graduated high school, she'd sat alongside me in the library when I studied for finals, but only because she was researching how to overpower a mummy. I told her to grab an end of muslin and pull really hard. She didn't think it was funny.

While I was mostly sure that she didn't believe in ghosts and goblins, I knew she had an irrational fear that couldn't be shaken. Ebony refused to go on a haunted hayride or attend a haunted house. She believed that the spirits would choose those settings to come alive and wreak havoc on the rest of us. I gave up trying to convince her those spirits were the same people who performed at the summer renaissance faire.

"This holiday is going to be the death of me," she said. "Do you know I went to Dig Allen's garage for an oil change and he was dressed up as a killer clown? I told him my brown sugar would be fine for another two weeks and I left rubber in his driveway."

"Ebony! Dig is probably still crying in his beer. You know he pictures himself as Shaft to your Foxy Brown."

"No killer clown is going to take me out to dinner on Saturday night, I know that much."

I laughed. "You've never said yes to Dig's dinner invitations in the past when he wasn't in costume."

She reached inside the neckline of her fitted blue blazer and fingered the chain that her medallion hung on. "Yes, but the option was there. I have standards. I'm not going out to dinner with a killer clown and that's that."

Sounded like Dig was going to have some explaining to do once the Halloween season was over.

"Have you had any luck finding a new location for the party?" I asked.

"That's another thing. Why am I in charge of making sure the undead of Proper City have a place to hang out? I would just as well put a bowl of candy on my front porch, lock the doors, and let the spirit world celebrate without me."

"Ebony, the ghosts and goblins deserve their night and you're the best person for the job. Are you going to let Halloween happen in a rented out fire hall? No, the Alexandria was just about perfect, but if it can't happen there, you have to find someplace else."

"You're as bad as the rest of them," she said.

"Well?"

"I'm working on it." She patted the combs that held the side of her hairstyle in place and left.

I helped my dad, Kirby, and the rest of the Elvis impersonators for the next few hours, and we closed up a little after seven. That was the thing about business in a small town like ours. We didn't stick to hard and fast store hours, and if customers wanted to shop, we kept the doors open.

This being our busy season, we were lucky not to stay open all night.

When the last of the customers left—finally settling on Little Red Riding Hood and the Big Bad Wolf—my dad locked the door and the Elvises collapsed. My dad looked at me, I looked at Kirby, and Kirby looked at them. "Pizza?" asked the one in the bedazzled white jumpsuit. Kirby looked back at me.

"Phone it in. They have my credit card on file."

"You go on upstairs, Margo. I'll take care of the store and the guys," my dad said.

On a normal day, I would have stayed with them, but today I had something else in mind. Before heading to the apartment, I stopped by the files of costume rentals and flipped through the alphabet until I found the one for Sol Girard. Not wanting to draw attention to myself, I took it with me and didn't open it until I reached the kitchen.

I dropped into one of the dining chairs and opened the file. Sol was a regular customer of ours, and the file was filled with rental slips dating back over the past few years. I closed the folder and started at the back. The last rental slip was for the Wolf Man costume I'd seen him in at the kickoff party.

The rental slip in front of it, dated two days earlier, was for Spider-Man.

Chapter 15

I CHECKED THE date on the rental slip and matched the credit card numbers to the file. It was the same information. Which meant that Sol Girard had rented two costumes from us, not one.

It wasn't odd for someone to rent more than one costume, especially this week. But I couldn't help think about the figure I'd seen scaling the wall of the Alexandria when I called for help. Or the fact that Spider-Man not only didn't help, but he took the opportunity to get away.

Not a single other person had mentioned Spider-Man scaling the side of the building in their statements to the police. Why not? More than one had pointed him out when I looked out the window. Why ignore a man in blue and red spandex against a dirty brick building?

I tucked everything back into the folder and closed the folder in front of me. It would have to go back downstairs tomorrow. My dad had never upgraded to a computerized system despite the work it would save, and the only way we could keep track of how many costumes we rented and who had what was to maintain a meticulous filing system. It wouldn't do anybody any good for me to be misplacing files now. Especially this one.

Then I got an idea. Detective Nichols was so sure I had something to do with the murder that she was sure to come back around. I'd only learned about Sol's land ownership today, but that information was vital to her investigation. I had to tell her what I'd found out. And with a few well-placed hints, she'd come to Disguise DeLimit and look through our files, and discover exactly what I just had and then she'd question Sol.

Could Sol really have been responsible for the murder of Paul Haverford?

I'd known Sol for years, ever since he'd turned his monthly poker party into a costumed affair. There'd been a *Maverick* theme, a football theme, and a pirate theme in recent memory. Sol came up with the theme, and the players were responsible for their costumes. I briefly wondered if the addition of the costumes helped or hurt the different players' poker faces.

I was still sitting in the kitchen thinking about Sol's file when my dad finally came upstairs carrying a large box.

"Hey, kiddo, you weren't waiting for me, were you? Some of the boxes that I shipped here arrived and I wanted to go through them."

"What did we get?" I asked.

"Band uniforms from a high school in New Jersey. They sent their mascot too. Look at this." He turned around and set the box down, pulled something brown and white out, and stuck it on his head. When he turned back to me, he was wearing a cow's head.

"Their mascot is a cow?"

"A Jersey cow, no less," he said. His voice was muffled by the interior of the cow head. Soot jumped on the table and stretched his head to sniff the cow. "Moo," my dad said. Soot swatted his paw at the cow's nose, got his claws stuck in the fur, and then jerked his paw a few times until he was free. He jumped down from the table and stood in front of his bowl.

"I think he wants some milk," I said.

"He's smart, but he's not that smart."

Soot meowed and then walked away.

"What are you doing with that file?" my dad asked. He sat next to me and took the head off, setting it on the table at a vacant place setting.

"I was sorting out some of the paperwork that hasn't been filed yet."

"Yes, things get a little behind schedule this time of year. Make sure you file it when you have it organized. The longer you let it go, the bigger job it'll be." He picked up the folder and opened it. "This is Sol's file." He looked directly at me. "He sure was excited about his costume," he said with a laugh.

"Was it his idea for the members of the Elks Lodge to dress up like the Universal Monsters?"

"Yes. He told everybody to keep an eye out for the Wolf Man." He closed the folder and tapped his finger on it. "That was a month ago. This file was already put away. Why did you really want to look at it?"

I sighed. "I found out today that Sol owns a lot of property in West Proper. He's been buying up lots as they become available and was planning on building lower income housing."

"What does that have to do with his Wolf Man costume?"

"It doesn't. But Sol was at the party, and he apparently had a beef with Paul Haverford."

"Margo, what have I told you? We don't just go around accusing people we know of things like murder."

"What about last time, Dad? We did know a murderer. Right under our noses too."

"Honey, I know that shook you up. I know that my heart attack did too. You've had a lot of changes in the past year. Giving up your job in Vegas, moving back to Proper to run the shop, starting over with your social life. I know you gave up a lot of your independence and privacy by moving in here too. I love having you here, but I think we should talk about a more permanent solution."

"Dad, I love being here. There's no reason we can't coexist."

"You say that now, but one of these days you're not going to want your father as your roommate." He stood up and rested his hand on my shoulder. He patted my shoulder twice and walked into the hallway. "I'm going to take a shower and then meet up with Don."

"You're going out?"

"There's a gathering of ghost hunters at Dillon's Steak and Ale. I can't let Don go without me."

I carried Sol's file downstairs and spent the next hour straightening the store. Half of the pinstriped suits were missing from the gangster rack and the flapper dresses were picked over. I combined the two and hung a gorilla suit on the wall. On the shelf above I placed a white plastic wig head with a short black wig, and then pulled a cheap *Planet of the Apes* mask over the front. The closer we got to Halloween, the more creative we had to get with the remaining costumes.

I moved on to filling in the colored hair spray from a case in the stockroom. Soot had left another mouse in one of the dark corners, and I had the unfortunate job of disposing of it. I carried it out front to the public garbage can on the corner. A car door shut out back, an engine started, and Dad pulled out of our cross street and turned right. Funny, it seemed like he was wearing a shirt and tie. I went back inside and locked the door just as the phone rang.

"Hi, Margo, it's Don. Is Jerry around?"

"He just left." The pungent smell of aftershave hung in the air. It stung my nose. "What is this meeting, anyway? Ghosts gone wild?"

"What meeting?"

"The thing you two are going to at Dillon's Steak and Ale. Dad said it was a meeting of ghost hunters."

"I'm not going to the thing at Dillon's. I was calling to see if he read this article about the Elvis sighting in Utah."

"Don, do you think if Elvis was alive and well he'd be hanging out in Utah?"

"Who said anything about him being alive? Tell Jerry to call me when he gets back."

I said that I would and then hung up. Something was up and it didn't have to do with the ghostly form of Elvis. I went to the office and powered up the computer, and did a search for Dillon's Steak and Ale. I ignored the specials and clicked on Events and my stomach dropped to my knees.

If my dad had been telling the truth about going to Dillon's Steak and Ale, then there was an even bigger problem than I'd anticipated. Tonight at eight thirty, Dillon's Steak and Ale was hosting an over-fifty singles' mixer.

Chapter 16

MY DAD WAS at a singles' mixer? He hadn't dated my whole life, and he'd never taken off his wedding ring either. It wasn't that women didn't notice him or even drop by with the occasional casserole, chocolate cake, or even, once, a rack of lamb. He'd always politely thanked them and returned their trays when the food was gone. He'd never followed up on their flirtations or innuendoes. So why now?

And then something else occurred to me. Was that the *real* reason he was hinting around that it wasn't a good idea for me to keep living here?

I knew he had every right to live his life, and if this was what he wanted, I would support him. But that didn't mean I wasn't going to need help dealing with it. I rummaged through a stack of business cards by the register and found the one I was looking for deep down in the pile. *Willow Summers. Talk Is Cheap.*

The card had a thick, bumpy texture thanks to the seeds that were infused into the paper. When I'd first met Willow, she was new to Proper and had been looking to rent costumes for a getting-to-know-you party. At the time, I'd thought she was inviting her neighbors. It turned out she was inviting her group—a collection of people who needed someone to share their burdens with. I didn't think I'd be willing to talk in front of a group of strangers, but the fact that Willow had rented a collection of Coneheads costumes in order to make her clients feel comfortable spoke volumes about the way she approached therapy.

I left her a message to call me, and then I called the police station.

"This is Margo Tamblyn. I'd like to speak to Detective Nichols. I have information regarding the murder of Paul Haverford."

TWENTY minutes later, I sat in the police station opposite the detective. She studied the contents of Sol Girard's rental agreement that I'd brought with me. I waited, silently, for her to put two and two together and come up with something other than "Margo Tamblyn is Guilty."

She shut the folder and pushed it a few inches away from her. "This is the rental agreement for Mr. Girard's costume."

"Yes. Both costumes."

"Both."

"Yes. He and the rest of the Elks were monsters, but he also rented a Spider-Man costume—did you see? And remember my statement from the night of the murder? I saw someone dressed as Spider-Man on the fire escape outside of the Alexandria Hotel right after I found Paul Haverford. And if you do some research into Sol's background, you'll find that he owns a bunch of property on the west side—property that would be worth nothing if the plans for Havetown came to fruition."

"You just happened upon this information?" she asked.

I tapped the folder in front of her. "There is a rental slip inside that folder that links Sol Girard to the Spider-Man costume. Somebody at the party had to have seen Spider-Man on the fire escape. When I yelled for help, someone thought it was an act and he yelled that Spider-Man would save me. You need to check it out. I know that much. If you receive a tip about an open investigation, you have to look into it."

"Ms. Tamblyn, let me show you something now." She opened up a black three-ring binder that she'd carried into the room when I first arrived. Inside was a clear plastic bag, and inside the bag were small pieces of torn up paper. She set the plastic bag in front of me. "We found this in Mr. Haverford's office. Do you know what it is?"

I knew what it was. The documents that I'd torn up and left scattered over Paul Haverford's desk the day he'd been murdered. It seemed from the tone of her voice that Detective Nichols knew it as well.

"Paul Haverford said he was going to go make an example out of Disguise DeLimit. I was mad. I tore up the documents and threw them on his desk and left. That doesn't mean I killed him."

"No, it doesn't, but it does give you motive and opportunity. Considering you own the costume shop, it would not be difficult for you to produce a rental slip to link Mr. Girard to the Spider-Man costume at the party."

"What about Camel Coat? The guy who was arguing with Mr. Haverford when I arrived at his office? Do you even know who he was? Because he was angry too. Maybe he had a real motive."

"Ms. Tamblyn, you are correct about one thing. If you provide us a tip, we have to investigate it. But I strongly suggest you reconsider your current strategy. Because if I find out that you're making up tips in order to distract us

from what really happened, I won't look the other way."
She picked up the manila folder that I'd brought and tapped
the fold on the desk a few times, and then held the folder
up to me. "Have a nice night."

Friday

The next morning I found myself sitting in Willow Summers's comfy makeshift living room. I was dressed in an
orange turtleneck, patchwork vest, brown tweed bell-
bottoms, and platform shoes with tights. A brown suede
floppy hat covered the top of my hair.

"I think Detective Nichols is out to get me," I said. Of
all of the issues that could have kicked off my first appointment with Willow, this seemed to be the most pressing.

Willow Summers's office was really a small Craftsman
house two miles past the Alexandria Hotel. The parking
lot was loose gravel, and the sidewalk was overgrown with
weeds. A stray cat had sat on a welcome mat in front of
the door but jumped down into the bushes that lined the
building as I approached. If the Zip-Two hadn't been running late, I would have taken a few extra minutes to try to
befriend him.

Willow had met me at the door and guided me into a
dark, wood-paneled room to the left inside of the interior.
Heavy floral curtains covered the windows from ceiling
to floor. The furniture was floral too, but not the same
print. I'd chosen an overstuffed pink and blue floral rock-
ing chair and Willow sat opposite me on the love seat. She
wore a long, flowing orange and brown dress with ivory
lace trim by the collar and sleeves, and ivory crocheted
tights over her legs, which were tucked up underneath her.
Brown leather clogs sat next to an empty metal cage next
to her sofa.

"Tell me why you think the detective is after you," she said.

"You probably heard about the murder at the Alexandria Hotel on Monday, right?" She nodded. "I was the one who found his body. It was a businessman, Paul Haverford. He and I had a fight earlier that day, and I shot the security camera with Silly String, and nobody was supposed to be up there anyway, and now she thinks I had something to do with it."

The curtains behind her moved. "Don't mind Thumper," Willow said. "I let him out of his cage this morning and he likes to hide behind the curtains."

"Thumper?"

"My rabbit."

I leaned forward. "There's a rabbit in here?"

She smiled. "There's a rabbit and a bird. I like to create a homey environment so people feel less nervous. Now let's get back to you. Have you ever experienced feelings of paranoia in the past, or is this the first time?"

I left Willow's office feeling better than I had since the murder. I headed back to the Zip. There was barely enough time to get back to the store before we opened the doors. Three days before Halloween and we still didn't know where the October 31 party would be. If it wasn't for the open homicide investigation, this would have qualified as one of our biggest crises.

There would be no getting away from the store today. The swim team had committed to another job long before Kirby connected them to us, so it would be my dad and I running the show. I powered up with a kale, banana, and peanut smoothie and joined my dad. He was standing by the sales counter examining the white lab rat head.

"Did you design this?" he asked.

"Yes. It's for Mr. Smythe, Kirby's chemistry teacher. He let his class choose his costume and this is what they came up with."

"Where'd you get the design?"

"I made it up."

He lifted the head with both hands and held it out in front of him. For the eyes, I'd found two round tap lights and had drawn pupils and irises on each. The lights had four cycles: white, strobe, red, and a slow swirl through every color of the rainbow. My dad had it set on swirl, and as the eye color morphed through red, yellow, pink, green, purple, orange, and blue, I had an off-kilter sensation, as if I were being hypnotized. Dad held the head up and looked inside.

"Eye holes?"

"Under the snout."

"Air holes?"

"Front of the neck."

"How do you know it won't move around once it's on?"

"There's a series of Velcro straps inside. They fit around the head and then over the top and secure in the back. Then the fur folds down on top of that. Watch." I took the head and folded the fur forward from a slit at the back of the head. Feeling around the interior, I located two straps of Velcro and pulled them around my head like a band. I lined up the Velcro and pressed the strips together. Next I found the piece of Velcro that ran over the top of my head and pulled it back, securing it to the pieces that were already in place. I draped the fur down over my head and shifted the entire thing slightly until my eyes were lined up with the eye holes. Then, I gently shook my head from side to side. The head stayed in place.

"Not bad," he said. "Not bad at all. You just made this up, you say?"

"Pretty much."

He put his arm around my shoulders. "Costumes are in your blood, Margo. When I go, I won't have to worry about the store."

"Go where? You just got back!"

He pointed to the ceiling. "Go."

I backed away and swatted his arm. "You're not going anywhere for a long time. And after that scare last April, don't even think about joking about your health."

It was just about eleven; time to open the store. Dad unlocked the front door while I looked into the mirror at the reflection of the rat head. I marked off two sections with pins where I could add ventilation. Behind me, my dad welcomed our first customers.

"Good morning and happy Halloween season!" he said. "I'm Jerry. Look around as long as you want, and let me know if you have something special in mind. If we don't have it, we can probably make it."

"Actually, I'm looking for Margo Tamblyn. Is she here?"

I turned to face the front door. "Cooper?" I said.

Chapter 17

MY VOICE CAME out muffed from under the white fur head.

Cooper looked at me. "Margo? Is that you in there?"

I tried to pull the head off, forgetting about the Velcro inside. I held up my finger in a wait-one-second gesture and then reached inside the head and undid the straps. When I finally pulled the head off, my hair flew up in a display of static electricity. I tried to smooth it down, too late. I grabbed my floppy suede '70s hat from the counter and pulled it on.

"Cooper, hi. What are you doing here? Are you looking for a costume?"

He scanned the room, lingering for a moment on the papier-mâché head of a devil next to a rack of red plastic pitchforks. "I came to see you." He smiled his aw-shucks smile. "I don't have a lot of time, but I wanted to give you a copy of the maps we were looking at." He held out a white cardboard tube.

"The quaternary maps," I said. "I didn't expect you to copy them so quickly. I hope it wasn't an inconvenience."

"Not at all. There's a town hall meeting tonight and the subject of what's going to happen to Paul Haverford's plans is on the agenda. These are a part of the conversation, so I was already working with them."

I took the tube, popped off the end cap, and stared inside. "Thank you," I said. Behind him, two couples entered the store and went different directions. My dad raised his eyebrows at me. "I'd love to offer you a cup of coffee and go over these right now, but I can't. In about an hour, this place will be full of customers and it's just my dad and I today."

"Don't worry about it." He looked at his watch. "I have to get back to the office anyway.

I walked him to the front door, mindful that I was being watched and that I'd most likely have questions to answer after he left. As we walked through the doors, a school bus pulled up in front of the store and a small army of children piled off and ran past us. Saved!

"Thanks again, Cooper. You didn't have to make the trip out here. I could have picked the maps up."

"This gave me a chance to surprise you." He reached up and tugged on the brim of my hat. "I thought you were mod?"

"I'm whatever strikes me when I wake up in the morning. The side effect of growing up in a costume shop."

"Sounds like a cool way to live." He grinned and pulled his keys out of his pocket. "You wouldn't— Would you— Do you have . . ." He cleared his throat. "Let me try this again. Do you have any interest in going to the town hall meeting tonight? Tak said you were interested in the Alexandria Hotel, and since that's going to be the hot subject . . ." His voice trailed off. "Normally those things can get a little boring, and I can't promise anything, but . . . Sorry. It's going to be boring. Just say no."

"Yes," I said without thinking too much about it. "I'd love to." As soon as the words were out of my mouth, I realized how much it sounded like Cooper had just asked me out on a date and I'd accepted. I felt my face flush red and glanced over my shoulder to see if anybody was watching. My dad was, but judging from the look on his face, he was more upset by the fact that I wasn't in the store helping with customers. "Where is it? What time should I arrive?"

"It's in the community center. It starts at seven thirty."

"I'll be there."

"Great. See you tonight." He walked around the corner and hopped into his SUV. I waved as he started up the engine and then drove away. Someone tugged on the back of my vest and I looked down.

"'Scuse me," said a small boy. "That man over there said to ask you where to find Batman in my size."

"Batman? Sure. Follow me."

EIGHT hours later, both my dad and I collapsed into plastic chairs that had been left around the store for customers who needed to sit. I kicked off the platform shoes and stared at my swollen feet. "I don't think I'm ever going to be able to wear regular shoes again," I said.

"One more day," he said. "I'm getting too old for this." He kicked his own shoes off, stuck his feet out in front of him, and wiggled his toes. "What's it going to be for dinner tonight? Take-out or a restaurant?"

I glanced at the clock. "You're on your own for dinner. I'm going to a town hall meeting."

He leaned forward. "Since when are you interested in

county politics? Did this have anything to do with your visitor earlier today?"

"That was Cooper. He's a friend—" I caught myself right before I said Tak's name. "He works in the Clark County Planning Office. I met him a couple of days ago."

"Does he know Tak?"

"Why do you ask that?"

"Because Tak used to work in the Clark County Planning Office." He looked at me as if I was slow.

"Oh, sure, yes, that makes sense. Yes, he knows Tak."

"Huh." My dad stood up and patted my head. "What time is this town hall meeting?"

"Seven thirty." I pushed myself up and followed him up the stairs. "You can figure out dinner on your own, right? Call Don, he'll bring you something."

"I'll be fine. Go, get ready for your meeting."

I took a quick shower and changed into a navy blue skirt suit, tights, and low-heeled pumps. I put on a little makeup and moved my wallet and phone into a small handbag that I could sling across my body while I drove the scooter. I pulled my door shut behind me and overheard my dad chuckle. I approached the kitchen. He was on the phone, his back to me.

"How about I come over at eight thirty?" he said. He paused for a moment, and then said, "Great. I'll see you then."

I set my handbag on the table. He turned quickly, surprised that I was standing there. "Did you take my advice and call Don? What are you two crazy kids going to do tonight?"

"Not Don. That was Marilyn Robinson. I ran into her last night. Nice lady." He patted the pockets of his wool blazer as if he was checking for something. "Well, this is a first," he said. "Both of us going out on dates."

Jeez. At this rate I was going to be seeing Willow Summers every single day.

* * *

I arrived at the community center a few minutes early. Cooper wasn't there. We hadn't made concrete plans to sit together or meet out front, so I took a seat in the back row. If he wanted to find me, he would.

The room was the kind of makeshift area that could be used for a number of different activities. Large squares of maple made up the walls, and mostly blue Berber carpeting covered the floor. Here and there, stains from spilled cups of coffee had turned the blue to a dismal shade of brown, but it appeared that no one had prioritized the act of cleaning the stains.

At the front of the room, two collapsible tables were set up on either side of a wooden podium. A handful of men and women filled the chairs behind the table, facing the audience. They talked among themselves in voices too low to overhear.

Cork bulletin boards hung at the front and alongside the room, advertising upcoming bingo games, carpools, local businesses, and pets up for adoption. An American flag from the time when Nevada became a state was framed and mounted on the wall next to a row of chipped bookcases. The shelves were filled with sets of leather-bound books. Scents of coffee and popcorn from a small snack table outside of the entrance filled the air as people arrived and helped themselves.

I wasn't sure what to expect, so I unscrewed the cap from a bottle of water and tried to relax. Whether it was my dad's date with the bank teller or my spontaneous plans to meet Cooper when I was somewhat dating Tak in private, I felt unsettled. As the clock ticked closer to seven thirty and I sat alone, it struck me how silly it was that I hadn't invited Tak. Had I wanted this to feel like a date? And if so, was I bummed that it appeared as though Cooper had stood me up?

I texted Tak. *At town hall meeting. Alexandria Hotel on agenda. Join?*

He replied a few minutes later. *Already have plans. Say hi to Coop for me.*

I stared at the phone. If I hadn't said anything, then Cooper must have. Which meant that Tak didn't care. Which meant maybe Tak had a different reason for keeping our relationship secret.

I was pulled away from my dating dilemma by the sound of the door closing. I looked up. Cooper stood next to my row.

"Sorry I'm late," he said.

"You're not late. The meeting hasn't started."

He looked confused. "I know. They were waiting for me." He had a laptop bag hanging from his shoulder, and he took it off and held it out. "Can you hold on to this for me? I have to get up front. If you have any questions, let me know and I'll try to answer them when it's all over."

I took the laptop bag and he walked down the center aisle and took a seat at the last vacant chair facing the room.

Maybe I'd been wrong about thinking this was a date.

A man in a dark suit moved to the podium. He called the meeting to order. Chatter dropped to nonexistent and he set the agenda for the evening.

"Ladies and gentlemen, we've set a specific agenda to discuss the property at 125 West Main Line Avenue, also known as the Alexandria Hotel. Under the ownership of Haverford Venture Capital, the hotel was to be demolished and the land used to construct a new development called"—he flipped through a few pages in front of him—"Havetown. Out of respect for the recently deceased Paul Haverford, we would like to settle this matter quickly and efficiently. We are aware that we will have people speaking for and against this project. Before we get started, I'd like our committee members to introduce themselves. Who wants to start?"

One by one, the seven people seated at the front of the room stood up, said their name and their job. The committee was comprised of two members of the city council, a recording secretary, two longtime residents of Proper City, the man who had made opening remarks, and Cooper, who was there on behalf of the planning commission.

The speaker returned to the podium. "Judging from the number of people here, I'm guessing a lot of you have something to say on this matter, so let's get started. First, we'll hear arguments for the demolition of the hotel and the construction of Havetown, and then against." He indicated a microphone stand between the two aisles of chairs and instructed anyone who wanted to talk to form a line behind it. Chairs shifted as people stood, jockeying for their position. Clearly the future of the Alexandria was a hot button for Proper.

The line quickly blocked my view, so I stood and moved to the back corner so I could see. It was then I saw that the first man in line was the man who'd been arguing with Paul Haverford the day I'd shown up at his offices. Camel Coat.

Chapter 18

"PLEASE STATE YOUR name, where you are from or who you are representing, and what your relationship to Proper City is prior to making your statement," instructed the proctor.

Camel Coat leaned toward the microphone. "My name is Bill Perth. Paul Haverford and I formed a partnership for the development of Havetown. His death, though untimely, should have no bearing on the timetables already established in the planning stages of Havetown. The demolition of the Alexandria Hotel has been a part of those plans all along. This meeting is a waste of time. There is no cause for this matter to be on the town hall agenda, and if a vote against our development plans is reached tonight, I will have no other choice but to seek legal action to protect my investment."

A rumble spilled out through the line and the crowd, the buzz of eighty or so people equaling that of a jackhammer. I watched Cooper. He kept his face from reacting but made a note on a tablet in front of him. The proctor, who had barely sat back down into his chair, returned to the podium. "Ladies and gentlemen, please," he said, trying to calm everybody down.

Another ripple tore through the crowd. Heads moved closer together as people made comments to one another. The proctor cleared his throat in the microphone in front of him. Someone hissed "Shhhhh!" loudly and the room quieted down.

"Mr. Perth, you may continue."

The tall man unbuttoned his camel coat and shrugged out of it. He folded it over itself and set it on the front row chair where he'd been sitting before the meeting started.

For the first time since I'd arrived, I scanned the crowd. I recognized a few people here and there: the sisters who owned Packin' Pistils, the manager of Catch-22, the landscaper for the Proper City Park. A family of six sat in the row in front of me. I recognized the father as Andy Caplan, the driver of the Zip-Two. His wife sat between two of their children, who ignored the activities in the courtroom because they were more interested in the games they could play on their phones.

When Bill Perth returned to the microphone, the room hushed down to near quiet. Without the polish that his topcoat provided, I could see that he lacked the air of successful businessman that Paul Haverford had probably been born with. Bill was stout, with most of his weight falling around his midsection. His suit jacket stretched across his back, leaving strained fabric by the seams of his sleeves. He had a white fringe of hair around an otherwise bald head, and his skin had a pinkish caste.

"Mr. Perth, please tell us the nature of your business with Paul Haverford and how it pertains to the Alexandria Hotel," the proctor said.

"Paul Haverford and I have been silent partners for the past seven years. We've invested in properties throughout

Nevada. The Alexandria Hotel is the first location we've purchased in Proper City. The town's proximity to the California/Nevada state line represents a unique location for housing."

"So you want to tear down the hotel and develop housing?" asked a voice from the audience.

Bill turned to the crowd and scanned the faces. "Our plans for development include leveling the hotel and neighboring structures, rezoning the area for residential, and building apartment buildings to draw new residents into Proper. Based on the expanded population, we have interested businesses and entertainment developers who will bring in additional restaurants, movie theaters, and shopping centers. Transportation to and from Las Vegas will be added, as will gambling establishments. The town will benefit from the additional tax revenue."

"And the small guys will be driven out of business," said the owner of Catch-22. Another rumble cycled through the crowd.

Bill pulled a white handkerchief out of his pants pocket and dragged it across his shiny forehead. His face had grown more red as he spoke, but his stammer had all but disappeared.

The proctor tapped a small gavel on the table at the front of the room. The buzz of voices quieted down. "Mr. Perth, the Alexandria Hotel is under consideration to become a historic landmark. Paul Haverford made it clear that he did not care about the town of Proper City in his development plans. If the petition to change the status of the building is granted, his plans will have to be halted."

That was strange. All this talk about leveling the property and building new apartments, and if Annette Crowley from the conservancy got her way, it would be a moot point.

"Haverford told me not to worry about the conservancy. He said he'd handle them."

The man to the left of Cooper gestured for the microphone. "You said that you and Paul Haverford were partners in this deal. If we could understand the nature of that partnership, we might be better prepared to address your concerns. Can you provide evidence of your business collaboration?"

"Unfortunately, I can't. Paul Haverford and I had a verbal agreement," Bill Perth said.

Chapter 19

THE WOMAN BEHIND me leaned down. "Not worth the paper it's written on," she said to me. Instantly I recognized the voice. I turned to confirm what I'd suspected. The newcomer was Francine Wheeler.

She wore a blue hooded jacket over a white shirt and dark trousers. Next to her was a small metal handcart with a box filled with notebooks, loose papers bound by a rubber band, and a carousel of slides. A long rolled tube of paper jutted out from one of the corners of the box. It looked suspiciously like the rolled map that Cooper had delivered to Disguise DeLimit.

"Find anything interesting the other morning?" she asked.

"The other morning?"

"At the hotel. You were there to do prep work for tonight's meeting, weren't you?"

Truth was that I'd been at the hotel for strictly selfish reasons. I wanted to get a look at the scene of the crime in broad daylight. But dressed as I'd been, in the uniform of a park ranger, I could see that I'd led Francine to her misassumption.

As I tried to figure out how to best explain my interest in the hotel and the town hall meeting, she leaned in again. "Perth is going to hijack this meeting if we don't do something about it." She stepped forward and cupped her hands around her mouth. "The only truth that Bill Perth said was that this meeting is a waste of time. I have evidence here that shows that the Alexandria Hotel is built on an active fault line. Demo that hotel and you risk the safety of the residents of Proper."

Heads turned to face us. Francine, not one to shy away from the center of attention, turned to me. "Help me with this, wouldya?" she said. She tipped the handle of the cart my direction and then walked up the aisle to the front of the room and grabbed the microphone from the stand.

"If any issue is to be resolved tonight, it should be this. The city council should acknowledge once and for all the work I've done in the field of seismology and the potential impact on the town of Proper City if this project is pursued. We can change the zoning laws so this doesn't become an issue again. You can affect change if you're willing to take your heads out of the dirt."

"Ms. Wheeler, you and your colleague will have your say. I will not have you derail this meeting."

"Perth's the one who derailed this meeting, not us. I have files, maps, test results. My colleague is bringing them up now—where is she?—that will prove the dangers."

Heat flushed my face. Francine had cast me on her side of the argument. Truth was, I would have taken any side opposite Paul Haverford. Besides that, I didn't want to see the Alexandria torn down long before I'd heard her speak of fault lines and tremors. Proper City had little left to remind us of the time when Pete Proper had founded it, but that little bit of history meant a lot.

I pulled the cart of information forward, only daring to make eye contact with Cooper when I reached the front of the room. He winked. I set the cart next to Francine and sat in a vacant seat in the front row. She dug through her cart for a binder and flipped through pages and pages of reports.

"I need a slide projector and a screen. And an extension cord. You didn't bring one, did you?" she asked me. I shook my head. "Next time be prepared. Okay, who's going to help me?"

The proctor stood up. "Ms. Wheeler, this is a town hall meeting. There are protocols to be followed. We are not here to discuss the geographic mapping you have been conducting in Proper."

"If construction is started on Havetown, the citizens are at risk. Anybody who lives in that housing will be taking their lives into their hands every single day."

"You cannot just charge the front of the room to make your case."

"This meeting shouldn't even be taking place! Paul Haverford is dead. Any plans to develop the west end of Proper City should have died with him."

The proctor spent the next thirteen minutes trying to regain control of the meeting. He finally gave up. Instead of hearing arguments for and opposed to the demolition of the Alexandria, the committee decided that the meeting would be rescheduled. People emptied out into the parking lot. Francine pulled her cart to the side of the room and a crowd formed around her. I scanned the audience for Bill Perth, but he was gone.

Although the meeting had been cut short, I'd already learned far more than I'd expected. Bill Perth claimed to be a partner in Paul Haverford's development deal, but I'd seen no mention of him in the paperwork I had at the store. Perth also claimed that Haverford said he'd take care of the conservancy. Interesting that Annette Crowley hadn't shown up for the meeting tonight. She said that the issue had been resolved. With murder?

And was what Francine Wheeler claimed actually true? Would construction on the Alexandria Hotel trigger an active fault line and put residents of Proper at risk? If so, then the argument about the future of the Alexandria boiled down to two things: money vs. safety. There were a whole lot of people invested in either pushing for or stopping the development of Havetown. And there was enough at risk that the stakes were high. Worth killing for?

I let the majority of the attendees leave the room first, hanging back until Cooper had separated himself from the committee.

"Wow," he said. "These things are usually pretty boring."

"I guess I should thank you for making sure my first town hall meeting was something special."

"Your first one? From the cheap seats up front, it looked like you had something to do with the chaos. You said you'd met Francine, but why did she call you a colleague?"

I looked down at my outfit, and then back at Cooper. "You know how I was dressed like a gangster the day we met? And at the planning office I was mod and today at the store I was a hippie?"

"This has to do with your clothes?"

"I wear costumes. Not just for Halloween, but for every day. Not masks, but the clothes. It started when I was growing up and my dad was raising me on his own. He didn't have a lot of time away from the store to shop for me, so my school clothes came from our inventory. I guess I got used to it. When I met Francine, I was dressed like a park ranger. She was too, only probably for real. She must have thought my clothes were official and assumed that I was a fellow seismologist."

"Because you were dressed like a park ranger. But seriously, a park ranger?" He looked at me like he didn't really believe me.

"The rest of the year it's more like an accessory here and there, but it's our busy season at the store so I step things up a bit."

"Why aren't you in a costume tonight?"

"I am." I glanced at my suit again. "This is my Normal Woman costume."

"Do you wear that one often?"

"I've never worn it before in my life."

Cooper laughed out loud. We were close to the exit, and a few stragglers passed us. Cooper stepped to the side to make room for them to pass. "I'm surprised Hosh didn't come with you. He usually likes these things."

I hadn't expected Cooper to bring up Tak, but now that he had, I relaxed a bit. "I did ask him, but he had other plans."

"Like I said, he's always got something going. You want to get a cup of coffee?"

There it was again, a comment about Tak's personal life. It reminded me that I didn't know where I stood. I looked away from Cooper into the parking lot. One by one cars pulled out of their spaces. One of them was a maroon sedan, like I'd seen parked in front of Haverford Venture Capital the day I'd gone to see Paul Haverford. I guessed that it belonged to Bill Perth.

"Margo?" Cooper said. "Coffee?"

"No, thank you. It's going to be late by the time I get home and I think it's best that I head back now."

"Okay, well, thanks for showing up. You brightened up the room, even if it was only for a little." He smiled.

I had the distinct impression that Cooper was feeling me out, trying to determine if I was interested in an actual date instead of the excuse of a town hall meeting. And I knew, very much so, that until I knew where things stood with Tak, any actions on my part would be for the wrong reasons. Cooper was nice and polite and interesting and attractive, but I wasn't a juggler. I wished I'd been honest from the beginning so this awkwardness wouldn't have taken place

"Thanks for dropping off the maps today," I said. I pulled my keys out of my bag and took a step toward the scooter.

"Bye, Margo."

The maroon car was still in the lot when I pulled out. I turned right, and then took an immediate left on the next street. I cut the engine and walked the scooter into a U-turn until I sat hidden by a row of shrubbery. I turned the engine off and parked the scooter, and then got off and crept forward until I had a clear view of the maroon sedan.

Fourteen minutes later, the lights to the car flickered. Bill Perth approached it and got inside. He pulled out and turned right. I ran back to the scooter, hopped on, and took off after him.

If home is where you park your car, then Bill Perth lived in one of the smaller houses in Christopher Robin Crossing. Named after the characters A. A. Milne had created, the development included streets like Piglet Lane and Eeyore Drive. I'd spent a little time here recently, when a client of the store had been murdered and I'd gotten involved in finding the killer. What I knew was that these houses didn't come cheap, and the owners controlled a large portion of the wealth that flowed through Proper. If Bill Perth lived here, he probably wasn't scrounging between sofa cushions to find spare change.

I followed him through the entrance to his development but felt too inconspicuous to stop, so I turned the opposite direction from him. Lucky for me, he left his car parked alongside of the curb of 241 Eeyore Drive. The address was easy enough to remember. I looped around the lot and headed home with far too many things on my mind to sleep.

Saturday

The next morning, I dressed in a white shirt, navy blue jacket, skirt, tights, and shoes. I knotted a turquoise neckerchief around my throat and pinned a small flight attendant cap to my head. I found a set of gold wings in my accessory box and pinned them to my lapel. The kitchen—the whole house—was suspiciously silent. I tapped on the door to my dad's bedroom. There was no answer.

"Dad? I'm heading out early. I'll be back before the store opens." I rapped my knuckles on the door again. "Dad?"

This time the door eased open. The bed was still made.

He hadn't come home from his date.

Chapter 20

THERE WASN'T A therapist in Nevada who would take my calls at seven in the morning, and this time I required more of a response than "Meow." I did the next best thing. I called Bobbie.

"If you're calling about yoga, you're too late. Half an hour ago I was totally calm and now these darn bears are making me crazy."

I'd never heard her get angry toward the bears and her reply temporarily sidetracked me. "What did the bears do?"

"I'm trying to make them costumes and it's not exactly working. I thought it would make for a nice window display."

"I could help you with that if you want," I said. "But first, you have to meet me for breakfast."

BOBBIE was already seated in the diner across the street from Money Changes Everything when I arrived. She wasn't alone. Teddy bears in various stages of dress filled the booth with her.

"I will not admit that I can't do this," she said.

"They're not—terrible," I said.

"They're not great either."

"I'll make you a deal. You play therapist for the next hour and I'll make the costumes."

"I'm your friend, Margo. If there's something you need to talk about, just tell me. You don't need a therapist."

"I need confidentiality. I need to know that what I tell you won't go any farther than this booth."

"Honestly, Margo, you didn't require this level of confidentiality in sixth grade. What gives?"

What she lacked in patience was countered by the army of teddy bears that surrounded us. Willow Summers may have had a bunny, a bird, and a cat, but it was hard to top a diner booth filled with teddy bears. I wasn't sure where to start, so I just jumped in.

"My dad is dating. For the first time in my life he's dating, and Tak might be cheating on me, and Bill Perth had a silent partnership with Paul Haverford, and Francine Wheeler thinks I'm a seismologist. Halloween is in two days and Ebony still hasn't found a place for the party. And Soot keeps bringing dead mice into the store and I think Detective Nichols wants to arrest me."

"Is that all?"

"The ghost of Pete Proper may have followed me out of the Alexandria Hotel the other night, but that's the least of my worries."

She stared at me for a couple of seconds. "You are one mixed-up chick."

"I resent that!"

"In about twenty seconds you covered everything from your dad's love life to a paranormal entity, and I can't get past the fact that you lied to me."

"About what?"

"About you and Tak. He can't cheat on you unless there's a collective 'you.' Is there a collective you?"

"There's a collective you. We. Us. Whatever. Yes. I lied to you, but you can't get upset about that right now. You promised!"

She picked her phone up from the table and tapped the screen a few times. "I agreed to that, what, like three minutes ago?"

"Something like that."

"Fine. When the alarm goes off, I'm back to being your friend and we will discuss this. But there's no way we can cover all of your issues in the next fifty-seven minutes, so as your temporary therapist, I'm making the executive decision to table all discussion of Tak until I'm off the clock."

"I should have made an appointment with a professional."

She crossed her arms and sat back against the booth.

"Okay, fine. Ever since the murder at the Alexandria Hotel, I feel like Detective Nichols is after me. So far I've found"—I looked up at the ceiling and counted names—"six suspects."

"You're opening with the murder? I thought for sure you'd open with your dad dating."

"I'm going to save that issue for Soot."

She rolled her eyes. "Okay. Talk me through the murders."

"The day I went to confront Haverford, he was arguing with another man. I found out last night that the man is Bill Perth. He claims to be a silent partner in Havetown, says that he and Haverford had a verbal agreement about the property. He's pushing for the demo of the hotel and the construction timetables to move forward even though Paul Haverford was murdered. That's a pretty hefty motive, right? If the development goes through, now it's all in his name."

"First he has to prove this verbal agreement. That's not going to be easy."

"I know. Okay, next there's Francine Wheeler. She works for the county in the geology department. She's a real dynamo. I found her testing the ground around the hotel Wednesday morning. She says that end of Proper is on top of a series of active fault lines, and if the hotel is leveled and construction starts, we'll set off a chain reaction that could cause people to die."

"She said that? People would die?"

"Maybe not right away, but she claims to have maps and charts and tests to back it all up. She is a very determined woman. She might have killed Haverford in order to stop Havetown from going forward. You know, sacrifice the one instead of putting the many at risk?"

"That's not really her decision to make."

"Exactly. But if she did . . . I mean, she could have. She was at the Alexandria Hotel two days after the murder. She said she was running tests, but maybe she was making sure she didn't leave any evidence behind."

"Who else?"

I chewed my lip for a moment. "Your friend Annette Crowley."

"From the conservancy?" She leaned forward. "Did you find something out about her?"

As pure of intention as Bobbie appeared to be, she enjoyed gossip as much as the next person. "I found an article from eight years ago. Before you volunteered for them. The historical society was trying to save the Peppermint House in Moxie. According to the article that I found, they had all but lost their chances because they couldn't afford to fight the rich title holders."

"That happens all the time, Mitty. There's no money to be made from a building that gets historical status, but depending on where the building is, there's lots of money to be made by developers."

"You didn't let me finish. The head of the company she was fighting took ill. He backed off, the historical society won, and Annette took a six month leave from the board."

"She fought a long battle and won. Maybe she just needed a break."

"Bobbie, the man who owned the Peppermint House was Paul Haverford."

"No way."

"Way. And remember what she said to us? *'The Alexandria Hotel is no longer an issue for the conservancy.'* Why not? And the other thing she said: no more Haverford, no more problem. It's like she knew that the issue would die with him."

"Mitty, I know you're looking for suspects, but be reasonable. The next thing you know, you're going to say you suspect everybody who was at the pre-party."

"Not everybody." A waitress came over to our table and dropped off a plate of waffles in front of me and a plate filled with scrambled eggs, sausage links, toast, and hash browns in front of Bobbie.

"What? I know what you like so I ordered when I got here." She cut her sausage into small rings, speared one, and popped it into her mouth.

I was going to need more than yoga to offset the caloric intake of a daily breakfast of waffles and smoothies. I used the back of my fork to spread the whipped butter across the surface of my waffles. As it melted, it pooled into the small squares, releasing the cozy fragrance of sweetness. We both stopped talking long enough to make a dent in the food in front of us. Two bites into the second half of my waffle, I set my fork down.

"Sol Girard has a motive," I said quietly.

Bobbie finished chewing her toast and washed her mouthful down with orange juice. I took her silence as an opportunity to keep talking. "He put all of his money into property out on the west end of Proper. He was planning on building low income apartments. It would have been in direct competition with Havetown. According to the planning office, if Havetown happens, Sol's property will lose all value."

"He would lose everything?"

"Pretty much."

"Huh. Sounds like you have some solid suspects. Why do you think Detective Nichols is after you?"

I told Bobbie about the argument I'd had with Paul Haverford when he came to Disguise DeLimit, how I'd torn up the contract and left it scattered across his desk, and how I'd obliterated the elevator security camera with Silly String from my spider costume.

At that moment, Bobbie's phone broke out in an instrumental version of Cyndi Lauper's "Money Changes Everything." Several patrons of the diner turned to find out where the noise was coming from. She crossed her arms and raised her eyebrows.

"Time's up."

"But we didn't make any progress. I'm no closer to knowing who committed murder."

"I think this is all too dangerous," she said. "You need to take what you know to Detective Nichols and let her handle it. She's the police. She's equipped to handle murderers. You're not."

"But you said—"

"I said I would listen and not judge. I said nothing about helping you find a murderer. Now, spill. It's time to pay the piper."

Chapter 21

IT FELT GOOD to tell Bobbie about my secret relationship with Tak, even if the relationship was less than I'd initially thought. Just the act of confessing that it had existed, that we'd set up clandestine meeting spots over the past few months, brought a glow back to the whole thing. And since Bobbie and I had been friends through elementary school, junior high, and high school, it felt like we were right back in the Proper City High library, whispering to each other about our prospective prom dates.

The subject got stickier when I brought up Cooper. "Twice now he's said something about Tak playing the field. And last night, I felt guilty about going to the town hall meeting with Cooper, so I texted Tak and he said he already had plans. Does that mean he's seeing other people?"

"Would it bother you if he was? I mean, it sounds like this Cooper guy is interested in you. What are you going to do if he asks you to something more than a town hall meeting?"

"I don't know. It's more complicated because they're friends."

"You know what I'm going to say, don't you?"

"I think so." I finished off the last of my waffles and set my silverware on the plate. "You're going to say I need to talk to Tak. Which means we're going to have one of those we-have-to-talk moments before we're even officially dating. Which is going to make me look like I'm needy and possessive and insecure. Who wants to look like they're needy and possessive and insecure when they're—you know—in the crush stages?"

"This is why normal people over the age of sixteen don't try to date in secret."

I balled my napkin up from my lap and threw it at her. She laughed.

"Talk to him," she said. "It doesn't have to be all serious, but you have a right to know where you stand. I'm sure it was totally innocent."

Everything Bobbie said made sense. I glanced at the wall clock. It was a little after eight. I needed to be back at the costume shop by ten to have a full hour to prep the store before opening. Today, the last Saturday before Halloween, would be filled with point-of-sale purchases. Colored hair spray, professional makeup, cheap wigs. The best of our costumes had been rented, but we could still turn out special costumes under pressure. If someone came in needing a costume, we'd come up with something.

"Do it now," Bobbie said.

Before I could choose the right words for a text, the door to the diner opened and Gina Cassavogli walked in, followed by a few of the women who worked at Candy Girls. She spotted Bobbie and me, pointed to a large round booth in the opposite corner, and split off from them. As the women made their way to the table, Gina headed toward us.

"Enjoy your freedom while it lasts, Margo," she said. "They don't serve waffles in prison."

"What's that supposed to mean?"

"You know what people are saying about you. You murdered Paul Haverford because his plans were going to destroy your little store. It's only a matter of time before Detective Nichols comes over with a pair of handcuffs. Real ones, not the plastic ones in your inventory."

My face felt hot. Gina's voice was too loud, her mannerisms too big, and her accusations too much for me to handle. I stood up and faced her. "You're just angry because there won't be any money coming into Candy Girls now that Paul Haverford is dead. You sold the store so you could be part of his big plans for expansion and those plans aren't going to happen."

"Shows what you know. I asked someone who used to work in the planning office about it and he said the murder wouldn't stop anything. Havetown is going to be built, new businesses are going to come to Proper, and Candy Girls is going to be the costume shop where everybody shops. We're going to expand and become a household name. Your little store will become a roadside attraction, at least until it files for bankruptcy."

"Who told you that?"

She put her hands on her hips. "Tak Hoshiyama."

"When?"

An evil smile crept across her face. "Yesterday when he and Nancy Nichols came to our store to pick out costumes. And Nancy said they were close to making an arrest."

ASIDE from the restaurants that served breakfast, there were very few businesses open at eight thirty in the morning. I left Bobbie with some money to pay my share of the bill and left. I wasn't ready to hear my dad talk about his date last night and I'd lost interest in talking to Tak. Instead of stopping, I drove past the store and continued on to the west side of Proper.

There was a noticeable change in the appearance of the properties the farther I went. Proper City was a desert town, so lush green lawns were nonexistent, even in wealthy areas like Christopher Robin Crossing. Professional landscaping included rock gardens, cacti, and the occasional bird feeder. But landscaping was a luxury not afforded the residents of West Proper. Yards were patchy with yellow grass and dirt. Bicycles were propped against houses, next to baskets of toys and dirt-coated, kicked-off shoes.

Main Line Road dead-ended into the base of a mountain. A double-ended arrow indicated that the narrow, dirt-covered road around the base of the mountain ran both ways, and a smaller, faded arrow underneath it indicated strawberries for sale to the left. I turned and followed the sign even though I wasn't in the market for strawberries. I hoped to find signs of life somewhere that direction. It was three miles before I did.

A string of rundown houses lined an unpaved road. The houses were all the same shade of concrete with black tar paper roofs. A shiny 1966 two-door Lincoln with a white hardtop and red vinyl interior sat in the third driveway on the right.

I knew that car. It belonged to Dig Allen.

I hadn't thought much about Dig since the party. I slowed down as I drove past and spotted him on the side of the house. I turned around at the end of the street and drove back, pulling into the driveway behind the Lincoln.

"Margo? What are you doing out this way?"

"I went for a drive and let my mind wander. Didn't

know I was going to end up here. Are you— You don't—
What are you doing here?" I asked.

"This was my mom's house," he said. "She passed away
a couple of years ago. My sister and her daughter needed
a place to stay so there was no rush to sell it."

"Doe she still live here?"

"No, she just needed a place to get back on her feet after
her divorce. The judge granted her custody based on this
address, and truth was I liked having her and the little one
around."

"Why'd she move?"

He crossed his arms and leaned back on the heels of
his black CAT boots. "Margo, don't try to be so polite.
This house isn't in the best condition. My sister got a job
in Moxie and moved six months ago."

"What are you going to do with the house?"

"Funny thing about that. This property has gone from
being the forgotten land of Proper City to a hot commodity.
You know Sol Girard?"

"Sure," I said, trying to keep the surprise out of my
voice. "I heard he owned some property out this way."

"He owns the rest of these houses. He's got some good
ideas about tearing them down and building newer houses
for lower income families."

"Do you oppose him?"

"Oppose? No. I like the idea. Proper City isn't about
the rich folks, it's a town for people who are getting started.
Families, neighbors, community. I respect what Sol wants
to do. The only reason I didn't sell to him was because my
sister was living here."

"What's going to happen now?"

"I'm not sure. That Haverford guy swooped in and
bought up ten times the property that Sol owns. His plans
are to tear all of this down and have it rezoned for

businesses and retail. What do we need retail for? There's a mall in Primm that'll sell you whatever you want. And for the people who want entertainment, they can drive into Vegas."

"So what's going to happen to Sol's plans?"

"Depends on what happens to the zoning petitions that were filed. Until a decision is reached, Sol's plans are on hold. He's sitting on the worst piece of real estate in Clark County and there's not a darn thing he can do about it."

Chapter 22

"**WHAT ABOUT YOU?** Are you going to sell to him now that your sister has moved out?"

"He stopped asking so I stopped answering. But between you and me, I like Sol's ideas a lot more than I like the concept of Havetown."

I thanked Dig and left. It was a quick drive back to the costume shop. When I arrived, my dad's car was parked in his space behind the shop. I locked my helmet to my scooter and felt the hood of his car. It was still warm.

I went inside and found him juggling a silver candelabra and two green glass bottles with corks in the top. I took the bottles from him.

"Good morning," he said. "You got up early."

"I met Bobbie for breakfast. You must not have heard me leave." I studied his face for his reaction. "How was your date last night?"

"I don't want to talk about it." He moved the candelabra from one hand to the other. "How was yours?"

"I don't want to talk about it either."

He turned his back on me and climbed into the store's front window. Someone had rented the Dr. Frankenstein and monster costumes, so my dad had returned to the Dracula theme, this time with Mina Harker. The table remained set, but now the pale female mannequin dined with Dracula. Don was inside the window. He dabbed two drops of bloodred nail polish on the mannequin's neck, and then aimed a hair dryer at it to direct the polish into the appearance of blood drops. When he was satisfied, he adjusted the silver candelabra on the table. Dad took the bottles from me and handed them to Don, who set them next to a domed silver serving tray.

"What's in the bottles?"

"Water," he said. "It didn't look right with empty bottles."

A marble cutting board filled with cheese, grapes, apples, and crackers sat on the table in front of the figure of Mina Harker. I picked up a grape and stuck it in my mouth. Immediately, I spat it out. It was plastic.

"You didn't think I'd use real food, did you?" he said. "Have I taught you nothing?" He reached to the side of the window and pulled on a hidden cord. Heavy plum velvet drapes closed behind the two figures. I climbed out and went to the sidewalk to get a better look. Instead, I found myself face-to-face with several mummies.

"Hi, Margo," said one.

"Kirby?" I asked, spotting his close-cropped red hair peeking through the wrappings around his head.

"Yep. Can I talk to you for a minute?" He stepped a few feet away from the other mummies and gestured for me to follow.

"What's up?" I asked.

"I know you've been buying us pizza for dinner every night, but do you think maybe tonight you can give us a gift card to The Cheat Sheet?"

"The bed and bath store? Sure. Why?"

"Well, we needed our sheets for the costumes and now none of us has anything to put on our beds."

Business started as soon as we opened the doors. Dad and I tasked out Kirby's friends to make our last-minute deliveries while we helped the procrastinators assemble costumes from the pieces we had left. Our racks of merchandise had thinned considerably, as had the stockroom. If Soot had left any mice in the stockroom, we would have turned them into costumes.

The cowbell over the door chimed just after noon. Ebony entered. She was dressed in a blond wig and a chain-mail dress with elaborately folded shoulders. The dress was cut high on each side, revealing toned thighs. Garters that matched the dress connected to chain-mail leggings. The same chain-like material covered thick gloves that came halfway up her forearms. She held a small bow and arrow in one hand and a bichon frise in the other. He yipped.

She towered above the mummies, who gave her a wide berth, except for one. He walked up to her, checked her out from head to feet and back. "*Mad Max Beyond Thunderdome.* Cool."

"Finally getting into the spirit of Halloween, are you?" I asked.

"If it's good enough for Tina Turner, it's good enough for me. Now, are you people hungry? I've been in the test kitchen all morning working on recipes for the party Monday. I need some tasters. Who's in?"

Cheers rose from the mummies around the store. The customers took the scene in with amusement. Two mummies cleared a table that held stacks of old rubber masks, and Ebony set her insulated bag on top. She made a few more trips to and from her car. When she was done, the table was set with a red crushed velvet table cloth and plates of pumpkin puffs, deviled eggs, meatballs in the shape of hearts on wooden skewers (she called them stakes), baked heads of garlic that had been cross sectioned and drizzled with olive oil, *pan de muerta*, and an assortment of finger sandwiches in the shapes of ghosts, coffins, and witches that she'd punched out with cookie cutters.

Shopping ceased as customers and employees lined up to get a sampling of Ebony's wares. It was no secret that when Ebony planned an event, she went all out. Shindig offered more than coordinated plates and napkins. The city of Proper had hired her to deliver Halloween, and even if she was scared of the spirit world, she wasn't going to let us down.

Ebony pulled me aside somewhere between my fourth and fifth pumpkin puff. "What'd you have to do to get these mummies to work for you?"

"Feed them pizza and promise them new sheets."

She started to reply, but then shifted her weight and put her hands on her hips. "Are you for real?"

"That's what Kirby said."

"Kids," she said, shaking her head. She turned her attention back to me. "Your dad tells me you went on a date last night. Anybody I know?"

"It wasn't a date. I went to a town hall meeting."

"With anybody special?" she prodded.

"Just a friend."

"Girl, you keep this up and you're going to have a whole lot of friends and nobody special."

"Who says friends aren't special?"

"That's not my point."

I'd been waiting for Ebony to make a comment about my love life, and this time I finally had a retort ready. I stood straight and looked her dead in the eyes. "You know, Dig Allen is a really good guy. The next time he asks you out, you should say yes."

We had a brief stare-off for a couple of seconds. Finally, she smiled. "Maybe I should."

BUSINESS slowed considerably after lunch. I straightened the racks and unpacked the last case of purple hair spray. You never could predict what the hot color would be from one year to the next. We had three cases of green unopened. I thought of Dig in his Incredible Hulk costume and got an idea.

While nobody was looking, I ducked upstairs with two cans of green hair spray, a cheap black dress, and a hula hoop. I sawed through the hoop with a serrated bread knife and fed it through the hem of the dress, changed into the dress, and sprayed my arms, legs, and face with the green hair spray. I went back downstairs and grabbed a cheap plastic toy ray gun from the accessories wall. I crept up behind Don and jabbed the ray gun into his back. When I pulled the trigger, whistles and beeps sounded from the gun. My dad, Kirby, and the last remaining customers turned around to see where the noise came from.

"Take me to your leader," I said in a robotic voice. Applause broke out around the store.

"Is that costume available?" asked one of the customers. "I'll take it."

I moved to the counter and wrote up a ticket for the dress, the gun, three cans of hair spray, and a lime-green wig. The woman added glow-in-the-dark fishnets, a headband with two white balls that jutted out from the top like antennae, and white plastic hoop earrings to the pile. Apparently in her world, aliens liked to accessorize.

EBONY'S surprise test kitchen offerings had kept the swim team appeased through lunch, but high school boys seemed to have a bottomless appetite. New sheets, while probably necessary, weren't going to curb it. Ebony ordered half a dozen pizzas for delivery and pulled me aside.

"Girl, I've been over this whole town in search of a place to throw this party. After what happened to Haverford, nobody wants to play ball. This town is more spooked than I am, and for a town of people who like to dress up in costume, that's not a good thing."

"Have you talked to Octavius at Roman Gardens?"

"He's booked with the Knights of Columbus."

"What about the Proper City Community Center?"

"Turned me down cold."

"The library?"

"Too much risk of damaging the books. Nope, I'm at a dead end."

The words *dead end* reminded me of the end of Main Line Road, where I'd been earlier today. Desolate properties that had been ignored for far too long would make convenient Halloween locations. Even better, the property was owned by Sol.

"Have you ever been to Dig's mother's house?"

Ebony put her hands on her hips. "Don't you go trying that show-me-what-it-feels-like nonsense on me. I can see what you're doing."

"What?" I said. "Dig inherited his mother's house in West Proper."

"He did, did he?"

"The neighboring houses are all vacant. I just thought it would make a good location for the party, that's all."

"How many houses are we talking about?"

"Four, I think. Maybe five."

"Singles?"

"Yes."

"We could do the food and beverage in one, turn one into a haunted house, host the costume contest in a third, and have party games in the fourth. Tie it all together with some kind of scavenger hunt so people have to go to each house. We've never done anything like that. Margo, that just might work. Who do I need to talk to?"

It might not have been common knowledge that Sol owned the property, but I'd already been told that fact by two different people. "Sol Girard. He's the property owner. But you might want to start with Dig, all things considered."

"All things considered, my fanny. You're up to something. I just don't know what." She wandered away and pulled out her phone. A few minutes later, she came back over to me.

"Dig said the decision is up to Sol. If Sol says yes, Dig's going to close his towing company tomorrow and help make it happen." She looked down at her Mad Max outfit. "Now I got two problems. One, I need to go back to Shindig to make the food. Two, I can't take a business meeting dressed like this."

"Solution: you go do what you have to do at Shindig. I'll talk to Sol." I'd been looking for an excuse to ask him about his investment, and here, one had presented itself.

"You better do it soon. It's already after seven, and I'm going to need an answer so I can make this thing happen. If he says no, we're going to be celebrating Halloween at the PCP."

Proper City had been known to stage celebrations at the PCP, most regularly the Sagebrush Festival that took place every summer. But while the park was the perfect central location for pop-up tents, games, rides, and the occasional musical performance, it wasn't right for Halloween and Ebony knew it. The houses in West Proper would be perfect as long as we could get permission, transform their appearance, and get the word out. A borderline impossible deadline, if it wasn't for Ebony.

"I'll make it happen. Trust me."

I went to the counter and found the file with Sol's phone number and address. Halfway through his phone number, I set the phone back down on the cradle. I didn't want to take a chance on him saying no over the phone.

Instead of Sol, I called Bobbie. "I'm heading out to talk to Sol Girard about Halloween. You want to join me?"

"I thought you were going to talk to Tak?"

"Not yet. The store has been busy and now there's this to deal with. I'll talk to him tomorrow."

"You're avoiding confrontation."

"I'm confronting the very real possibility that Proper City isn't going to have Halloween because of a murder investigation."

"Tomato, tomahto." She laughed. "Are you sure it's a good idea to go to West Proper? That area can be a little rough."

"It's ten after seven. We'll be there by seven thirty and home by eight."

"I can't get away for another ten minutes. Where do you want to meet?"

"Main Line Road dead-ends into the mountain. Let's meet there and then drive to Sol's together."

"Okay, see you soon."

I went upstairs and found a navy blue quilted nylon coat that fit over my flight attendant outfit. Ivory chased Soot from room to room. Soot stopped in the middle of the kitchen, turned around, and hissed at Ivory. The white puffball of dog whimpered for a moment, looked up at me with his big brown eyes, and then back at Soot. My grumpy gray cat stuck his paw out and swiped at the air between the two of them, but even I could see that his claws were retracted. It was clear that Soot enjoyed the chase as much as Ivory.

I scooped up Soot and cradled him like a baby. His front

paws jutted straight out and crossed slightly. His back legs twitched and sought for something to leverage himself against. I ruffled the fur on his ample belly, and then leaned down and kissed him square on top of his head. His hind legs caught my arm, he pushed until he was sitting up, and stuck his paws over my shoulder. Ivory hopped around my ankles and Soot looked down at him and meowed. He hopped from my shoulder to the top of the refrigerator, then moved down to the counter and the floor. The second he hit the ground, Ivory took off after him.

Kids.

I went back downstairs and told my dad where I was going. "Are you going to be here when I get home?" I asked.

"Sure I will." He looked at me funny. "Are you sure you don't want to stay out later? Maybe see one of your friends?"

"No. Tomorrow's a big day. I'll be home within the hour."

For the first time in my life, I couldn't read the expression on his face.

THE scooter was low on gas, so I topped it off and then continued on my drive. Like earlier that day, traffic on this side of town was slight. I spent more time stuck at an out-of-service traffic light than any other part of the job. Whoever was in charge of road maintenance needed to know about that.

Streetlamps illuminated the drive down Main Line Road. The farther I went, the more desolate it appeared. I was glad that I'd asked Bobbie to meet me. I slowed as I approached the dead end at the end of Main Line and looked for Bobbie's car. There were no signs of her. I pulled off to the side of the street and raised the visor from my helmet. Behind me, a pair of headlights approached. I hopped off my scooter and pushed it behind the sign advertising strawberries. It would make more sense for us to arrive together.

As the headlights grew closer, I realized that the car approaching wasn't Bobbie at all. I was at a dead end in West Proper—completely vulnerable and alone.

Chapter 23

TAK PULLED HIS SUV up alongside me and rolled down the window. "Long time no see," he said.

"Two whole days."

"You've been avoiding me," he said.

It wasn't so much avoiding him as it was trying to understand where we stood. Cooper's comments about Tak playing the field and keeping relationships secret and Gina's comments that he and Detective Nichols had been to Candy Girls to rent their costumes for the party would have been enough. But there was something else. I didn't like the sneaking around. I didn't like how we pretended to barely know each other in public. If he was embarrassed to be seen with me, then there was no point pretending.

"I've been busy." I cringed at the sound of my voice. It had a note of distance to it, as if I were talking to a stranger. "The store, and the murder, and . . . stuff."

"I've been busy too," he said. "The restaurant, and my parents, and . . . stuff."

"That's what I figured."

His engine idled for a few seconds. He sat in the SUV and I stood on the street. I was still wearing my helmet, and if Bobbie wasn't going to get here soon, I was going to have to drive off alone. I looked down the road behind his truck. There were no other cars in sight.

"You told Bobbie about us," he said.

Realization dawned on me. She'd set me up. I was going to get her when I had a chance.

"Climb in. I'll take you to Sol's house and we can come back and get your scooter when we're done."

"How do you know I'm going to see Sol?"

"Bobbie told me that too."

Oh, yeah, I was definitely not letting her off the hook.

"You can take your helmet off if you want," he joked when I got in the car.

I unbuckled the loops under my chin and set the helmet on the floor by my feet. I pulled the flight attendant hat from the pocket of my coat and pulled it on over my flat hair.

"How was the town hall meeting last night?" he asked. His voice was light and cautious.

"Fine. Interesting. Francine Wheeler was there. So was Paul Haverford's business partner. What do you know about silent partners and verbal agreements?"

"Silent partners put money into businesses but have no say in the company. Verbal agreements are shaky at best. They have to be proven in a court of law."

"Bill Perth—that's Haverford's partner—said he and Haverford had a verbal agreement on the development of Havetown. And now that Haverford is dead, if the agreement is proven, wouldn't Perth benefit from all of the plans for Havetown? So instead of halving the profits, he'll be the sole owner of the property?"

"It's possible, I guess, but it's going to be a long road for him to prove it. You're not— Wait—this isn't about

your interest in the Alexandria Hotel, is it? You're trying
to find out who killed Paul Haverford. That's the real reason you're going to visit Sol."

"You heard Cooper. He said that Sol owns the property
out here. I was talking to Dig Allen this morning, and he
said Havetown will make Sol's property worth nothing. I
just want to talk to Sol and hear from him."

"I thought you were here to talk to him about using his
property for Halloween?"

"Bobbie told you that too?"

"Ebony told me that."

A rush of heat climbed my face. "Oh yeah? Well, Cooper
told me that you date around, and Gina Cassavogli told me
you and Detective Nichols came into Candy Girls to pick
out costumes together. Want to compare any other notes?"
I glared at him for a second and then faced forward.

Tak slowed the truck down and pulled into the driveway
of a white stone house. The mailbox said *Girard*. The lawn
had been landscaped in small river rocks with a pathway
of pavers surrounded by tiny orange pebbles leading up to
the front door. I was out of the car before Tak had it in
park. He caught up to me by the time I rang the bell.

Sol Girard was less imposing in regular clothes than he
was when dressed like a monster. He was about the same
height as me, which was short for a man. His hairline had
gradually receded from the forehead back, and somewhere
along the line he'd taken to parting what was left on the
side and combing it over the top. The comb-over had gotten
thinner and thinner, and was now only enough strands to
barely conceal the shiny skin underneath.

What he lacked in hair on his head was more than made
up for with big thick eyebrows in a dark shade of almost
black. His natural expression was sour, which probably
helped him during the monthly poker game. During the
years when he'd been a client of the store, I'd gotten to see

a softer side of Sol, that of the man who enjoyed throwing costume parties, complained about his wife without really meaning anything by it, and bragged about his grandchildren on a regular basis.

"Margo, come on in." He held the door open. "What brings you out this way? Car trouble?"

"No, actually, I—we—came out here to talk to you about Halloween." Sol looked back and forth between Tak's and my faces. "Do you know Tak Hoshiyama?" I said. "We're trying to find a location for the annual Proper City Halloween party." I shot a look at Tak, who seemed surprised by my answer. I looked back at Sol. "I was talking to Dig Allen this morning, and he said you own some property out this way."

Sol wasn't paying much attention to me. He stared at Tak. "Your parents own that sushi restaurant, don't they?"

"It's not sushi. It's teppanyaki."

"Yeah, that's right. Cook it in front of you. Make a volcano out of an onion."

I felt Tak go rigid next to me. He stood straighter and squared off his shoulders. "My father is an award-winning chef. He and my mother have fused Japanese and Hawaiian foods on their menu."

"Sure. Just don't let them stop with the onion volcano. It's a hit with my grandkids."

Sol smiled at Tak, but it didn't seem genuine. I reached down and squeezed Tak's hand. He squeezed back. Whatever was going on between us, I wanted him to know that I was on his side.

Sol turned back to me. "You said something about the Halloween party? What did you have in mind?"

We followed him into his living room. Overstuffed chenille sofas faced each other with a worn wooden table between them. A fire burned in the fireplace at the end of the room, lending a cozy atmosphere. A plug-in room freshener sat on the mantle above the fireplace next to a row of photos of Sol's extended family. It looked like every other living room in Proper.

Tak and I sat on one sofa and Sol faced us. I didn't waste time with small talk. "As you probably know, the Alexandria Hotel was supposed to be the location of the annual Halloween festivities this year. Because of what happened on Monday, the hotel is off-limits. Ebony Welles—you know Ebony, of Shindig Party Planning, right?—she's been trying to find another location, with no luck. After talking to Dig, I thought— I wanted to ask— Would you consider—"

"Dig Allen told you about my property?" Sol said. He leaned forward. He had one hand in a fist with the other hand wrapped around it. His knuckles turned white. "What else did he tell you?"

Tak pressed his thigh against mine. Even without the cue, I knew to proceed with caution. Everything I knew had come from Cooper or Dig. Rumor and innuendo. If Sol was keeping secrets, he wouldn't be eager to know that the rest of us had been talking about his finances.

"He didn't say much. Just that he inherited his mother's house, and that the houses on either side of it were owned by you. I didn't know that you invested in property."

"It's not common knowledge," he said. "And I'd like to keep it that way."

"We don't need to tell people that you own the property, we only need your permission to be able to come in and use the buildings. But if you wanted people to know, it would be a nice gesture to the town. Proper City hasn't missed a Halloween in decades, and it's either this or the PCP."

Sol leaned forward and propped his forearms on his thighs. He looked down at the carpet, giving me a square look at the bald dome of his head. When he looked up, he shook his head back and forth. "I'm afraid I can't say yes."

"But why? You're a member of the community. You know what it means to everybody."

"It doesn't have much to do with me. That property is in probate."

"But I thought you owned it?"

"I did. Until Paul Haverford made me an offer I couldn't refuse."

Chapter 24

"PAUL HAVERFORD BOUGHT your property?" I asked. "When?"

"Haverford has been after me for that stretch of land for a while. I had my own plans and didn't want to sell. But the more property he bought up, the more it seemed that the only way to recoup my investment was to sell to him."

"But I thought you wanted to develop a stretch of lower income houses for families just moving to Proper? Have-town is the opposite of all of that. It's about bringing in expensive stores and loud businesses and gambling. It's about changing everything Proper City stands for."

Sol leaned back against the sofa and his eyes narrowed. "You know more than you let on. Who have you really been talking to?"

Tak cleared his throat. "She's been talking to me. I used to work in the Clark County Planning Office. We went out to visit a friend earlier this week and it came up in conversation."

"I'd appreciate it if you leave me and my investments out of your conversations."

"But you investments are a matter of public record, aren't they?" I asked.

Sol reached forward and picked up a wooden serving tray that sat on the coffee table. He slammed the tray down. We jumped at the sudden, violent action. Tea from a mug that sat nearby sloshed out upon impact.

"You didn't come out here to ask me about Halloween, did you?" he asked. "You're on a fishing expedition. Well, cast your net somewhere else. My business is my own." He stood up and walked to the door. We followed. I had never seen this side of Sol, this private, angry, closed-up man. He wanted us gone, and suddenly that seemed like a very good idea.

Tak and I didn't talk until we got back to where I'd left my scooter. He parked his RAV4 behind it and let the engine idle.

"Do you think—" we both said at the same time. And then, "I don't know."

He turned the engine off and unclipped his seat belt. "Are you in a rush to get home?"

"Not really." I unclipped my seat belt too. "What do you think got Sol so angry back there?"

Tak glided his fingertips over the steering wheel, and then let his hands drop into his lap. "It sounded to me that he doesn't want word to get out that he was doing business with Paul Haverford."

"But that can't be a secret, can it? Like I said to him, it must be a matter of public record."

"There's a lot of ground between public record and common knowledge," he said.

"Okay, so there's an even bigger connection between him and Haverford. The only thing is, if Haverford made him a good offer, then he'd have no motive. Wouldn't he want the deal to go through?"

"Depends. With Haverford out of the picture, the deal falls through. Sol not only keeps his property, but he has an inside track on the rest of the land that Haverford owned. Perfect timing to grow his own piece of the Proper pie."

I giggled. Tak laughed too. The pent-up tension we'd both felt in Sol's living room manifested in a wave of silliness. This wasn't the first time I'd dissolved into giggles around Tak, and he knew once I started it took me a while to get control of myself. When I finally had, he reached over and threaded his fingers through mine.

"I like it when you laugh," he said. "It's been a while."

And then the concerns, about Tak keeping me at a distance, about his costume shopping with Detective Nichols, about him playing the field all came back. I heard Bobbie's voice in my head.

"There's nobody else," he said, reading my mind.

"But Cooper said—"

"Cooper likes you," Tak said. "He probably wanted to clear the playing field."

"I thought you two were friends?"

"All's fair in love and war."

Under the cloak of darkness, I smiled to myself. Bobbie had been right. All I'd needed was to talk to Tak face-to-face. My concerns dissipated and I felt like I was cocooned in a warm glow of security. Except for one thing . . .

"So you weren't at Candy Girls renting a costume with Detective Nichols?"

Tak's expression changed. "Actually, that part was true."

I pulled my hand away from his and got out of the truck. He scooped up my helmet from the floor before I could grab it. He got out of his side and caught up with me as I was wrestling my scooter out from behind the STRAWBERRIES FOR SALE sign. "Margo, don't be mad. It's not what you think."

"Really? Because what I think is that you went to our main competitor to rent a costume with your ex-girlfriend."

"Okay, it is what you think. But hear me out."

"I don't think so, Tak. It's going to take something big to make me see things differently. But maybe I'm not wrong. Maybe the fact that we aren't willing to be seen in public means something. Maybe we're just fooling ourselves."

We stared at each other for a few moments, no words spoken. I wanted to be wrong. I wanted to go back to the beginning and forget about trying to keep our relationship a secret. I wanted him to tell me that we got a do-over.

Silently, he held out my helmet. I took it and left.

IT was well after nine when I got back to Disguise DeLimit. The night had been a bust. Sol hadn't agreed to my plan, and Tak and I had split up before we were even together. On a scale of one to ten, today had been a two. I remembered spraying myself green and dressing up in an alien costume. Okay, maybe it had been a four.

I let myself in through the back door. Soot sat inside like he was trying to catch me breaking curfew. I carried him upstairs. My dad and Don sat in the dining room with a series of maps laid out in front of them.

"What are you two up to?" I asked.

"Planning a road trip," said Don.

"Where are you headed?"

"Blues country."

"Chicago?"

"Memphis," said my dad.

"Mississippi," said Don.

Suddenly the assortment of maps made sense.

I scratched Soot's ears until a low rumble emanated from him. "Dad, I think we might want to call someone about the mouse problem in the stockroom. Soot has been working overtime."

"We don't want to put him out of a job, do we, fella?" He held Soot's paw and jiggled it up and down.

Soot wriggled around and jumped out of my arms onto the map. He swatted at a pen that sat on the table, and then flopped onto his side and stretched.

"You have a good night?" my dad asked.

"I've had better."

"Anything you want to talk about?"

"Nope. Good night."

Sunday

The next morning, I dressed in a pair of ripped jeans over black tights, a white T-shirt, and a black leather motorcycle jacket that said DAUGHTERS OF THE REVOLUTION on the back. I'd created the stencil myself and painted it on with Wite-Out. The letters had dried and cracked and a few had mostly peeled off. I clipped my wallet to a silver chain and hooked it onto my belt. The chain dangled down alongside my right thigh. I snapped on fingerless black leather gloves with silver studs and used a heavy hand on my eyeliner.

I found my dad in almost the same spot where I'd left him. Instead of a map, he was studying the classified section of the newspaper. I filled the blender with blueberries, almond milk, kale, and protein powder, hit blend, and then poured it all into a large plastic Big Gulp cup.

"Looking for a job?" I joked, peeking over his shoulder.

"An apartment." He closed the newspaper and folded it in half. "The last time we lived under this roof, you were just a girl. Now you're grown-up. When you came back here after my heart attack, I know you wanted to be close at hand to take care of me, and I appreciate that, but maybe it's time to find another place."

"You mean not live here anymore?" I asked.

"It was just a thought." He stood up. "You've been pretty interested in that old Alexandria Hotel, right? There's an article in here about it." He left the newspaper on the table and refilled his coffee, and then went downstairs to the shop.

As if I needed this! On top of everything else, my dad was evicting me. I unfolded the newspaper and scanned the apartment listings, and then folded it closed again. I flipped through the rest of the newspaper until I found the article he'd mentioned. It was small bulletin in the Lifestyle section, about the hotel's pending status as a historic monument. The conservancy was hosting a signature drive in order to gain more names on their petition. The event was being held all day in the parking lot outside of the hotel. It started in twenty minutes.

I went downstairs and found my dad rooting through boxes in the stockroom.

"I'm going to take the money from the safe and make a deposit. Okay?"

"Sure," he said. "You think anybody will want to dress up like a cigarette girl?" he asked, holding out a tray.

"Give it a shot. I'll be back in about an hour."

DESPITE what I'd told my dad, I drove to the Alexandria Hotel first. I couldn't justify the information I'd uncovered at the library with the person I'd met at Catch-22 with Bobbie. Annette was passionate about saving the Alexandria Hotel. I could respect that. But was there more here than a passion to save historic buildings? What had happened eight years ago when she and Paul Haverford went head to head over the historical status of the Peppermint House?

I parked my scooter in the lot. Annette wrestled with a folding table. Her hair had been pulled back into a pony-tail, and her bangs looked even shorter than I remembered them. Today she wore red cat-eye sunglasses and a triple strand of pearls over a floral cardigan and gray wool skirt. I joined her and grabbed one end of the table while she locked the legs into position.

"Thank you," she said. "You're Bobbie's friend, aren't you?"

"Yes. Margo. We met at Catch-22."

"That's right. Have you signed our petition yet?" She picked up a clipboard and thrust it at me. Annette was not one to waste time on pleasantries.

I took the clipboard and scanned over the form. The first available space was about halfway down the page.

"The hotel sure has been in the news a lot these days," I said. "I imagine it's difficult to get people to separate the idea of saving the hotel from what happened here the other night. Is that good or bad for your mission?"

"The recent publicity was the best thing that could have happened to the Alexandria Hotel. Now people are aware of it. They understand what's at stake. Paul Haverford turned out to be my biggest ally."

"But I thought he was your opponent? He wanted to bulldoze the hotel and use the land to develop Havetown."

She straightened up and adjusted her glasses. "You misunderstood me. What I meant was, the best thing to happen to my cause was Paul Haverford's *murder*."

Chapter 25

ANNETTE'S RUDENESS SHOCKED me no less today. I dropped the clipboard, and the pen came detached and landed by her feet. She bent down and picked up both, and then held them back out toward me. Annette was a woman with singular focus, and until my signature went on that page, she was on the clock.

"Did you sign yet?" she asked.

I believed in the preservation of our small town's history. If there hadn't been a murder attached to the historic hotel, I would have signed without question. So I did. I tucked the pen onto the clipboard and handed it back to Annette. She glanced at my signature, cocked her head, and then, as if satisfied, set it down on the table. She removed a pin from her cardigan and held it out to me. "Your token of appreciation."

"Oh, no thank you," I said. "I can't take your pin."

"I have two thousand of them in my car. I haven't had a chance to finish setting up yet."

I took the pin. It was a small gold image of a building

with red enamel decorating the façade. In a circle around the image were the words *Preserve and Conserve. Our buildings are our future.*

I stuck the pin onto the collar of my white T-shirt. "Is the petition still necessary?"

"I'm not taking any chances. It would be just like Haverford to find a way to shut me down from beyond the grave. That man has caused me nothing but trouble since the day I met him."

"This wasn't the first time you and Paul Haverford had fought over property, was it?" I asked.

"We fought all the time. It's hard to believe that there once was a time when we saw eye to eye. These days it's like countries at war trying to stake claim to our territories. Only I'm trying to protect the land around here. He wanted to exploit it for his own financial benefit."

"Have you spoken to Detective Nichols about his murder?"

She looked surprised by the question. "I gave her a statement on behalf of the conservancy. 'Despite the fact that Paul Haverford was pushing for zoning changes to Proper City that were diametrically opposed to the mission statement of the Clark County Conservancy, we deeply regret his passing.'" She straightened the edges of a few of the papers in front of her. "That sounds as good now as it did the day I said it to Detective Nichols."

"You don't sound upset that he's dead."

"That's the way it is in the preservationist's world. There's a handful of rich developers who make a nuisance of themselves. Pretty soon, they all start to run together into one big enemy. One less enemy, one more saved building."

"Is that how you felt when he took ill during the fight for the Peppermint House out in Moxie?"

Annette reached both hands up and adjusted her cat-eye glasses. "Just what are you getting at?"

"He was going to win that round. The house was all set for demolition. And then he got sick. Funny timing. The demolition was first postponed and then canceled. And you took a six month hiatus from your position as president of the historical society."

She pushed her cat-eye glasses up the bridge of her nose with her index finger and looked out at the parking lot. A couple of cars headed our direction. She focused her attention on the items on the table, straightening the edges and lining up the pens.

"People are starting to arrive. I have to finish setting up." She left me by the table and went to her truck.

Behind me, the sound of tires on gravel announced the arrival of either helpers or petition signers. I turned and looked. A stream of cars was driving toward the parking lot. Annette returned to the table with a blue plastic tub. She pulled a stack of blank forms and a bag of pins from inside and then set the tub under the table. She separated the forms into smaller clumps, and clipped each to a different clipboard. By the time the newcomers arrived at her table, she'd become a one-woman force of nature for change. I doubted that she even saw me leave.

Halloween season being what it was, the bank had extended their hours of operation to include Sundays during the month of October. I kept to narrow streets off Main Line Road instead of fighting traffic. That was one of the benefits of driving the scooter. I might not be able to go faster than thirty-five miles an hour, but during rush hour, I could get from point A to point B faster than any car on the road. I parked, locked my helmet to the seat, and went inside.

Marilyn Robinson was the only teller at the window. She smiled brightly, I assumed, because of her recent change in relationship with my dad. I braced myself and approached.

"Another big deposit?" she asked. "This is probably it, though, right? Tomorrow is go time."

I pulled the stack of checks, cash, and credit card slips from the inside pocket of my motorcycle jacket. "This should be the last deposit until after it's all over. Between last minute customers and deliveries, I won't have a lot of time for errands."

She fed the bills and checks into her machine like before. They fluttered like angry butterflies trapped in a net. A number flashed onto her small screen, and she punched the number into a machine in front of her. Her fingernails were long, dark, and expertly manicured. She used the tips of them instead of the skin of her fingertips, letting off a series of clicks and clacks as the two made contact with each other. After a few minutes, she hit the big key and a long slip of paper ejected out of the top.

"I see Annette got to you too," she said. At my confused look, she pointed to her lapel. A small gold pin just like the one I'd gotten this morning punctured the fabric.

"It seemed like a good cause," I said. "I'd rather we preserve our history than bulldoze what we have and build a new landscape."

"Between you and me, Paul Haverford's plans for Proper were far from being green-lighted. He had too many loans and made too many investments. His business partner filed a lawsuit against him for half ownership of the LLC, and don't even get me started on his problems with the zoning board. I was as surprised as anybody when he went public with his plans."

"Why would he?" I asked. At her confused look, I clarified. "He made a lot of enemies when he announced what he was planning on doing. Why say anything before it was official?"

"Nobody knows for sure, but my theory is that he was trying to force someone's hand. The additional press would attract other investors, and once they were on board, he would have had a lot more ammunition to take to the zoning board. Think of the additional tax revenue that would come into our city. Think of the tourists. You and me, we might like the small town feel of Proper, but the city council could have a lot more power with that kind of money at their disposal."

"But then why would he have trouble with the zoning board in the first place? If that's the case, wouldn't they ignore everything else and approve his application?"

Marilyn handled the money and credit card slips as if she was a robot on autopilot. Drawers opened and closed, bills were paper-clipped together, and blank slips were fed into her machine to print out the totals. All the while she kept up a steady stream of conversation.

"The only thing the city council cares about more than money is reelection. Havetown represented a sticky wicket for them. Bring in more tax dollars and change the face of Proper City, or maintain the status quo until after the elections. Six of one, half a dozen of the other."

She picked up the checks and tapped them to line up the bottom edges, clamped them together with a metallic pink binder clip, and set them in a small cash drawer below the counter. When she was finished, she click-clacked a few more keys on her machine and then fed a deposit slip into it. After it had circled through the printing feature, she handed the slip to me.

"I guess your dad will be at the big party tomorrow?"

"We haven't talked much about it. Did he say something to you?"

"To me? Why would he say something to me?" she asked.

I shrugged. Apparently she wanted to talk about dating my dad as much as I did.

"Tell your dad I said hi, would you?"

"Why don't you tell him yourself the next time you see him?"

"Who knows when that'll be?"

Before I could think of another question to ask, my phone buzzed with a message. Almost immediately, it rang. I looked at the display. "This is him now. Are we done?"

She nodded. I excused myself and turned away from Marilyn.

"Hi, Dad," I answered.

"Where are you?"

"I'm at the bank."

"Forget the bank. You need to come back to the store. Right now."

"Okay. Is everything okay?"

"Margo, I don't know what you got yourself involved in, but Detective Nichols is here and she wants to talk to you."

DETECTIVE Nichols was dressed in her standard outfit: black pantsuit, white collared shirt. Today she'd added small gold hoop earrings. Her hair was parted on the side and tucked behind her ear. Unlike at the opening night at the Alexandria Hotel when she'd slicked it back and passed for a man, today it hung in waves on either side of her face. Any softness that her hair conveyed was quickly countered by the appearance of her gun on her belt.

"Ms. Tamblyn, I've recently been made aware that you've been spending time at the Alexandria Hotel."

"That's where Halloween was going to take place."

"Yes, but you knew your store was being barred from participation." She held up a piece of paper encased in a clear plastic sleeve. Immediately I recognized the logo of Haverford Venture Capital on the front. It was a copy of the document Paul Haverford delivered to the store the day he was murdered. The same document I'd torn up and thrown on his desk.

"You only recently took over the day-to-day running of Disguise DeLimit, didn't you?"

"Yes."

"After your father ran it successfully for forty years."

"Yes, but—"

"Six months after you took over, you're facing a lawsuit that's going to threaten the future of the store. Aren't you?"

"What are you trying to say?"

"Help me understand. Why did you go to the Alexandria Hotel on Monday night? That was a private party for the businesses that Paul Haverford owned."

"That party has always been the pre-party for the businesses involved in Halloween. Paul Haverford never said I couldn't attend."

"Why have you continued to return to the Alexandria over the course of the next several days?"

"I've taken an interest in the hotel's history."

She studied me for an uncomfortable moment, and then turned to one of the officers with her and held out a hand. He reached into a bag and pulled out another plastic bag. This one contained several long sticks that looked like candles. Painted on the side in stenciled white lettering were the words: *Caution: Explosive.*

"Do you know what this is?"

"No."

"It's dynamite. We found it buried next to the foundation of the Alexandria. If someone had lit it, there's a strong possibility that it would have damaged the building."

"Detective, I wouldn't know the first thing about how to get dynamite and set it off."

Just then a loud *BOOM!* came from the stockroom.

Chapter 26

WE ALL JUMPED at the sound. The stockroom door opened and a cloud of smoke poured out. Emerging from the smoke was Kirby. He looked as surprised as I felt. Nichols and the two uniformed officers went into the stockroom.

"Oh, hey, I didn't know anybody was out here. Did I scare you?" he asked.

"Kirby, what were you doing in there?" I asked.

"Experimenting. Remember how we talked about having something extra to go with our costumes? Upgrades?"

"I remember you mentioning something."

Detective Nichols returned from the stockroom. "Were you responsible for that explosion?" she asked Kirby.

"It wasn't really an explosion. You thought it was? Cool. That's what I wanted."

"Walk me through what just happened back there."

"Sure. Come with me," he said.

We followed him into the stockroom. The backstock had thinned considerably. Kirby had set up a six-foot table by the back wall of the stockroom. On it sat a stereo and a microphone to the left, and several Styrofoam coolers on the right. Holes had been cut into the sides of the coolers, and metal pipe had been threaded through them. Detective Nichols slowly walked around the table, touching nothing. When she completed her circle, she stood in front of the table again.

"Go ahead," she said.

Kirby screwed a plastic cap on the end of the pipe that jutted out of the last cooler. He lifted each lid and poured water from a pitcher into them one by one. When he was finished, he moved to the table and fiddled with the stereo.

"Brace yourself," he said. He pressed play and held the microphone in front of the small speakers. A few seconds later, a loud *BOOM!* sounded again. He yanked a handful of strings that were tied to each of the cooler lids and they came off, releasing clouds of smoke. "Cool!" he said. "It worked again!"

Nichols waved her hand back and forth through the smoke. It floated into clouds around us, dissipating as it rose. Her men looked at her. She looked at Kirby. Kirby had a giant smile on his face.

"Out front," Nichols said. "Everybody."

Truth be told, I was a little curious to find out how he'd done it myself.

AFTER the scare of the unexpected explosion, Kirby's explanation of how he did it was anticlimactic: coolers to build up the pressure of the dry ice inside and an iTunes download of special effects magnified with a handheld microphone borrowed from the drama club. I didn't know if he had the best timing in the world or the worst, but at least, for a few moments, he'd diverted Detective Nichols's attention from me.

"Ms. Tamblyn, I'd like to continue our conversation."
She and I stepped to the front portion of the store, right
behind the door that led to the window display. "I don't
know how this ties in to my investigation, but one thing is
clear. You have motive. Maybe you arranged for that little
display to throw me off. I don't know. What I do know is
that Disguise DeLimit is at the center of this homicide
investigation."

I pointed to the document in the clear plastic sleeve.
"You already know I tore my copy up and left it in Paul
Haverford's office, so you know I was angry when I left
there. But I'm not the only person who was angry with him
that day. Have you spoken to his partner, Bill Perth? He
was at the town hall meeting the other night."

"Ms. Tamblyn, make things easy for yourself. Stay
away from the Alexandria Hotel. Stay away from anything
that has to do with the Alexandria Hotel. And if you do
plan to go out for Halloween, do yourself a favor and stay
among friends. If for some reason I need to check your
whereabouts, that'll make it easier for all parties involved."

"You don't believe anything I've told you, do you? You
don't believe that I saw Spider-Man on the fire escape, or
that Paul Haverford was in the elevator when I found him.
You haven't followed up on anything I've told you about
what I saw. But that doesn't mean I didn't see it. Just
because you don't believe me doesn't mean what I'm saying isn't true. I already told you that Sol Girard rented a
Spider-Man costume. And Annette Crowley has a history
with Paul Haverford. What about Francine Wheeler? She
was poking around the foundation of the Alexandria House
Wednesday morning. She could have planted that stuff to
make it look like someone was going to harm the hotel."

She crossed her arms over her chest. "It's starting to
appear as if you're conducting your own investigation into
this murder. I'm going to strongly advise against that too."

Detective Nichols and her team of cops left. Their cars pulled away from the curb out front and were quickly replaced with Ebony's late-'70s coffee-colored Cadillac Coupe de Ville. It not only put every other car in Proper to shame, it put a few of them off the road too. Inside, I could see Ivory on the passenger side. He was on his hind legs, his paws on the window. His little black nose pressed up against the glass. Ebony climbed out of the car and stared at the police cars, and then turned to me.

Today Ebony was dressed like herself. Brushed-out afro, large gold hoop earrings, crocheted poncho, patchwork bell-bottom jeans, and platform shoes. She reached into the car and called to Ivory. He left the window and went to her, and she scooped him up and tucked him under her arm. Her poncho bunched up on the side where she held Ivory, but neither seemed to mind.

She stared again at the receding cop cars. "You in some kind of trouble?" she asked me.

"I'm not sure," I said. We watched in silence as they all but dissolved into tiny dots in the distance. "What's up? You usually don't venture out this close to Halloween."

"The way things are going, there isn't going to be a Halloween." She looked up at the sky and waved her hands around over her head like she was swatting away an angry, invisible bee. "That ghost of Pete Proper has been haunting me for the past week, making a mockery of me. I can feel him watching me. Go away, ghost!"

A trim couple in matching tennis clothes exited the frozen yogurt store across the street and stared at us. I grabbed Ebony's wrists. "Shhhhhh! You're scaring away the customers."

"What do you need customers for? Didn't you hear me? Unless somebody figures something out soon, there's not going to be a Halloween."

I kept my grip on Ebony's wrist and pulled her into

Disguise DeLimit behind me. Kirby and his pals were clustered around a small boom box. Kirby held the microphone that he'd used to magnify the explosion, but this time he held it up to his mouth and made beatbox sounds. Another one jumped in with a rap about swimming laps.

If they hadn't been so dependable over the past week, I would have had them declared mentally unstable.

I dragged Ebony upstairs to the kitchen. She dropped into one of the diner chairs and held her head in her hands. From where I stood, all I saw was the top of her giant, brushed-out afro.

"Why me?" she said. "This is not my holiday. I'm tellin' you, give me St. Patrick's Day. I'll give you a pot of gold and a rainbow. Heck, I'd even import a leprechaun. Or July Fourth! I could rock that holiday. Nothing says patriotism like the stars, stripes, and soul food. I could deck this place out with sparklers and flags and rockets bursting in red air."

"It's the rocket's red glare, the bombs bursting in air."

"Doesn't matter. I could do that holiday. I just can't do this one."

I didn't mind focusing on a different problem for the moment. In fact, I welcomed the distraction. Detective Nichols was not going to ruin Halloween for me.

"Why is this your problem?" I asked.

"Because when Paul Haverford was killed, his funds were frozen. Everything that had been planned was put on hold. Now you're got businesses all over town who thought they were getting paid to participate this year, some who thought they were guaranteed thousands of dollars in media exposure, and they aren't willing to move forward without their big payoff."

"But the annual Halloween party has never had private funding in the past. What happened to the money that was earmarked for the celebration?"

"There's money. There's just not the kind of money these people were expecting. Last year, the cupcake store on the corner of Thumbelina and Main Line donated twenty dozen cupcakes. This year, they said they'd provide them at a twenty percent discount. If I agreed to that, I wouldn't have any money for decorations, setup, beverages, or any other food. We'd be a bunch of people wandering the streets in costumes eating cupcakes. Not that there's anything wrong with that, but it's nothing like the kind of Halloween that this town expects."

"Not every business in Proper was bought out by Paul Haverford. There have to be some who are willing to participate."

"Yes, but how am I supposed to know who to approach?"

"Wait here."

I ran downstairs, past Kirby and his friends (were they doing the "Thriller" dance?) to the office. The envelopes from Haverford Venture Capital were where I'd left them. I took the whole stack back upstairs and shut the connecting door behind me.

"Open these. There's a list of the businesses Haverford Venture Capital purchased."

"No," Ebony said. She slid a fingernail under the sealed envelope and pulled out the paper. "Yes!" She set the papers down. "Now what?"

"Remember you said if you didn't figure something out the party was going to be held at the PCP?"

"That was a joke."

"Why? It's a central location. It's owned by the city. Nobody's going to say we played favorites. And once we make it official, we can ask the other businesses—the ones not owned by Paul Haverford—to pitch in and be a part of it. Proper City has always been about community. Haverford wanted to ruin that by dividing us into the Haves and the Have-Nots."

"Girl, you make a good point. But it's a little late to contact the zoning office and get approval to throw a massive public party there tomorrow night."

"Not if you know the right people, it's not."

I picked up my cell and flipped through the recent calls until I found what I was looking for. Cooper's number. I stared at it for a moment before checking to see if Ebony was watching me. She was.

"I'll be right back."

I left her in the kitchen and moved to my bedroom. There was absolutely no reason I should be nervous about calling Cooper. The way Tak and I had left things, it was clear that he was resuming his relationship with Detective Nichols. And it wasn't like I was calling Cooper for a date, I was calling him to make arrangements with the city of Proper. It was all very on the up and up.

Before I had a chance to second guess my actions, I hit dial. Maybe he was a call screener. Maybe he was driving and would let it go to voice mail. Maybe he left his phone on his desk. Maybe—

"Cooper Price," he answered.

"Cooper, hi, this is Margo Tamblyn. From the costume shop?"

"Margo. Hi." He paused. "This is a surprise. I wasn't sure I'd be hearing from you after you gave me the brush-off."

"That wasn't the brush-off," I said quickly. "I had a lot on my mind that night. I wouldn't have been good company."

"You should have let me be the judge of that."

If I'd doubted whether or not Tak was right when he said Cooper liked me, I didn't doubt it anymore. His friendly banter had just enough flirtation to it to let me know if I was interested, so was he. And between Detective Nichols's accusations and Tak's choice of her over me, my ego was wounded, and Cooper's attention felt good. Maybe relationships weren't supposed to be clandestine and difficult and fraught with secrets.

"I have a feeling your call isn't purely social," he said.

"You're right, it's not. I'm conducting official Halloween business."

"Official Halloween business? Sounds important."

"It is." I hesitated for only a moment. Turning to Cooper instead of Tak definitely said something about how I felt about our relationship, but there were bigger things at stake here than my love life. "Remember how I told you we might need help finding a new location for Halloween? Paul Haverford had made arrangements for the annual Halloween festivities to take place at the Alexandria Hotel. Part of his plans were that only businesses that he owned could benefit from anything connected to the party."

"Let me guess. The murder has taken the Alexandria off the market as a potential place to party and you need a new location."

"Bingo. Ebony Welles, the owner of Shindig, has been trying to coordinate some kind of party on short notice. I don't know how well you know Proper, but we always have a Halloween party. Now it's crunch time and we don't have a venue."

"Why call me? Shouldn't you be calling every restaurant and banquet hall in your town?"

"Nobody is willing to say yes on such short notice. In the past, everybody chipped in and made it happen. This year, Paul Haverford bought a bunch of businesses and promised them a big payoff. Those very businesses aren't willing to donate their food and drink anymore. Ebony's calling the ones who aren't affiliated with him, but it would probably go a lot more smoothly if we knew where we could hold the party."

"Back to my question. Why call me?"

"Because you work in the planning office, and you might be able to get us the authorization to hold the party in the Proper City Park." The words rushed out of me in a gush of syllables and hope. As soon as I'd finished my request, I held my breath and crossed every set of fingers I had.

"The PCP? You want to hold the party there?"

"It was a thought."

He was silent. I don't know what I'd been hoping—not true, I'd been hoping that he'd immediately say it was a great idea and that he'd pull whatever strings were necessary—but his lack of response said the opposite. I'd asked for too much, and now I'd burned a bridge.

"Maybe it wasn't a very good thought. I don't know what I was thinking. Forget I asked."

"Hold on. I'm just thinking things through. It might work. It's a public area, so there's nothing to restrict people from coming together there. I'll have to ask around about food and beverage. What else would there be?"

"We usually have some kind of haunted house, which I don't think we could do, but maybe a maze? We could set it up with partitions from the hardware store. There are also games for the kids and a costume contest at the end of the night. Other than that, it's mostly mingling."

"Tell you what. Let me call my supervisor at home and see what he thinks."

"Thank you," I said.

"Don't thank me yet."

After I hung up, I went back to the kitchen. Ebony was on the phone. "We're still working out the location, but rest assured, the party is going to happen." She looked up at me. I crossed my fingers and held them up. "So, can I count on you? Great. How many? Great. I'll call you back as soon as I have more details." She hung up. "Cheesus Crust is in for twenty pizzas. They said you've been a good customer this week and they want to help you out."

"Remind me to thank Kirby for that." I lowered myself into the chair next to hers. "Who else? I can make some of the phone calls for you."

"Sure. Take this one." She handed me the phone number for Hoshiyama Kobe Steak House.

Chapter 27

I STARED AT the number, even though I already knew it by heart. "Have the Hoshiyamas ever participated in the Halloween party in the past?"

"Nope."

"Then maybe since this year is such a crisis, we should concentrate on businesses with a track record."

She jabbed her pointy fingernail on the scattered papers in front of her. "So far four of those businesses belong to Paul Haverford. Say good-bye to your falafel station, your cake pops, and your slider burgers."

"That's only three."

"Love 'em or hate 'em, Candy Girls used to donate props for the photo booth."

"We can do that."

"Margo, I need you to donate the fog machines and juice. And to wrangle that swim team into helping pull this whole thing together. Even Disguise DeLimit has a limit. You can't do everything."

I slumped down a few inches. Even if Cooper did call

back with the go-ahead, we had a lot of work to do in a short amount of time. And even though I'd be willing to pull an all-nighter, I knew that once the moon came out, Ebony would be as far away from the PCP as possible. Even if I did arm her with silver bullets and a garlic necklace.

She tapped the paper in front of me. "Make the call. We need every yes we can get."

I tapped the number out on my phone.

"Hoshiyama Kobe Steak House, how may I help you?" said a female voice. In the background, I could hear the snappy notes of the koto being played. It was a harplike instrument that I'd come to associate with hibachi chicken, miso soup, and Hoshiyama fried rice. Even though the sounds were faint, my mouth started to water all the same.

"Hi, this is Margo Tamblyn, from Disguise DeLimit."

"Margo, are you calling for Tak? Hold on, he's in the kitchen."

"No!" I said too quickly. Ebony looked up at me. I stood up and turned my back to her. "Is this Mrs. Hoshiyama?"

"Yes, but please, call me Lynn. Is something wrong?"

"No— I mean, yes, but it doesn't have to do with Tak. Did I call at a bad time?" I snuck a look over my shoulder at Ebony. She had her chin propped on her hand and was watching me as if I were the nightly entertainment. I rolled my eyes and turned my back to her again. There was no point in leaving the room this time. Even if I did hole up inside of my bedroom for the duration of the call, I knew she'd grab a glass and hold it to the door so she could hear our conversation.

"I'm working with Ebony Welles from Shindig to coordinate the Proper City Halloween party for tomorrow night. I don't know how much you know about it, but the businesses in the city donate food and beverages to the party, usually something specific to Halloween. I know it's last minute, but I was wondering if you would be interested?"

"One moment, please." She placed me on hold for a few

seconds. When she returned a few seconds later, the music was absent from the background. "I am familiar with the Proper City Halloween party, but we have never been approached to participate in the past. I have always assumed that it was because people still consider us outsiders."

"Mrs. Hoshi—Lynn—please don't think that. I can't speak for the people who organized the party in previous years. I've been living in Las Vegas for the past seven and wasn't here to participate in the party. But this year is different."

"I understand from my son that this year's party was supposed to be a private affair."

"Yes, it was. A businessman had purchased several businesses around town and was going to restrict participation in the event solely to them."

"I'm familiar with this man. He made an offer on our restaurant."

"Paul Haverford bought Hoshiyama Steak House?" I asked, stunned. Why had Tak not mentioned that?

"No. My husband would not sell. This is a family business, and in our world, family is more important than money. From what I've learned about you, I believe you understand."

"Yes, I do."

"Tell me, Margo, why are you calling so close to the event? What do you expect us to be able to contribute?"

Until that moment, it hadn't occurred to me that my phone call could be misconstrued as an insult. I felt a tap on my shoulder and whirled around. Ebony stood opposite me. She held out a piece of paper, which I scanned quickly.

"Until a few hours ago, we didn't think there was a chance that we could have a Halloween party this year, but a bunch of us—the people who know how much it means to everybody here—are doing whatever we can to make sure the party happens. Please consider saying you'll participate. It would mean the world to all of the families who look forward to this event every year. It will send a clear message to anybody who thinks our town is for sale that we believe more in who we are and what we can offer each other than how many movie theaters we have or whether or not we can increase city revenue by bringing in gambling."

"I need to talk to my husband about this. You'll have our answer by the end of the day."

"Thank you."

I ended the call and looked at Ebony. "Where did you come up with that?" I asked, waving toward the paper.

"There are two types of people in this town. The ones who were on board with Haverford, and the rest of us. If the Hoshiyamas said no to him, then they're good people. I know how to make my case with good people. You speak from the heart. It's worked on six other businesses already."

I looked over her shoulder. She had left her lined notepad on the table. A list of restaurants, caterers, retail shops, and entertainment had been written under the word *YES*. The second column that said *NO* was empty.

I hugged her. "What would Proper City do without you?" I asked.

"Girl, I'm just building up good karma so the spirit world won't mess with me tomorrow night."

My cell phone rang. I looked at the number and then at Ebony. "Let's hope your karma spills over onto me. We're about to find out if the park is a go."

I took the call. "Did you talk to your boss?" I asked instead of saying hello.

He laughed. "I did. He's drawing up city permission documents as we speak."

I let out a *whoo-hoo!* Ebony caught my enthusiasm and did a couple of dance moves out of *Saturday Night Fever*.

Ivory, who had been sleeping on one of the dining chairs, woke up, climbed onto the table, and let out a howl. We sure knew how to party.

"Thank you, Cooper. This is big—huge. I don't know how to repay you."

"I do. How about we go to the party together? And just in case there's any confusion, I want to be clear. I'm asking you out on a date."

"Sure," I said. I mean, after all that, how could I say no?

ONCE Ebony was able to leverage the information about the PCP to the businesses around town, the yeses came flooding in. Within an hour, she had a full lineup of contributors. Food stations and party games were on the agenda, as was the annual costume contest. She even had a list of more than fifty people willing to turn out tomorrow and help assemble the whole thing. At the rate she was going, she was going to help Proper City have its best Halloween yet.

I excused myself from the kitchen and went downstairs to the store to work on the teddy bear costumes I'd promised Bobbie. I cut out the fabric needed for ten pairs of small black trousers, and then added small patches from scraps of plaid, polka dot, and tweed to them. When I was done, I assembled the pants and set them into a pile. Miniature hobo pants, like the ones I'd worn the day Paul Haverford came into the store and delivered those papers. As comfortable a costume as it was, I remember how awkward I'd felt, sitting in his office while he and Bill Perth had argued while dressed in their own rich businessman costumes.

I hadn't thought much about that argument in the past few days. Bill Perth had been at the town hall meeting, and he had claimed to be an equal owner in Haverford Venture Capital and Havetown. In fact, while a whole lot of other people were pushing to shut it down—Francine Wheeler and Annette Crowley leading that charge—if what Bill Perth claimed was true, then he stood to benefit a great deal from the plans going forward.

But what had he said? They had a verbal agreement. How did he plan to prove that anything he said was true? Maybe it wasn't. The one person who could deny his claims was dead. And if Havetown went forward as planned and Bill Perth could establish his initial 50 percent investment, he'd be a very rich man. With no partner to split the profits with.

It seemed that perhaps Bill Perth had as much of a motive as the people who wanted to stop Paul Haverford.

I'd followed Bill home from the town hall meeting, so I knew he lived in Christopher Robin Crossing. I knew one person who lived in that development. Grady O'Toole. I hadn't talked to him much since his best friend had been murdered a few months ago and I'd helped expose the killer, but things had been left on a friendly note. I found his number and called.

"Is this *the* Margo Tamblyn?" he said when he answered. "The queen of Halloween? The countess of costumes? The lady of a thousand faces?"

"I only have one face," I said.

"So it is you. When the phone didn't ring and the postman didn't deliver a letter, I started to think you had left all this behind. Gone, forgotten, it's a tough thing to live with."

Grady O'Toole was twenty-six to my thirty-two, six years that felt like the Grand Canyon of age differences to me. He was rich and cocky with just enough charm to get away with almost anything he wanted. He had hair the color of a freshly minted penny, freckles across his nose, and the healthiest dose of self-confidence I'd ever encountered. But despite all of that, I liked him. He and his friend had been like brothers to each other: healthy competition, but with an innate loyalty.

"I have a sneaking suspicion that you figured out a way to go on," I said.

"True. I bounce back from adversity remarkably well. To what do I owe the pleasure of this conversation?"

Until he asked, I hadn't known how I was going to approach the question of asking him to spy on Bill Perth. I should have planned this better before making the call.

I went with the direct approach. "Would you be willing to give me dirt on one of your neighbors?"

"Anyone in particular or just the general population of Christopher Robin Crossing?"

"One in particular. Bill Perth."

"Ah, so what I heard is true."

"What did you hear?"

"That you're digging around the murder of Paul Haverford. Is that your thing? Thrill seeker?"

"More like truth seeker. I was the one who found his body, and the police have suggested that they don't believe my account of what happened."

"You're a suspect?" He laughed. In a way, it cheered me up. If the idea of me as murderer made someone laugh, then things couldn't be as dire as Detective Nichols had led me to believe, right?

"I prefer person of interest," I said. "And I'm not a thrill seeker. This is Halloween season, and I would like nothing better than to concentrate on business."

"But you don't trust Detective Nichols to do her job."

"I didn't say that."

"You don't have to. She wasn't right about Blitz's murder either. I wouldn't trust her. Now, what do you want to know about Bill? He doesn't recycle and he waters his lawn every day even when there's a water crisis. He doesn't pick up after his dog, and he leaves his trash can in the street so people can't park in front of his house. And on the full moon, you can find him naked in the yard, turning into a werewolf. Anything else?"

"Grady, this is serious."

"Maybe I'm exaggerating about the howling-at-the-moon thing, but everything else I said was true. He's offered to pay every kid in this neighborhood to pick up after his dog. Even my six-year-old sister won't pick up dog poop for five dollars."

"I don't blame her."

Grady laughed. "What is it you really want to know?"

"What kind of person is he?"

"He's the kind of person who takes what he can and thinks nobody else notices. Last year, someone circulated a petition to have the street lamp timers reset. They wanted to add an extra hour so the streets of Chris Cross would be more safe."

"Chris Cross?"

"Christopher Robin Crossing. Keep up with me, Margo."

I should have known the rich would figure out a way to hippify their neighborhood name. "Continue."

"Perth refused to sign the petition. He said the additional cost would filter down to our property taxes and the expense would outweigh any potential benefit."

"Maybe that's true."

"Maybe it was, but there were enough signatures on the petition to get the bill on the ballot and to win the vote. Proper City goes dark when the sun goes down, except in Chris Cross, where we have our own city-funded daylight."

"What does this have to do with Bill Perth?"

"Turns out the reason he didn't want the bill to pass is because he waits until the sun goes down so he can hook his hose up to his neighbor's house and wash his car. Every single night."

"He washes his car every night?"

"Ever since the timers changed. And he doesn't wash it himself, just oversees the process."

"Who washes it?"

"The kids in the neighborhood. He offered them ten dollars for that."

I glanced at the clock. "What time does this nightly car washing take place?"

"Let's see. The sun sets around six, right? He'll wait until it gets dark and he hooks his hose up to his neighbor's house. Ol' Perthy probably uses more water than anybody else in this whole development."

I got an idea. If what Grady said was right, then Bill Perth would be busy with his car washing routine when the sun went down. I didn't know if Bill Perth was the type to work on a weekend, but it sounded like he was a creature of habit. That meant if I wanted some alone time to poke around Haverford Venture Capital, I'd have a solid window of time.

"Grady, if I ask you to do me a favor and I don't want to tell you why, will you do it?"

"On one condition. You find me a costume for tomorrow night."

AFTER hanging up with Grady, I spent the rest of the day in the workroom. First, I assembled the balance of the teddy bear costumes for Bobbie. When I was done, I had stacks of miniature hobo outfits, clown jumpers in brightly colored polka-dotted fabric, and white fur yeti costumes. Fitting a teddy bear into a yeti costume had been the funniest thing I'd done in a long time.

Kirby and his pals came in and out of the store, working

through the balance of the last minute costume deliveries.
Today they were dressed in black clothes. They'd each
slicked back their hair and dusted baby powder on their
skin to appear more pale. Dark kohl rimmed their eyes,
and plastic vampire teeth were the final accessory. I mostly
ignored their comings and goings and worked on the final
touches of the lab rat costume. It was down to the wire,
but after seeing the laboratory that Kirby set up with the
explosion, I knew that particular costume had a chance to
blow everybody away—not to mention what it would do
for Kirby and his chemistry grade.

At a quarter to five, Kirby returned to the store alone.
"Are you almost done? Mr. Smythe was expecting me by
five thirty."

"Just about. How does it look?" I pulled the rat head
over my own. Additional ventilation by the neck area kept
it cooler than it had originally been. I'd also increased the
size of the eye holes, so Mr. Smythe would be able to see
more clearly. I reached up and tapped both of the tap lights
that were secured to the inside of the head.

"Whoa," Kirby said. "That's going to blow everybody's
mind."

I turned to the mirror. Yep, it was definitely a winner.
I pulled the head off and set it on the counter while Kirby
assembled the white fur rat suit and furry white feet into
a large garment bag. He lowered the head into a cardboard
box, sealed it, and carried the whole thing out to the small
Disguise DeLimit van. Seconds later he pulled away from
the curb and headed west.

Getting together the last of the costumes had kept me
from worrying about Detective Nichols and her warnings,
but now that I was alone in the store, it was hard to think
of anything else. I wandered the aisles and pulled out a
pinstriped double-breasted suit, a plastic tommy gun, a
fedora, and a pair of spats for Grady. He'd probably

substitute a designer suit for the one I was supplying, but the rest of the accessories would pull his costume together. Besides, didn't every twenty-six-year-old guy want to dress like a gangster?

The text message came through at 6:17. *Perth car wash has started.*

I changed into the black zip-front jumpsuit that I'd worn under the spider costume and filled a small black backpack with gloves, flashlight, camera, baseball hat, and a ring filled with castoff keys. Lastly, I switched my phone to silent and left.

It was time to do some stealthy snooping around Paul Haverford's offices.

Chapter 28

HAVERFORD VENTURE CAPITAL occupied a one-story building that extended the length of the parking lot. Spaces by the door had been marked for visitors and employees. I was neither. I also didn't have to worry about parking a car, since I'd ridden a bike and stashed it behind a row of hedges two blocks back.

The parking lot was empty. I approached the building from the side and kept to the shadows. When I reached the front doors, I pressed my face up to the glass and looked inside. The lobby area where Bill Perth and Paul Haverford had argued was as it had been. Two sofas perpendicular to each other, with a square coffee table in the center. A carefully lined-up row of magazines in the middle of the table.

To the right of the lobby was the door to Haverford's office. I pulled my flashlight out of my backpack and shined it through the glass doors. Haverford's office door was ajar. A sliver of light spilled out from the crack. Who would have been in here since the murder? Why leave on a light, and why leave the door open?

The light inside the office went dark for a moment, and then returned. A chill washed over me, like I'd been blasted with fog from Kirby's dry ice chest. The reason the door was open and the light was on was because someone was in there. Right now.

I turned my flashlight off and backed into the shadows. Whoever was inside had had the same idea that I'd had, but why? And how had they gotten in without a key? Gingerly, I tested the front door. Locked. There had to be another entrance.

Stealthy behavior came easily with the costume. I crept backward until I was pressed against the front of the building, and then turned and jogged silently around the side, and then to the back. A service door had been propped open with a concrete block. Before I could decide whether to enter or call the police, a woman in a khaki uniform came out.

Francine Wheeler.

She looked the opposite direction first, and then bent down to move the concrete block. As the door was closing, she stopped and slowly turned to face me. I was two feet away from her.

She pulled an electronic device out of her pocket and aimed it at me. I jumped backward and screamed. She dropped the device and grabbed my arm, and then pulled me into the dark interior of the office.

"Margo, right? You scared the crap out of me. Are you here for the maps?"

"What maps?"

"For Havetown. These clowns think they're going forward with that development. Ha! Not while I'm around."

I looked at the door behind her and back at her. "How did you get in here?"

She held up a set of keys. "If anybody asks, Haverford gave them to me."

"But why would he— Oh," I said. I didn't like the implication, but seeing as I was alone with her in a building and nobody knew where I was, it didn't seem the time for accusations.

I tried a different course of action. "Francine, at the town hall meeting, you said something about changing zoning laws so the Alexandria wouldn't be an issue. You said you had evidence of the active fault lines that ran under Proper City. Was that all true?"

She looked at me as if talking to a child. "There is a real risk here. I've been running tests in West Proper for years. If builders come in here with jackhammers, they're going to trigger a quake. It's that simple. That project cannot happen, and I'll do whatever I have to do to stop it."

"Why are you here?"

"To find the maps for Havetown." She gestured to a stack of round cardboard shipping tubes behind her. Next to the tubes were labels with HVC and a return address. "I'll drop these in the post office drop box tonight and they'll be delivered to me tomorrow."

"What are you going to do with them?"

"Don't worry about me." She tapped her head. "I have a plan."

The last thing I'd expected when I headed out to snoop around HVC was to find Francine Wheeler breaking and entering. Even if she did have a set of keys—of questionable origin, as far as I was concerned—her presence inside the building after dark seemed less on the up and up than mine. I had dueling thoughts racing through my head. *Get out of here and notify the police*, and *Do some snooping yourself now that you're inside*.

The police won. Not because I called them, but because suddenly, the lobby of the building was awash in blue and red lights that splashed through the front glass doors thanks to the police cruisers in the parking lot.

"Come on. We have to get out of here," Francine said. She stooped down and grabbed the cardboard mailing tubes and headed toward the back door. I ducked behind the receptionist's desk and looked for something— anything—that might make my trip worthwhile. The desk was neat in the way that only an employee who plans to be gone for a few days will leave it. I grabbed a small black spiral-bound calendar from under the telephone and followed Francine out the back. As the door closed behind me, I watched a hybrid hatchback leave a parking spot down the street. Francine had gotten away undetected.

I was not so lucky.

"MS. Tamblyn, do you know what a crime of moral turpitude is?" Detective Nichols asked. We were back at the fairy-tale police station, only it was rapidly losing its charm. The detective and I were seated in the same room as before, and once again, she'd chosen a chair directly opposite me. I felt exposed, vulnerable. Especially since this way gave her a full view of what could easily be described as my stealthy black burglar costume.

"No."

"It's the intent to commit burglary."

"I wasn't burglarizing Haverford Venture Capital."

"Then why don't you tell me what you were doing there?"

"I must have walked over every inch of Proper City from the time I grew up. I've never been picked up by the police before. Why tonight?"

She let my question go unanswered. I sensed that she wanted me to talk more, but I fought the urge to converse.

I was sitting in a room with the woman who was going to attend the annual Halloween party with my secret boyfriend. There was a slight possibility that whatever I said wouldn't have anything to do with her case.

Minutes ticked by on the clock on the wall. The longer the silence spread, the more aware I became of the subtle tick of the passing seconds. *Thunk. Thunk. Thunk.* Which quickly started to sound like *Think. Think. Think.* We spent the most awkward two minutes and sixteen seconds together that I could have imagined. I was surprised when she broke the silence first.

"Help me out here. I'm investigating a murder. I have video of you destroying the security camera in the elevator where the body was found. I have evidence that places you in the victim's office, and evidence that shows that you were angry when you were there. Now, thanks to an anonymous tip, my officers find you casing the victim's place of business. You keep telling me you're not guilty of anything, but that doesn't match up with your actions. Which do you want me to believe? What you say or what you do?"

Her softened tone of voice was different from how she'd spoken to me in the past. This time it felt like she really did want to listen to what I had to say. "I wasn't the only person at HVC tonight. Yes, I went there to snoop. But I found Francine Wheeler inside. You remember her, right? The seismologist? She said Paul Haverford gave her keys, so maybe she had a right to be there. I don't know. But if I were you, I'd look into her alibi. She is opposed to Havetown and told me she'd do anything to stop it. Anything," I stressed again.

"So by your count, I have at least five other people I should be investigating: Francine Wheeler, Annette Crowley, Bill Perth, Sol Girard, and Spider-Man. Did I get that right?"

My face flushed hot with deception. "I'm trying to help you here."

"So are your friends." She picked up another piece of paper. "Bobbie Kay called and said she would vouch for you as a character witness. Don Digby said that Paul Haverford may have been involved in funding secret government experiments and was taken out because someone thought he was a risk to national security. And Ms. Ebony Welles called earlier today and said we shouldn't discount the ghost of Pete Proper."

It was good to have friends. Even if they were all a little crazy.

"Everything I have told you since I discovered the body of Paul Haverford has been true. If you would follow up on that statement and use it as the foundation to your investigation instead of focusing on me, you might have answers right now. Yes, I was mad when Haverford came to the costume shop last week. And yes, I went to his office to try to reason with him. But I didn't kill him. And for you to think for a moment that I did, well, that says a lot about you." I was angry. I stood up. "Are you going to arrest me or put me in a holding cell? Because tomorrow is Halloween, and I have a lot to do. So if you've got some kind of master plan here, let's get on with it."

Detective Nichols stood with me. "You're free to go, Ms. Tamblyn." We walked out to the lobby. "Do you need a ride home? We didn't find your scooter in the parking lot, and the Zip lines are done running for the night."

I would rather walk the two miles home than arrive in a cop car. I pulled my cell out of my pocket. There were several missed texts from Grady. I put the phone back into my pocket. "Dead battery," I lied. "Can I use your phone to call a friend?"

"No need," I heard from behind. I turned around and saw Tak leaning against the inside door, arms crossed over his chest.

Chapter 29

"WHERE DID YOU come from?" Detective Nichols and I asked at the same time. Even thought the situation called for it, it would have been wrong to say "Jinx."

"Are you done here?" Tak asked the detective. She nodded. He held his arm out. "I'll take you home, Margo."

I followed him out of the police station to his SUV. He remote unlocked it and I climbed in. Neither of us spoke until he pulled up in front of Disguise DeLimit.

"My father and I came here tonight. He wanted to talk to you directly about the Halloween party at Proper City Park."

"But I wasn't here."

"I know. I called Ebony, but she didn't know where you went. I called Bobbie. I even called Coop. It didn't seem like you to blow off a meeting with my dad."

"I thought he or your mom were going to call. I didn't know he was going to come personally."

"My father believes in handling business face-to-face.

While we were here, Grady O'Toole showed up. He said you were in trouble, something about Bill Perth not washing his car like he was supposed to, and that you were about to do something risky. I called Nancy and the dispatch officer told me she was with someone they picked up at Haverford Venture Capital. Talk to me, Margo. What's going on?"

"I can't talk to you, Tak. Not anymore."

"I think you owe me an explanation." He looked out his window. The moonlight illuminated the straight line of his nose and accented his defined cheekbones. The shadows in the hollows of his cheeks only served to pronounce them more. His black hair was pushed back, though one side fell forward and hung over his dark brown eyes. Even though he wasn't facing me, I could see pain in his face.

I reached out and put my hand on his arm. "It's not what you think," I said.

He looked at me. "Then tell me what it is, because that's how it looks."

I pulled my hand back and curled my hands up in each other. "I've been in charge of Disguise DeLimit for only a few months now, and we're at risk of losing it because of the plans for Havetown. Somebody else wanted to stop Paul Haverford even more than I did. But Bill Perth is going forward with the plans for Havetown even though Paul Haverford was murdered. Not only is he moving forward, but he's claiming that he was a fifty percent silent partner in the business and that now he's entitled to one hundred percent of the profits. That's a lot of money if he can prove it."

"Can he?"

"I don't know. It would be hard to prove a partnership that even he admits was made by verbal contract, but then again, the only person who could deny it isn't around to deny anything."

"What did Grady mean about Bill Perth's car and you doing something risky?"

"I followed Perth home from the town hall meeting the other night. He lives in Christopher Robin Crossing. So does Grady. I called him—Grady, not Perth—and asked what he could tell me about him."

"And somehow you ended up with the idea that Perth was washing his car and you could break into his office and snoop around."

"No! Okay, yes, I went to HVC to snoop, but I didn't plan to break in. Francine Wheeler was there. Inside. She broke in, not me. And when she found me, she pulled me in, and that's where I was when the police found me."

"You got lucky this time. You might not be so lucky the next."

"I was picked up by the police. How is that lucky?"

"I asked Grady if he knew where you were and he said yes. I told him to call the police and report suspicious activity at that location. They sent a car, and you were taken to the station. Bill Perth doesn't even know that you were there."

"But—"

"But nothing. Grady was right. What you did was risky. Nobody knew where you were going. What if something had happened to you? How would your dad feel? Or Ebony? Or Bobbie? Did you stop to think about what it would do to your friends if you became the next victim?"

I thought back to the police station, to the various suspects that my friends had suggested that Detective Nichols investigate. Don's government agents and Ebony's ghost-of-Pete-Proper theory. And even Bobbie, a pillar of the community because of her nonprofit work with Money Changes Everything. She was willing to stake that reputation on me and serve as a character witness.

For as long as I could remember, I'd been too afraid of taking chances to fully live my life. I cherished the familiar and did what I could to keep people safe. Even the seven years that I'd spent working in Las Vegas had been a challenge. Being on my own for the first time, making new friends and adopting Soot, it had served the dual purpose of showing me what life would be like if everybody and everything I knew went away and I had to start over. Ultimately, I'd chosen to return to Proper City and take over the family business. I wanted to be a part of the community. Tak's words stung, if only because they showed how clearly I valued everybody else more than I thought they valued me.

"Tak, I never meant to insult your father, and I never meant to be a burden to you."

"Who said you were a burden?"

"You came to the police station to run interference between Detective Nichols and me. I can't think of many more awkward situations."

"Why?"

"Because you're dating her again. I wish I hadn't heard about it from Gina Cassavogli, but it is what it is."

"That's what's bothering you."

"Thank you for helping me out tonight, but I can take it from here."

I climbed down out of his SUV and let myself into the store. I found Soot asleep behind the rack of feather boas. He growled at me—no doubt because I woke him up—and then stretched his paws out in front and slowly stood up.

"Come on, Soot, we don't have time for you to do yoga. I need to talk."

He looked up at me and meowed again. Instead of carrying him upstairs with me, I sat down on the cold concrete floor next to him. "Okay, fine, we can talk here. What do you think I should think about Tak? Twice now I've brought up him dating the detective. He doesn't deny it. But he showed up at the police station to help me. Why? Is he trying to string me along while he dates her? Or is it over?" I bent my knees and wrapped my arms around my legs. Soot ducked underneath like he was going through a tunnel, and came out the other side. He brushed his head against my hip and nuzzled my elbow. I rubbed his fur by his ears.

"And now there's this thing with his father. Did I offend him? And if so, how do I make it up to him? I don't know what he wanted to say when he came here, and now it's too late to call. Even if it wasn't too late, I can't just call. You heard what Tak said. I have to go there and talk to him face-to-face. And it's not just about Halloween anymore."

Soot turned around and meowed again.

"You think I'm making this into too big of a deal? As far as I know, Tak is dating his ex-girlfriend, who just so happens to be the lead detective on the murder case where I'm being investigated. His father thinks I insulted him, and Ebony needs his father to agree to participate in the PCP Halloween party. How would you feel?"

Soot ducked back under my knees and walked in front of me. He turned around, sat on his gray haunches, and let out a howl that the employees of the frozen yogurt store across the street probably heard.

"Soot!"

And then, as if nothing had happened, he lowered his head, licked his paw, and started washing his face. I pushed myself up, and then squatted down in front of him. "You made your point." I ruffled his freshly cleaned fur and went upstairs. The house was once again quiet. I tiptoed past my dad's room, not sure if he was in there, and not sure how I'd explain my night if he was.

*   *   *

Monday/Halloween

The next morning, I dressed like the devil. Red dress, red tights, red boots. Red gloves. Red wig. Red horns, red pitchfork, and red forked tail that hung from a red patent leather belt. Instead of a smoothie, I poured a glass of tomato juice, which matched my outfit, and carried it downstairs. I unlocked the front doors and stepped outside.

It was Halloween day.

Some towns had started to celebrate trick-or-treating on the Saturday or Sunday night that was closest to October 31, but not us. We built the event around the date. Most of the residents dressed in costume first thing in the morning and kept them on all day.

Across the street, the staff of Froyo was dressed in bellhop uniforms. Purple velvet jackets, pinstriped pants, and small matching hats with tassels from the top. I raised my glass of tomato juice to them and they waved back. A mobile home pulled up to the curb in front of me and blocked my view.

This was no place to park a mobile home. I walked around the back of the vehicle. The logo on the side said *Minnie Winnie*, followed by *Winnebago*. The temporary paper license was from Nevada, and the plastic frame to the plate said *Moxie Winnebago*. Whoever the owner was, they'd just recently made their purchase.

The doors to the Winnie opened up while I was standing around back. A man dressed in a long black cape lined in red satin climbed out of the driver's side. His gray hair was combed away from his face and slicked down. He walked around the front of the Winnebago. Cars zipped past. I went back to the sidewalk.

"Excuse me, you can't park that thing here," I said. "This is my store and you're blocking the entrance."

The man joined me on the sidewalk. He was easily over six feet tall. A prominent widow's peak on his forehead pointed down toward thick gray brows that framed out bloodshot red eyes. Under his cape was a white shirt, black waistcoat, and gold cross that hung on a thick gold chain. He walked right up to me and raised his hand to my face. Even though I appreciated the intricacies of his costume, I pulled back for a split second.

"Margo, it's me," he said.

"Dad?"

He reached up and poked his finger into his eye. Out came a red contact lens. He repeated on the other eye and held both in the palm of his hand, and then removed a set of false upper teeth. "Those things were driving me crazy," he said.

First thing I did was hug him. Second thing I did was cross my arms and tap my foot. "What's with the car? Last I checked, Dracula didn't drive a Winnebago."

"It's my new car. What do you think?"

"It's your— What?" I stared at the large mobile home. "What do you need this thing for?"

He pulled out a rag and wiped at an invisible spot on the side. Now that the contacts were out, his eyes were bright and shiny with joy. I couldn't remember the last time I'd seen such enthusiasm on my dad's face. "I got the idea when I was snowed in. Who wants to rely on airplanes when you can travel at your own pace? I'm going to take her around the country. There's room for me to sleep in the back and plenty of space for any costume purchases I might make."

"Her?"

"Celeste. I named her after your mother."

That's when I knew. My dad hadn't been going to

singles mixers. He hadn't been dating Marilyn Robinson. He hadn't been looking for a new relationship. He'd been giving me privacy while figuring out a way to follow his own lifelong dream of traveling the country scouting for unique items for the store. And he'd found a way for my mother to be a part of that dream.

"Dad, I've never been more proud of you than I am right now," I said.

"And I've never been more proud of you than when you called this your store. Come on, let me show you the inside."

The tour of the Winnebago took ten minutes, but we turned it into an hour. My dad brewed two cups of instant coffee in his miniscule kitchen. I told him how the rat costume had turned out, the party that was taking place at Proper City Park, and how Ebony was reaching out to local businesses to help set the whole thing up.

"Then what are we sitting around here for? We should be at the PCP helping her. Are you ready to go?"

"You go first. I'll join you shortly. First, there's something I have to take care of."

HOSHIYAMA Kobe Steak House sat on an otherwise vacant lot on the west end of Proper. The building was long and low, with a flat roof that was set off by curved wooden beams. I drove past the parking lot and pulled my scooter behind the bank. Unlike other cities, Proper businesses didn't mind if you used their parking during off hours, and this allowed me the chance to check my reflection in the glass doors of the bank before entering the restaurant. Perhaps I should have rethought my devil costume.

Inside the restaurant, employees were bustling around

with carts filled with silver bowls, rice, and meats. I scanned the interior, looking for Mr. Hoshiyama. I spotted him in the back by the doors that led to their private dining room. Before I determined how to approach him, I felt a hand on my arm. I turned and found myself face-to-face with Tak's mother.

"He is a proud man, Margo, but he is generous. Treat him with respect and you will receive it back. But understand that he is the one who has been slighted. Not you."

Chapter 30

I NODDED MY understanding. She held her hand out toward the private room and smiled. I thanked her and followed Mr. Hoshiyama into the back room.

The last time I'd been back here, I'd been Tak's dining guest. We had sat next to each other on thick pillows that surrounded the low table. Paper lanterns had provided the soft glow of light around us while we ate, laughed, and shared a moment.

Today, the pillows had been moved to a stack along one wall. The table was covered with large, curved blades. Not the kind used for cutting food, but the kind used for battle. The assortment alone was intimidating.

I tapped the door frame. "Mr. Hoshiyama," I said. "I'm Margo Tamblyn. I came to apologize for not being at the store last night."

The older gentleman stood straight and turned to face me. He had a full head of hair, parted on the side and trimmed neatly into a classic style. It was easy to see the resemblance between him and Tak: the cheekbones, the dark eyebrows, the naturally rosy red lips. His face was tanned, and the effects of the sun had turned his skin papery. But still, he was an attractive man, albeit at the moment, a very serious one.

He bowed slightly in my direction and I returned the gesture, even though I wasn't sure if it was appropriate. "Miss Margo," he said. "My son tells me that you are responsible for the Halloween party taking place in the park this year."

"All I did was call a friend and ask him to see if he could gain approvals for us."

"This friend, he works in the Clark County Planning Office? Where my son used to work?"

"Yes."

"You are friendly with my son, no?"

"Yes, Tak and I are"—I hesitated—"friendly."

"But you no longer spend time with him now that he is a restaurant employee and not a city planner."

"That's not true!" I said quickly. "Tak and I—we met a few months ago when I moved back here. It had nothing to do with his job or with mine." I thought of the one thing I could say to make him understand. "I moved back to Proper City to run my family's costume shop, Mr. Hoshiyama. It was my parents' dream to have that shop, and my mother died when I was born. My father's been running it by himself my whole life. I think it's noble for Tak to work here. He respects what you and his mother have created, and he wants to be a part of that."

"My son has an engineering degree from Princeton. He graduated in the top of his class. He is wasting himself here."

"Mr. Hoshiyama, my family is me and my dad. I never had the chance to meet my own mother. But I know that they built that business together out of love, and now, I'm going to play a part in helping it succeed. I think you should recognize that Tak is trying to do the exact same thing for you."

Tak's dad turned away from me. He picked up two knives from a pile behind him. When he looked up at me, he crossed the blades on top of each other in front of him. "These knives are from my family in Japan. They have been in storage for a long time. No one has seen them for decades."

"What made you bring them out?"

"We have lived in Proper City for ten years and have never been invited to participate in the Halloween party. It has felt as though the city views us as outsiders. When you asked us to participate in the Halloween events at the park, I thought this would make a nice display and would allow us to bring our own history to the city. Takenouchi and I will dress in traditional samurai costumes and allow children to view Japanese weapons. Perhaps we can stage a demonstration."

It was a beautiful idea and the children of Proper City would love it. Not just the children either. Grady and his friends would too. There had never been anything like that here. And it was time for us to expand on what the celebration had been to the town and to include everybody, not just families who had lived here for generations.

"I hope my actions last night won't make you reconsider your idea. It's perfect, and everybody will love it. I know it."

He bowed again. "Then it will be."

"Thank you."

I said good-bye and stepped out of the private room. As I was sliding the door shut behind me, Mr. Hoshiyama stopped me.

"Miss Margo, my son cares for you a great deal. He thinks that I won't approve of you because you are not Japanese. He must only look at my choice of wife to know how far from the truth that could be." He looked past me at Lynn Hoshiyama. I looked at her too. She seemed to sense that she was the focus of our attention. She paused next to a table where she was delivering mugs of hot green tea and looked at us with concern in her eyes. Quickly her expression changed to a smile. I snuck a glance at Mr. Hoshiyama. From the look on his face, I could see that he was completely in love with her.

"Thank you, Mr. Hoshiyama. This has been very enlightening." I held out my hand and he shook it.

I left the restaurant and drove to the park. The climate in Nevada was dry and arid. Plants didn't grow unless heavily watered, which went against the water rationing laws that were in place. Our public park was a stretch of mostly dirt peppered with the occasional patch of yellow grass. Picnic tables and benches sat under an aluminum roof off to the side and public charcoal pits sat every twenty or so feet. It wasn't unusual to find families out for a day at the park, even though there was little else to do other than eat and throw a Frisbee.

Already, cars were lined up around the perimeter. I recognized business owners and neighbors mingled with people who must have moved to town during the time I was in Las Vegas. Ebony stood at the center of the park, waving people forward and pointing out where they should go. I strode across the dirt and joined her.

"Girl, we're gonna have a party!" She held her fingers up on either side of her head and snapped them as she slowly moved her hips from side to side. It was as if Ebony had her own private soundtrack playing.

"So the city is on board?"

"The hotel is restricted from entry. As far as the city is concerned, there wasn't going to be a party this year. Do you know how happy they were when I called with this solution? I've got ads lined up to run on the radio station. The Proper City Chamber of Commerce even did an e-mail blast for us, and they said the phones have been ringing ever since. You think we can get those swim team boys to go door to door?"

"Judging from the number of people here to help set up, everybody already knows."

WE worked on party setup for the next several hours. Beef-Cake, the local burger joint, showed up with platters of hamburgers and hot dogs for the volunteers, and Catch-22 provided baskets of fried shrimp. Even vegans were accommodated when Hummina Hummina Hummus made a delivery of pita bread, falafel, a portable raw vegetable station, and, of course, hummus.

Packin' Pistils unloaded a truck filled with pumpkins and set up a jack-o'-lantern carving station in the corner of the park, and then surprised us all with several dozen vases filled with orange floral arrangements, which Ebony used to line the stage where the costume contest was to take place.

As happy as I was that Ebony had gotten past her fears about the new party, I couldn't quite ignore my own concerns based on the murder at the kickoff party. Were we being foolish by going forward with the annual activities? Or would something else happen? And if it did, would it happen at the PCP, where our party was to take place, or was it going to happen at the Alexandria Hotel?

As the morning moved into afternoon, the landscape of the park transitioned from a wide expanse of dirt and trees to a series of vignettes. In addition to the pumpkin carving and the stage for the costume contest, there was an area designated for witch makeovers and another section cordoned off for a makeshift outdoor haunted house. The hand-painted sign over the entrance read *Trash-land*. Men, women, and children dragged giant black plastic trash bags into their work space. I wasn't sure how it would turn out, but they seemed enthusiastic, so I let them be.

Dig stood by the end of the stage with a hammer in one hand and a fist full of nails in the other. He had a red bandana tied around his forehead and pulled low.

"You look like you're solving quantum physics in your head," I said, approaching him.

"This is a field. It's supposed to be scary. It doesn't look scary now."

"That's because it's daylight. Remember the Alexandria? It looked scary the other night, right?"

"Yeah, but it had all of those cauldrons around it, and the fog. We're in the middle of a public park. No electricity. We need light and we need fog. It's like we got ourselves some undeveloped land here, and we have to turn it into Halloween Town by tonight."

"You're right. And I know just the person to help you. Give me five minutes."

The truth was, I'd been looking for an opportunity to call Tak and get him involved. He hadn't been at Hoshiyama Steak House when I was there, so maybe he didn't know what was going on. I called him.

"Hi, Private Number," he answered.

"Hi," I said. "I'm with Dig Allen, and it turns out he's in need of a city planner who can turn the PCP into Halloween Town by tonight. Do you know anybody who might be interested in the job?"

"Depends on what it pays."

"If you hurry, you'll get a burger or hot dog from Beef-Cake. Maybe even a shrimp basket from Catch-22."

"My family owns the best restaurant in Proper City and

you're offering me food as a payoff? Cooper might go for that, but my experience is worth more."

"What do you want?"

"How about a date for the party tonight?'

"I thought you had a date for the party."

"Not as far as I know. You know anybody who would be interested?"

I did. I also knew someone who had already accepted a date with Tak's friend, Cooper. Unfortunately both of the people I knew were me.

"I already told Cooper I'd come to the party with him."

There was a silent beat. "I should have expected that. He asked me if I minded if he asked you out."

"What did you say?"

"He asked you out, didn't he?"

I felt a tap on my shoulder. It was Dig. He raised his eyebrows, and they disappeared under the bandana.

"Dig wants to talk to you," I said, and shoved the phone at Dig. "Tak Hoshiyama. Former city planner. Make him an offer he can't refuse and he'll help you with Halloween Town."

Dig took the phone and I walked away. I found Bobbie assembling a large bookcase.

"For the bears," she said. "You remembered the costumes, didn't you?"

"Yes and no. I made them, but they're sitting on the workstation at Disguise DeLimit. Will you be here for a little while?"

"Sure. As long as it takes for me to build this thing."

"Perfect. I'll get them and come right back."

I headed toward my scooter while the air filled with the sounds of hammers, grunts, and laughter. The scent of the food had faded, and in its place was the comingled fragrance of pumpkins, apple cider, and flowers. It was around four thirty. We had an hour and a half before guests would arrive.

Behind me, Dig yelled my name. When I turned around, he pointed at my phone. I jerked a thumb toward my scooter, and then pointed at where I stood. He seemed to understand my pantomime for "I'm going but I'll be back," shrugged, and put my phone in the pocket of his shirt.

The roads were mostly clear. The few people who weren't at the park helping to set up the party were either finishing up their day jobs or at home getting into costume. I giggled for a second at the thought of people primping like they were about to attend the prom.

I arrived at Disguise DeLimit in minutes and parked out front. Inside, I packed the stacks of teddy bear costumes into a red backpack, squashing them to make them all fit, and then zipped it closed. I pulled both straps on over my shoulders and left. A sliver of paper slipped out of the door frame to the sidewalk. *Package delivery left around back,* it said.

My dad had mentioned that he'd sent himself packages from the road. As much fun as Halloween was, there was always the possibility of mischief too. If I didn't make it back to the store tonight, those packages might sit out overnight. There was a chance they might even get stolen.

I drove my scooter to the end of the block and turned into the narrow alley behind the store. Cardboard tubes like the ones Francine Wheeler had had at HVC were scattered on the ground by the back door. I put the scooter on the kickstand and picked one up. It was empty. The address label said *Disguise DeLimit.*

What?

I picked up another. It was empty too. And then I heard something behind me. I turned around and saw Francine Wheeler lying on the ground with a trickle of blood running down the side of her head.

Chapter 31

I DROPPED THE cardboard containers and the backpack and raced over to her. "Francine? Talk to me."

Her eyes fluttered open. She looked like she was trying to focus on me. "You!" she said, and raised her hands to her face.

Her sudden motion scared me and I moved away from her. I felt my pockets for my phone, and then realized that I'd left my cell with Dig. "I'll be right back. I'm calling the police," I said.

I went into the shop and called 911. "There's been an accident at Disguise DeLimit. Please send paramedics."

"Are you hurt?" the operator asked.

"Not me. Francine Wheeler. Yes, she's hurt. Please send help."

I stayed on the line long enough to give my name and the store's address, and then grabbed a bottle of water from the refrigerator and went back outside to Francine. I held the bottle to her lips. Water trickled down the front of her khaki shirt.

I rooted through my backpack and pulled out a pair of the teddy bear hobo pants. I poured water on them and then held them to her head. She flinched at first, but then took the compress and held it in place. The tiny garment absorbed the blood from her wound. Once she was cleaned up, I could see that the gash was not nearly as bad as I'd originally thought. It was smaller than the size of a dime.

"Help is coming," I said to her. "Talk to me. What's your name?"

"You know my name."

"Say it anyway."

"Francine." It took her great effort to get the word out.

"Where do you live?" I asked, more to keep her talking than from any real interest. In the distance, I heard sirens.

"Small house," she said. "Quakeproof."

"I'm sure it is. Francine, who did this to you?"

Her eyes fluttered open a second time. She seemed to have trouble focusing on me. "You did."

Before I could ask her what she meant, an ambulance pulled up to the curb. Paramedics jumped out and pulled me away from her. I stood by the back of the shop with my arms wrapped around myself. What had she meant?

Detective Nichols pulled her navy blue sedan up behind the ambulance. When she got out, she ran her fingers through her hair and approached.

"What happened here?"

"I came back to the store to pick up some costumes for Bobbie—she's setting up her bears at the PCP with everybody else, I've been there all day working—and when I left out front, a piece of paper fell from the door and said there was a package delivery out back. I thought it was something my dad sent to himself—he does that when he's out buying costumes—but when I came back here, I found her on the ground."

"Did you touch her?"

"Yes. I brought her a bottle of water and then cleaned the blood off her head so I could see the wound."

She took two steps toward Francine and said something I didn't hear to the paramedic. He gently pushed Francine's hair back. The wound had turned dark and purple. The compress had controlled the blood flow, so the only sign was the circular mark. Detective Nichols looked around the ground for something that could have caused the injury. Scattered around were the empty shipping tubes and plastic lids, but nothing else. Her eyes rested on my backpack.

"What's that?"

"That's mine. It's filled with the teddy bear costumes I was taking to Bobbie."

"Open it."

I unzipped the bag and held it open for her to see the bear costumes.

"You're serious."

"Like I told you, I came home, filled the backpack with teddy bear costumes, and was about to leave when I saw the note about packages. I went around back and found the empty shipping containers and saw Francine. After I checked to make sure she was still alive, I came in and called you."

"Let's go inside. I have more questions."

We moved to the workroom of Disguise DeLimit. The long, narrow room was convenient for the wall of sewing machines that my dad had installed, but not so much for a one-on-one with the detective. The lights were bright, and the sterile white walls held little to distract me from what had happened. The only comforting thing in sight was the Bobbie Bear who had served as my fit model. He sat on the back of the counter, dressed in a pink and blue clown suit with a ruffle around his neck. More than just about anything, I wanted to reach out and hug him.

"Why did you come inside to call me? Why not use your cell?"

"Dig Allen has it. He's at the PCP. He'll verify that."

She made a note. "Do you know what was in the shipping containers?"

"I think they were quaternary maps. Maps of the fault lines that run underground."

She showed surprise. "How would a costume shop owner come to know about quaternary maps?"

"I learned about them the other day when I went to the Clark County Planning Office. I wanted to know more about the Alexandria Hotel, and Cooper Price—do you know him?" She nodded. "He told me about them. And then the next day he brought me a set."

"He brought them to you?"

"Yes. They're inside."

"Did you ask him to make another copy for you?"

"No."

She sat back and tapped the end of her mechanical pencil on the table. "Why would an employee of the planning office take the time to copy a map of fault lines for you?"

I felt heat climb my throat and cheeks. "I think he wanted an excuse to ask me out."

Her pencil tapping stopped. She set the pencil down and lined it up with her notepad.

"Do you still have these quaternary maps?" she asked.

"They're behind the register out front."

"Let's go."

IF I'd expected the detective to take me into custody, I would have been let down. After I handed over the maps, she went over my statement one more time. The only thing I left out was Francine's answer to my question. I had not done this to her. But someone had led her to believe that I had.

It would have been easy for another woman to masquerade as me, especially today of all days. I was dressed head to toe in red. But the only other woman who I'd connected to Paul Haverford was Annette Crowley. She'd done battle with Haverford in the past and had won. If she had been guilty of causing the illness that forced him to drop his development plans for Peppermint House, had she escalated her tactics to include murder—this time to eliminate her opposition for good? But if so, why go after Francine too? To throw the police off her trail and implicate me further, or was there something I was missing?

But maybe Francine was trying to say something else. I'd been with her when she stole the maps from the Haverford offices. Was she saying that my involvement had brought on her attack? That she'd flown under the radar until I'd gotten involved?

The other thing that seemed apparent from the detective's visit was that she was no longer warning me to mind my own business. Conversely, she wasn't warning me to be careful either. I wasn't sure how to interpret either omission.

It was closing in on six. I drove back to the PCP and found Bobbie dressing bears.

"Do you want to tell me why Detective Nichols delivered the teddy bear costumes to me instead of you? Not the person I'd expect you to call for a favor."

"Did she say anything else? Did she ask you any questions about me?"

"No. She gave me the costumes and asked where she could find Dig. I thought you said the costumes were at the shop. What was the detective doing there?"

"I found Francine Wheeler knocked out behind Disguise DeLimit. Detective Nichols came over to find out what happened. She asked me a lot of questions, but this time she didn't make it sound like she suspected me of anything. I don't know why either, because the attack happened behind my store. If she was going to turn something innocent into evidence that implicated me, she had a pretty good opportunity."

Bobbie tucked the legs of the last bear into a white fur yeti costume and pushed his head until he was all the way in. When she was done, she whipstitched the front and back of the head of the costume together with a length of white ribbon that I'd pinned on for that purpose, and then knotted each side off. The bear's tiny little face peeked through the opening, his mouth hidden behind white plastic vampire teeth that I'd hand sewn to the fur. She turned him to her and then to me. "He really is pretty adorable," she said.

"I know. What are you planning on doing with them tonight?"

"These bears speak for themselves. Make a donation, get a bear. Simple as that.'

"And your costume?"

She lifted a hanger from the back of the bookcase and held up a giant brown fur jumpsuit. "What else? I'll be dressed like one of them too."

I left Bobbie to rearrange the bears on her bookcase and paint her sign and found Dig helping Ebony with the stage. The vases of orange flowers were in place next to braids of glow-in-the-dark cords that illuminated the edge of the platform. Above us, strands of white twinkle lights were draped from tree to tree, creating our own starry night. I followed the strands until I found one that draped out of the tree toward the ground.

"How are they lit? Like you said, there are no outlets out here."

"Gas generator. Filled up, it'll last for about five hours."

"It's genius."

"It was Tak's idea. If it wasn't for him and his friend, we'd be trying to run the world's longest extension cord."

"His friend?"

"Cooper. Nice guy. He showed up after Tak got here. They work pretty well together. You should check out what they did in Have-Not Town."

"Who's idea was that?"

"Sol Girard. That reminds me. He said you dropped something when you were at his place the other night."

"I don't remember leaving anything behind," I said.

"Here," he pulled out a socket wrench. The circle on the end was approximately the same size as the wound on Francine's head.

Chapter 32

I BACKED AWAY from Dig. "That's not mine," I said.

He laughed. "It's not gonna bite, Margo. It's just a socket wrench."

"Where's my phone? I have to call Detective Nichols."

Dig must have recognized the urgency in my voice, because instead of teasing me, he pulled my phone out of his pocket. I grabbed it from him and called her.

"Detective Nichols," she answered.

"This is Margo Tamblyn. I think I have the weapon that was used to knock out Francine."

"What is it?"

"A socket wrench. The circle thingie on the end looks to be about the same size as the wound on her head."

"You have it with you?"

"Sol Girard gave it to Dig Allen to give to me. I think it was a message. I think he's trying to tell me not to get involved."

"Where are you?"

"The Proper City Park."

"I'll send a car out to his house to have a talk with him."

I hung up the phone, feeling like someone had painted a target on my back. Worse, I knew that as long as I was at the Halloween party, I was putting a lot of other people at risk. It wasn't worth it.

I turned to Ebony. "Whatever this thing is with Paul Haverford, it's gotten too big and I've gotten too involved. I'm going home. I don't want anybody here to be put in the middle of something I started."

"Girl, you're scaring me. It's bad enough I have to deal with the spirit world this time of year. What happened?"

I looked back and forth between her and Dig's faces. Behind them, Tak stood on top of a six-foot ladder, positioning strands of twinkle lights. Tak was dressed in Japanese attire: Wide-legged black pants, a close fitting black top, and blue kimono that had been bound at the waist with thick black fabric. I'd seen costumes intended to represent Japanese warriors, but they had been mass produced out of cheap red and gold fabrics. His had a quiet authenticity to it. Until now, I'd only seen him in the kind of clothes that other guys wore, but he didn't appear uncomfortable in costume—in fact, it was the opposite. He moved with grace and confidence. It was Cooper, next to him, dressed as Robin Hood in green tights, brown tattered outfit, and a quiver on his back, who fussed with his hem and seemed ill at ease with his appearance.

Tak paused for a moment and looked at me. Nothing from the evening, not the incredible setup of his booth or the stage lined with pumpkins or the bookshelf of teddy bears in costume could take away the sense of doom that pervaded the night. My eyes filled with tears, and they spilled, leaving tracks down my cheeks that dripped onto my red devil outfit.

Tak scrambled down the ladder and said something to

Cooper, who turned around. He set down the strand of twinkle lights he'd been holding and the two of them jogged over to where I stood.

"What's wrong?" Tak asked.

"That's what we're trying to find out," Dig said.

I took a deep breath and swiped the tears from my face. "Francine Wheeler was knocked out behind Disguise DeLimit. She's at the hospital now." I looked at Cooper. "She broke into Haverford Venture Capital last night and stole the quaternary maps. She said Paul Haverford's murder had to do with the expansion plans in West Proper, and she needed them to prove the risk of development."

"How do you know she stole the maps?" Cooper asked.

I looked at Tak. He knew I'd been at HVC last night. He must not have told Cooper about it. "I was there. I didn't— I wasn't helping her. I went to see if I could find something out about Bill Perth's involvement with Haverford. Honestly, I was going to snoop around the outside, try to look through the widows. And I did. The door to Haverford's office was open and a light was moving around. I went around the back of the building and Francine came out. We scared each other."

"What about the maps?" he asked.

"She had these long shipping tubes with her. She said she was going to send them to herself."

"What are these maps?" Dig asked.

Tak answered. "They show the network of fault lines that run under Proper and the neighboring communities. Seismologists like Francine rely on them pretty heavily to determine where there might be risk and to predict when the next earthquakes might take place. Paul Haverford would have had a set because of his development plans of West Proper."

"Why would this Francine person want to steal them?" Ebony asked.

"She made no secret of the fact that she opposed Have-town. She disrupted the town hall meeting the other night and tried to make her point. Even you two said that she's been a nuisance to the planning office for years."

Cooper rubbed a stain of grease from his fingers. "She's passionate about what she does. But those maps are public record." He looked at me. "That's why I was able to make you a copy. If Francine wanted them, she knew she could come down to the office and request them. She has in the past. I don't know why she'd break into the Haverford offices and steal them when she could just as easily obtain them through legal means."

"We're forgetting one thing," I said. "Francine isn't the bad guy here. She was knocked out. She's in the hospital. Somebody else didn't like the fact that she got those maps. Somebody else who is connected to Havetown."

"You went white as a ghost when I mentioned Sol Girard's name," Dig said. "You think he has something to do with this?"

"He owns property in West Proper. And he struck a deal with Haverford to benefit from the development. That happened right before Paul Haverford was murdered."

Ebony turned around and cursed. For the first time in my life, she didn't apologize immediately after. She put her hands on the platform in front of her and hung her head down. Thick dreadlocks draped to the sides of her head, hiding her face. Even though she didn't say it, I knew what she was thinning.

"It's too dangerous for me to be here tonight," I said. "I can't risk putting the rest of the people here in the line of fire because someone's keeping an eye on me." I looked at their faces and felt a little like Dorothy saying good-bye to the Scarecrow, the Tin Woodman, and the Cowardly Lion. "It'll be okay. You should all celebrate Halloween without me." I forced a shrug. "It's not so special. I wear costumes every day."

In the background, the Minnie Winnie pulled up to the curb. My dad climbed out and opened the back doors. Kirby climbed out of the passenger-side doors and met up with him. Together, with the help of two additional swim team members who must have been in the back, they unloaded the laboratory backdrop that went with Mr. Smythe's rat costume. The four of them carried it across the park and set it down next to Bobbie's bear display.

"I'll be right back." I left the group and approached my dad.

"Margo, didn't Kirby outdo himself?" Dad asked.

"It's incredible. Dad, I need to talk to you."

His expression changed from joy to concern. He instructed the boys to continue without him and we walked a few feet away from the display. I told him about the attack on Francine, the missing maps, and the socket wrench from Sol Girard. In less than two minutes, I briefed him on everything that had been happening, including my decision to leave.

He put his hand on my shoulder. "I don't want you to be alone tonight."

"She won't be, sir," Cooper said. He looked at me. "I know I asked you to be my date tonight, but I just wanted to spend time with you. The Cineplex is showing a double feature of *Halloween* and *Gremlins*." He glanced down at his green Robin Hood costume. "If I'm willing to be seen wearing tights in public, would you be willing to join me?"

"If you're willing to make that sacrifice, then I guess I should be willing to make my own. Let me get my things."

I didn't spend time on saying good-bye to everybody. Cooper checked the movie times on his phone, and I grabbed my now-mostly-empty backpack from Bobbie's booth.

"Are you sure you know what you're doing? I don't want

to make a big thing out of this, but every time Tak looks at you, it's pretty obvious how he feels."

"Bobbie, I don't have a clue, but Cooper asked me here and I said yes. We'll see how it goes. Maybe we'll crash and burn before we even buy popcorn."

"Before you leave, you might want to take a peek in the Hoshiyama booth. It's pretty incredible."

I walked back to Cooper. "Do you mind if I take a peek at the other displays before we leave? This is the only chance I'm going to get."

"Sure," he said. "Do you want me to pack your scooter up in my SUV?"

I hadn't given much thought to my scooter, but it was a good idea. Leaving it behind would indicate that I was at the party and would negate the whole point of me leaving. I pulled my keys out of the exterior pocket of the backpack and handed them to him. "Turn the key to the right a quarter circle to unlock the steering. You should be able to maneuver it easily after that."

"Okay. I'm parked over there." He pointed to the corner of the park. "You only have about ten minutes if we want to catch the previews."

"I can do ten minutes."

We went separate directions. In the corner of the park was a small striped tent. The fabric walls on one side had been removed, and in their place were two screens painted with cherry blossoms on rice paper. I stepped between the screens and gasped at the magnificent display in front of me.

The walls of the tent had been lined in black velvet, and pairs of swords and knives had been mounted. I stepped closer and reached my hand out toward the bright jade handle of a knife.

"No touching," Tak said from behind me.

Again I was struck by how comfortable he was in his outfit. Where Coop had been fussing with his almost nonstop, Tak inhabited these clothes the same way he wore a shirt and khakis. Even his black hair, normally falling to the side of his face, had been tied back, making his features more pronounced than ever. Dressed as he was, he might as well have been a warrior from another time, here to fight for his cause.

"What do you call this?" I asked, touching his sleeve.

"Which part? That's *Gi*. The pants are *Hakama*." He pointed to his waist. "*Do*."

"We should have something like that at the store," I said. "Authentic. Not like the samurai costumes at Candy Girls." I stepped back and pretended to assess him. "Not bad. It's part of the Tak Hoshiyama costume collection. It's you. It works."

"But we don't." He stepped closer. "I made a mistake. I should have told Cooper that we were seeing each other. Now—now you're going out with him and there's nothing I can do about it."

"He already told me about how you like to play the field. It's better this way. We both know where we stand and nobody's going to get hurt." I smiled. "Have fun tonight. Make your dad proud." Before he could say anything else, I turned around and left.

Cooper had my scooter loaded into the back of his car by the time I reached it. "Ready?"

"As I'll ever be," I said. I climbed into the passenger side and watched out the window as the final touches were put on the Halloween party decorations. Across the PCP, I saw Tak watching me. As mature as I'd acted, I didn't like how things had ended. I pulled out my phone and ran my finger over *Private Number* on my recently called list, and then pressed dial. Cooper climbed into the car and I hung up before Tak had a chance to answer. Maybe it was better this way.

Cooper pulled away from the curb, leaving the park and the Halloween celebrations behind us.

The Cineplex was on the northwest side of Proper, about a mile past the Alexandria Hotel. It sat among restaurants and nightclubs that had hung on for decades but constantly seemed *this close* to going out of business. Part of the Havetown plans had included a new thirty-two-screen movie house, which would have no doubt driven the Cineplex—and probably the other businesses in that area—out of business. But they were as much a part of our town's history as the hotel. I made a note to come out this way more frequently to show my support.

"How much do you know about the Havetown expansion?" I asked Cooper.

"You really want to talk about that?"

"It's the only thing anybody's talking about anymore."

He rolled down his window and waved to a group of children dressed as ghosts carrying plastic pumpkins to hold their candy. "I don't know much," he said. "Paul Haverford bought up a couple of miles of property in West Proper. His plans for that included housing. He also bought local businesses that he planned to exploit to bring in tourists."

"But if he wanted to expand so badly, why didn't he buy out the businesses where we're heading? Those restaurants and nightclubs can't be making any money."

"That's just it. Phase one of his plan was to develop housing. Phase two was to dump money into the businesses he bought. Phase three was to wait for the existing businesses that he didn't own to close on their own. Once they were closed, he could get them for a fraction of the cost."

"You know more about this than you let on."

"I learned a little from working in the planning office and a little from being on the city council."

"Which side were you on? Pro Havetown or against?"

Cooper didn't get a chance to answer. The truck started to shudder, and then the shudder turned into a shake. He fought to control the steering wheel. It jerked to the right. He grabbed it with both hands to straighten the truck out, but to no avail.

"Something's wrong." He pulled over to the shoulder. "Wait here. I'm going to check it out."

He hopped out and walked around to my side. He bent down and I felt the truck shake. I rolled down my window. "Is everything okay?"

"No. Somebody loosened the lug nuts on this wheel. If we'd gone any faster than we were, the tire might have come off."

"Can you fix it?"

"Maybe, but I'll need better light. I'm going to try to get us to the Alexandria parking lot. It's only about a hundred feet ahead."

A shiver went up my spine. The last place I wanted to be was the Alexandria Hotel. Cooper climbed back into the driver's seat and started the truck. He kept it at a crawl and we inched forward. The whole vehicle shuddered. Instinctively, I put my hands on the dashboard, as if I could hold it steady.

Had Sol vandalized Cooper's truck before giving Dig the wrench? It didn't make sense. How would he have known to vandalize that particular car? And why? Cooper hadn't done anything to him. As far as Sol knew, Cooper and I didn't even know each other.

But something else did make sense. Something I wanted desperately to ignore. Something that, no matter how ridiculous it seemed, I couldn't shake.

"You need a socket wrench to loosen the lug nuts, don't you?" I asked.

"Yes. Whoever knocked out Francine Wheeler at your store must have done this too."

Slowly, I pulled my hands away from the dashboard and looked at Cooper. "I never told you about the socket wrench," I said.

"No, you sure didn't." He threw the car in park and engaged the child safety locks inside the car.

Chapter 33

MY MIND RACED with questions, accusations, and suspicions. Cooper was the killer?

Cooper was the killer.

Cooper was the killer! And I was supposedly on a date with him. At a double feature. Nobody would think to look for me anywhere for at least four hours. And who knows what could happen in that amount of time?

I unbuckled my seat belt and faced him. "Why did you do it?" I asked. My voice shook.

"Maybe working in the city planner's office is enough for some people, but it's not enough for me. Paul Haverford and I had an agreement. I'd help him acquire the land he needed to turn this town into something meaningful, and he'd back me for city council." While he talked, he reached down and pulled the green felt shoe covers off of his feet, revealing clean white sneakers.

"But you're already on the city council."

"That's right. First time a city planner is in the seat reserved for a member of the DA's office. Technically, I qualify. Once Haverford backed me, nobody went against him. That's when I first realized the kind of power he had because of his money."

"You killed him."

"I thought we were partners."

"Bill Perth was his partner."

"Bill Perth was a patsy. Haverford needed someone to take the fall if there was any pushback from the community. And there was. The only way Perth would see a dime of the money he gave Haverford to invest was to convince all of those businesses that they were better off in than out. That's why he was at the town hall meeting. Even with Haverford dead, Perth needed to see a return on his investment."

"So where did you fit into the Haverford plan?"

"Every town needs a mayor, even Proper City. That was the agreement. I substituted some documents so Haverford's plans would get the green light, and he'd get me into office as the next mayor of Proper City."

"The maps of the fault lines," I said. "That's why Francine was so interested in seeing the ones at the Haverford offices. She's been monitoring the seismic activity out this way for over a decade. She knew the reports weren't right."

"She's been a thorn in my side since the beginning. In a way, she's lucky. I thought if I took care of her, we'd be home free. But then Haverford told me he had everything he needed from me and tried to cut ties. Everything he promised me was off the table. He'd been meeting with the city council behind my back and they were on board with his plans. The additional revenue stream would have given them leverage within Clark County that Proper City never even dreamed of."

The windows of the SUV had fogged up. Bright spots from where the light from the streetlamps hit the windshield told me where we were in relation to the old hotel.

Cooper had said a hundred feet in front of us. If I could get out of the truck, I could make a run for it. But could I outrun Cooper? Probably not. But if I got inside the hotel, and if they hadn't dismantled the props that had been set up last week, I had a chance at hiding, which was better odds than I had right now.

My mostly empty backpack sat at my feet. The only thing inside was my cell. I'd handed the keys to my scooter to Cooper so he could put it inside the back of the truck. Unless I could disengage the childproof locks, I was at his mercy. But watching him, listening to him, I became aware of his self-absorption. I needed to play into that, to keep him talking.

"Tell me how you faked the maps."

He laughed. "That's just the thing. I never had to fake anything. I just had to go back far enough in the archives until I found maps where the fault lines were inactive. The plans passed a vote easily. Nobody would have thought anything about it. Nobody but Francine. And then you showed up asking questions about the Alexandria. I knew you were going to be trouble. I just didn't know your angle."

"I didn't have an angle. I wanted to find out the truth."

"Don't get all *X-Files* on me. The truth is that this city is going down the tank. If it continues like it is, in five years, it's going to be a handful of families and a corner market. The Proper City infrastructure can't survive on the minimal income it produces. You want your way of life to continue, you're going to have to make changes. Havetown would have been the beginning."

"But if the development happened on top of active fault lines, a lot of lives would be at risk. What would you do if the construction crew died in a quake? Or if your first tenants did? How would that look for your administration?"

"Shut up!" he said. "You're as much of a problem as Francine. Good thing nobody will be looking for you for a while." He reached across the seat and clamped plastic handcuffs around my wrists. I struggled, too little too late.

Cooper got out of his side of the car and went to the back of his SUV. A minute later, he came around to mine and yanked the door open. He'd pulled a sweatshirt and jeans on over the Robin Hood costume. If anybody saw him now, they wouldn't put two and two together. They'd see a guy dressed like every other guy in Proper City. They probably wouldn't even notice him.

He pulled me out of the truck by my upper arm. The bite of his hand would leave a bruise tomorrow. If I had a tomorrow. I stumbled down from the truck. He pushed me from behind. "Walk."

My mind raced. I was in red patent leather boots with a slippery plastic sole. Cooper was in sneakers. No match. I twisted my wrists. The handcuffs were the same ones we sold at the store. With enough tension, I could break the chain from the plastic. But first, I wanted to know Cooper's plan.

We reached the grounds for the hotel. The large, plastic cauldrons that had been filled with dry ice and water still sat around the entrance. Were they still filled with water? Maybe—

I stopped next to one and turned to him. "So you and me, this"—I gestured with my handcuffed hands back and forth between us—"it's all been an act?"

He laughed. "You're an exciting woman, Margo. The costumes, they add to the package. It's easy to see what Tak sees in you."

"Tak and I aren't—"

"Save it. I saw your text to him the first night we met. Fake flat tire so you could rendezvous by the side of the road. I just got to you first." He laughed. "Secrets give people power, Margo. As soon as I figured out that you and Tak wanted to keep your relationship secret, I knew I had power over both of you. And I used it. You both made

it easy. Nice relationship. You both gave me permission."
He leaned forward and lowered his voice. "You don't get
what you want out of life by waiting to get permission.
You get it by taking advantage of opportunities."

"Is that how you justify murdering someone? Taking
advantage of an opportunity?"

"It didn't have to be this way. If Haverford kept his end
of the bargain, nothing would have happened to him."

"But it did. How did you—" I thought about the transi-
tion he'd made tonight, from Robin Hood to Casual Every-
man. He must have done the same thing that first night.
"The Spider-Man costume," I said.

"I didn't think you'd figure that out. I wore it under my
suit. Haverford arranged for the police to be at the party,
dressed like G-men. He followed me upstairs because he
thought I was one of them. When he wouldn't play ball, I took
him out, ditched the suit, and climbed out the window."

"I saw you. Nobody believed me, but I saw you."

"Come on, Margo, you should know better than anybody
that the right costume can make a person disappear."

He was overconfident. It was the moment I needed. I
braced myself for pain and brought my handcuffed hands
down across the top of my raised knee. The chains popped
out of the plastic and broke apart into bracelets. Cooper's
eyes went wide. I reached for the plastic cauldron and tried
to lift it. It was too heavy. I tipped it over and cold water
gushed over the dry dirt around his feet.

He jumped backward and I took off for the front doors
to the hotel. If they were locked, I'd dive through a window.
I didn't care about the property destruction. The only
chance I had was to get inside and away from him long
enough to call for help.

The door was locked. I used my elbow to shatter the
glass. Cooper was right behind me. I tipped two more
plastic cauldrons of water in my path. He slipped on the

wet dirt-turned-mud and fell. I reached inside the broken
glass, flipped the lock, and hurled myself inside. I ran to
the elevator. When it opened, I pushed as many buttons as
I could hit, and then hid behind a sofa. Cooper skidded
across the wet marble floor and dove into the elevator as
the doors shut.

The illuminated arrow above the elevator slowly rose
from one to two, two to three. I didn't know how long I
had before the car would return to my floor. I ran to the
former hotel desk where skeletons in bellhop uniforms sat
behind the desk, and grabbed the receiver from the phone.

No dial tone.

I didn't know where else to go. The arrow on the elevator paused on the fourth floor, and then the arrow moved
backward to three. There was no more time to think.

I raced past the skeleton bellhops toward the lobby. I
had to get away.

But where would I go? There was no safe place. If I
escaped Cooper tonight, he'd come after me tomorrow. He
knew that I knew that he was a murderer. I'd spend the rest
of my life looking over my shoulder. I had to find a way
to stop him.

Moonlight and streetlamps from outside provided light.
What little illumination fell through the windows created
weird shadows and haunting illusions. The bell over the
elevator announced that it had arrived on the first floor. I
ran into the ballroom and ducked behind the blue blob that
hovered over the piano. Cooper came out of the elevator
and went straight for the front doors. He must have thought
I would run if given the chance.

Up close, I saw that the blob had been made of spray
foam insulation and painted with an iridescent, luminous
paint. Crepe paper arms finished with flat hands cut out
from cardboard were attached to the blob, the hands on
the piano keys. Invisible wires suspended the whole thing

from the ceiling, and several yards of cheesecloth had been draped over it. A small portable fan sat on the piano bench, aimed up. That must be what gave it its movement.

Like most illusions, it was silly up close. No wonder Agent Smith—whichever police officer that was—had instructed me to stay out of the ballroom. The party planners hadn't wanted us to know the secrets behind the animated installations.

Animated. That meant power. Of course there was power—the elevators were running. I reached forward and hit the on switch to the fan. The blade started up and the cheesecloth hovered magically. The crepe paper arms moved as if actually playing.

The front door opened. I ducked back, behind the thick, heavy velvet curtains. Only the faintest movement was visible through the fabric.

Cooper looked into the ballroom. He held my backpack in one hand. When he caught the motion of the blob, he froze. I stood as still as I could, hoping that he would not see me. His phone rang. He held it up to his ear. "Hey, man. We're on our way. Margo wanted to stop off at the Alexandria first. Sure, no problem." His voice was so casual, so calm, that whoever was on the other end of that call would never know that he was hunting me down inside the abandoned property.

Something from the wall pressed into my side. I ran one hand up the wooden wall to see what it was. Another switch. I flipped it. The piano music started up, at first slow and distorted. The chandelier above the blob lit too, flicker candles giving the appearance of flames dancing. Cooper looked up, then around the room, and then behind him. It was my only chance.

I came out from behind the curtain and pushed on the blob as hard as I could. It swung away from me. One of the invisible wires snapped and it swung farther, knocking into Cooper. He stumbled back. The crepe paper that attached the hands to the piano tore. The cheesecloth fluttered in the air like an apparition.

The sudden movement had caught Cooper off guard. The blob swung back toward me and I pushed it again, this time even harder. The second wire snapped and it hit him like a giant bowling ball, knocking him down. I yanked the cheesecloth from the ceiling and threw it over Cooper like a fisherman casting a net. He cursed and struggled against it, too late. I grabbed my backpack and pulled out my phone. I fumbled with the screen, trying to unlock it and dial. Cooper reached up from the ground and swatted the phone out of my hands. I ran for it and dialed again. This time the call connected. "Alexandria Hotel," I said. "Hurry. It's an emergency." Cooper sat up. I dropped the phone and picked up the blue blob and pinned him under it with all my might.

Help arrived faster than I expected. Police cars, ambulances, and at least two samurai warriors burst into the hotel. One of the warriors pulled me away from the blob and held me in a tight embrace. The other held Cooper Price captive with a well-trained sword.

Chapter 34

I WAS QUICKLY removed from the chaos and checked for injuries. A paramedic used industrial cutters to remove the broken plastic handcuffs from each of my wrists even though I told him it I had the key back at the costume shop.

I sat in the back of Tak's SUV with my legs dangling down. He stood next to me, one hand on the small of my back, the other on my knee. There was no secret to his body language. Anybody who looked over at us could tell we were more than friends.

"How did you happen to be here?" I asked Tak. "You were at the party. You should have been in the middle of a demonstration with your father."

"I was. Dig had my phone. When we were done, he handed it back and said some private number was trying to reach me. Your dad overheard him and made a comment that you'd been getting calls from a private number too. I tried to call you back but it was busy. You were supposed to be at a movie with Cooper. Your phone would have been off."

"You called him next."

He nodded. "I didn't want to but I did. You left the park because you were afraid someone was going to come after you. Coop said you wanted to stop off at the Alexandria on the way to the theater. Your call went to Nancy right after I talked to Coop. He acted so calm that I almost didn't figure it out. I'm supposed to be analytical. I should have put two and two together a lot faster than I did."

"He didn't just fool you. He fooled us all." I thought about Cooper's attentions over the past week. He'd known from the start that Tak and I were hiding a relationship, and he'd used that against us. Secrets give people power, he'd said. And that's what he had wanted. Power. I leaned toward Tak, put my hands on his face, and kissed him.

"Ahem."

We pulled apart. Detective Nichols stood in front of us. My dad was behind her. "Ms. Tamblyn," she said. Her eyes cut to Tak's face, to his hand on my knee, and then back to my face. "The last time we spoke, you gave me information that implicated Sol Girard. Do you want to tell me what happened between then and now?"

And that's how I came to tell my audience about Cooper Price's political ambitions, the decades-old quaternary maps that Cooper had passed as current that allowed Paul Haverford to push the plans for Havetown past city council, and how the city of Proper was no longer at risk for a hostile takeover. Sol Girard, Annette Crowley, Bill Perth, and Francine Wheeler had each been fighting to protect what they felt was theirs, but it turned out to be a different type of greed that had driven Cooper beyond normal actions to murder.

After the detective gave me license to leave, Tak took me home, and my dad followed in the Minnie Winnebago. Even if I could have convinced one of them to take me to the PCP—which I tried, to no avail—it would have been too late to experience Halloween. I told myself there would always be next year.

Tuesday–Thursday

My celebrity started to die down after a couple of days and business returned to normal. Slowly, costume rentals came back to the store. Kirby and I took turns operating the industrial steamer to remove any odors on the costumes, and the empty spaces in our inventory were filled. The week after Halloween always felt like a bit of a letdown from the energy of the month leading up to it, but this time it was different. I reminded myself over and over that things would return to normal as soon as the next themed birthday party came about. Sol's poker game was only a few nights away, but there was a chance we'd lost his business for good, thanks to my accusations.

Not a single person—my dad, Ebony, Don, or Dig—had commented on the apparent change in Tak's and my relationship. When the phone rang on Wednesday, my dad simply said, "Phone call for you." He resumed his task of removing Mina Harker and Dracula from the window display, replacing them with the cow costume he'd found on his recent trip to New Jersey.

"I know this is last minute, but I was wondering if you were available for dinner at the restaurant tonight?" Tak asked. "Seven thirty?"

"I'd love to."

"I'm going to be busy until then, so I can't pick you up."

"Considering you live there, that would be silly. I'll bring the scooter."

When I hung up, I looked at my dad to see if he'd been listening. "I'm going to meet Tak Hoshiyama for dinner," I announced.

"Sounds like fun." He packed the plastic fruit and turkey from his display into a cardboard box and sealed it with a tape gun. "What time are you leaving?"

His lack of reaction was suspicious. "He said to be there at seven thirty. I'll close up and head over after."

AFTER closing the store, I changed into an orange sweater and skirt and pulled on a vintage kimono from my mother's wardrobe. The delicate fabric had a green, orange, and yellow floral pattern to it that fit the '60s, when she must have purchased it. Although I'd never had the chance to meet her, I'd gotten to know her through what she'd left behind: the memories my father had, and the garments I'd inherited. When I wanted to feel her presence, I turned to her closet.

I freshened up my hair and touched up my makeup. Soot watched me from the bed. "Do I look okay?" I asked. He curled his paws underneath his body and rested his head on them. Apparently, he had no concerns.

The benefit of dining with someone who is part owner of a restaurant is that there's little concern at seeing a full parking lot. I pulled into the bank lot and parked by the front doors, locked my helmet to the seat, and checked my reflection in the bank door windows. I was surprisingly nervous.

I made my way across the parking lot to the entrance to Hoshiyama. Two men dressed in garb similar to Tak and his father's samurai costumes flanked the entrance. They bowed down as I approached. When they stood back up, they pulled the heavy doors open and let me inside.

Tak hadn't invited me to dinner. He'd invited me to Halloween.

The interior of the restaurant had been partitioned and decorated like the park had been. On the far left side was

Bobbie and her bookcase of bears (though her inventory was significantly depleted), and to the right was a bevy of witches who stirred bubbling cauldrons that sat on top of the teppanyaki cook station. A small platform had been built in the center of the restaurant and lined with the pumpkins and orange floral arrangements that Packin' Pistils had delivered to the PCP. Some of the petals had browned around the edges, but they were mostly intact.

To the right of the interior was the laboratory that Kirby had built. A life-sized lab rat—Mr. Smythe, I sure hoped—stood behind it. His eyes glowed red. He pawed at the air, and then tinkered with a few of the test tubes and beakers in front of him. A large pitcher of blue liquid sat in front of him. Kirby, dressed in a white lab coat, poured the blue liquid into a glass and drank it. He tipped his head back and laughed maniacally. An explosion sounded and plumes of smoke billowed from around the table. Everybody applauded.

I felt someone behind me and turned. Ebony and Dig stood together, dressed as Ike and Tina Turner. Ebony hugged me, and then pushed me away and held her finger up. "Don't you ever go doing anything like that to Ebony again."

I looked at Dig. "What?" he said. "I'm just trying to pull off an Ike Turner costume and make it look cool."

"Girl, you better turn around or you're going to miss the main event."

I turned back to the interior of the restaurant. Mr. Hoshiyama and Tak stood in the center of the floor, dressed in their samurai costumes. They both bowed toward me, and then bowed toward each other. In an act that must have been expertly choreographed, they raised swords and clanked them against each other, moving forward and backward. I wasn't the only spectator who was mesmerized by the poetry of their motions.

When they finished, the place erupted in applause. They bowed toward each other, and then bowed toward us. Tak handed his blade to his father and said something to him. His father nodded once. He watched Tak walk to me. There was pride in his father's expression.

"What do you think?" Tak asked.

"I think you brought me Halloween." I couldn't keep the smile from my face. "It's the best present ever."

"Ever?" he asked. "I'm going to have to outdo this for your birthday."

"You've got time. My birthday isn't until July."

He took my hand. "That's nine months away. A lot can change in nine months."

"Tell me about it."

We walked together through the restaurant. Tak's mother, Lynn, stood by a food station handing out servings of Hoshiyama fried rice, skewers of yakitori, and small cups of miso soup. If anybody here had been among the people who had not included the Hoshiyamas in the Proper City events in the past, they would have a hard time ignoring their contribution today.

"Tak, you didn't do this by yourself. Who else was in on it?"

"I think the question you meant to ask was who wasn't in on it. Ebony set the place up with the help of Dig, Don, and your dad. Kirby and his teacher handled the lab rat. My parents provided the food and the restaurant. Everybody else chipped in to help move the fixtures from the park to here."

"What about you?"

"My job was to make sure you didn't suspect anything."

"People have been returning their costumes all week. Where did these come from?"

"Look around. I think you'll figure it out for yourself."

I scanned the crowd. For the first time, I noticed the large assortment of witches, princesses, and generic gangsters. A couple of pimps in purple velvet suits with dollar signs around their necks. These costumes didn't come from Disguise DeLimit. They were the store-bought kind that came from Candy Girls. Which reminded me of something I didn't yet understand.

"Why were you and Detective Nichols picking out costumes at Candy Girls?"

He looked embarrassed. "She asked me to help her pick out a costume. I didn't realize until we were there that she meant a couple's costume, and then it was too late to say anything. Besides, you were showing interest in Coop. I wasn't sure where we stood."

"I don't know which is worse: that you picked out a couples costume with Detective Nichols, or that you went to Candy Girls."

"Before you say anything else, you should know that Candy Girls helped make this happen tonight."

Across the room, I caught eyes with one of the witches. Gina Cassavogli separated from her coven and walked toward us. "Give me a second," I said to Tak.

"Be nice," he said. He let go of my hand and stepped back.

Gina wore the same witches costume she'd worn at the Alexandria Hotel the night Paul Haverford was murdered. The cheap black plastic cape was knotted at her neck. Underneath she wore a tight, strapless dress that ended mid-thigh, and high-heeled platform pumps with square buckles clipped onto the front.

"You provided the costumes so everybody could keep this a secret from me," I said. "I don't know what to say."

"Forget about it. Once those maps came out, all plans for Havetown fell through. The only way Candy Girls was going to get any money out of this whole situation was to sell more costumes. I was happy to take their money."

"You used Tak's idea as a business opportunity?"

"Yep. And I don't regret it for a second." We had a stare-off. I don't know what she was thinking, but I was conveying some pretty judgmental thoughts. "Fine. I'll make a donation to Bobbie." She turned around, her plastic cape snapping behind her.

THE party wound down around midnight. An impromptu costume contest led to Mr. Smythe collecting a small gold trophy that had been donated by a member of the swim team. Don and my dad held court in a corner, discussing a recent flurry of suspicious UFO activity in a canyon in Salt Lake City, Utah. By the time the party broke up, they'd organized a road trip for the weekend. That Minnie Winnie was going to get a lot of use.

Despite other offers, I prepared to drive myself home. I'd felt like Cinderella at the ball tonight, but that didn't change a lot of things. The store still had competition. Kirby's break was over. He had to return to school, and it would be up to me to run the store. My dad was ready to move on with the next phase of his life, and probably I should too.

My phone pinged with a text message. *Happy Halloween, Margo. See you tomorrow.*

The screen said it was from Tak. He'd reprogrammed it from Private Number.

I had a feeling Soot and I would be talking about what that meant for a long time.

Recipes

—

MARGO'S GANGSTER
BLUEBERRY SMOOTHIE

1 cup plain yogurt
1 cup milk (almond, soy, or regular will work)
½ cup blueberries
1 banana
1 tbsp. protein powder
¼ tsp. vanilla seasoning

1. Toss all ingredients into a blender.

2. Blend for 30 seconds to 1 minute.

3. Pour into a glass and enjoy!

—

MUMMY DOGS

1 package hot dogs

1 tube of uncooked croissant dough
(must be the kind that comes flat)

1. Preheat oven to temperature marked on croissant dough package.

2. Unroll one sheet of croissant dough and lay flat on cutting board.

3. Using a sharp knife or pizza cutter, slice croissant dough into ¼–½-inch strips.

4. Wind strips of dough around each hotdog, starting at one end. Wrap loosely until hot dog is covered.

5. Place wrapped hot dogs on a baking sheet and follow baking direction on croissant packaging.

6. Remove and serve!

———

HALLOWEEN-THEMED TORTILLA CHIPS

Warning: making these is almost as much fun as making a Halloween costume for a teddy bear.

1 package corn tortillas
1 bottle of vegetable oil
Salt

COOKING SUPPLIES:

Shallow skillet
Halloween-themed cookie cutters

Wooden skewer
Slotted spoon
Paper towels for draining

1. Pour the oil into a large skillet and turn on medium-high heat.

2. While the oil is heating, take two tortillas from package and set on cutting board.

3. Punch your shapes out with Halloween cookie cutters and set aside.

4. Check if your oil is hot enough. (Insert a wooden skewer into the center of the skillet. If the oil bubbles around the wood, you're good to go.)

5. Add your punched tortilla shapes to the oil. (If you're nervous about your first batch and want a practice round, use the pieces of tortilla that were left over after the shapes were punched. This is equally good for quality control.)

6. Remove shapes as they harden (you'll feel this with the spoon). They will be in and out in less than 30 seconds.

7. Transfer shapes onto paper towels to drain.

8. Lightly salt.

9. Start next batch and continue until all shapes are fried. When you're done with all of your cut-out shapes, fry the pieces that are left from the punched tortillas. They'll taste just as good as the shaped ones, and trust me . . . you'll want something to snack on.

10. Serve with pico de gallo or salsa.

HALLOWEEN PICO DE GALLO

1 bunch cilantro
1 tomato
1 onion
1 carrot (optional, adds Halloween color)
1 can black olives (optional, adds Halloween color)
1 jalapeño

1. Chop the cilantro, discarding stems.

2. Dice tomato, onion, carrot, black olives.

3. Mix.

4. Mince a little of the jalapeño and toss in if you want your pico to have a little kick.

Costumes

KIRBY AND THE SWIM TEAM'S
EASY "EGGS SUNNY-SIDE UP" COSTUME

White sheet
Yellow swim cap

1. Cut a small slit in the center of the white sheet. Hole should be just big enough to let your head fit through.

2. Pull sheet over head and let it drape over shoulders.

3. Put on yellow swim cap.

OPTIONAL ACCESSORIES

Bottle of ketchup or Tabasco
Oversized fork (since this is a prop, be sure to either
make one out of cardboard or buy a plastic one from a
Halloween shop. Metal forks will most likely not make
it through metal detectors at public parties!)

EASY (AND INEXPENSIVE!)
MUMMY COSTUME

Water
Tea bags
Five yards of muslin
White long-sleeve T-shirt or turtleneck
White leggings or thermal long johns
White socks

1. Boil a large pot of water and add several tea bags. Let tea steep for 30 minutes.

2. Soak muslin in tea. This will dye it and give it an aged appearance.

3. Remove muslin after about 30 minutes and hang to dry.

4. When dry, make 1-inch cuts every 2 inches along non-selvedge edge.

5. Using hands, tear the muslin into long strips.

6. Dress in white T-shirt, long johns, and socks.

7. Wrap the end of one strip around the toe of left foot and knot it to itself. Wind rest of strip around foot, covering sock.

8. When end of strip is reached, knot end to the end of a new strip. Continue winding around foot.

9. Continue winding up leg.

10. Repeat on right leg.

11. Wrap strips around hips and torso.

12. Wrap strips around left arm and then right (if you are left handed, do right hand and then left).

13. Wrap strips around neck.

14. Wrap strips around face, leaving opening around mouth and eyes.

15. Knot extra strips onto body at intervals, leaving the ends loose.

———

10 SLIGHTLY SCARY COSTUME IDEAS

1. Witch
2. Cruella de Vil
3. Tippi Hedren's character from *The Birds*
4. Mummy
5. Zombie
6. Alien
7. Jack the Ripper
8. Evil Doll
9. Giant Spider
10. Headless Horseman

———

GROUP COSTUME IDEA: M&M'S

2 yards of felt
1 square of white felt
Marker or chalk
Scissors
Computer/Printer

Pins
Sewing Machine (or needle and thread)
White tights
White turtleneck
White boots/sneakers/shoes

1. Fold felt in half.

2. Draw a giant circle on the felt.

3. Cut out circles (cut through two layers of felt).

4. On computer, type lower case letter *m* onto Word document. Set the font to Times New Roman, 750 pt.

5. Print letter.

6. Lay printout UPSIDE DOWN on white felt and pin together.

7. Cut out letter *m* from felt, using printout as guide.

8. Center white felt *m* on one giant felt circle.

9. Pin.

10. Stitch white felt *m* to felt circle around edge of letter.

11. Imagining the circles as the face of a clock, stitch them together (*m* side in) from 1:00–2:00, 4:00–5:00, 7:00–8:00, and 10:00–11:00.

12. Flip inside out (*m* will be on the outside).

13. Dress in white tights and turtleneck.

14. Step into giant M&M.

DON'T MISS DIANE VALLERE'S
MATERIAL WITNESS MYSTERIES!
KEEP READING FOR AN EXCERPT
FROM THE LATEST BOOK . . .

SILK STALKINGS

AVAILABLE FROM BERKLEY PRIME CRIME!

THE CLOCK WOULD strike midnight in two minutes. This was important for a few reasons, not the least of which was that the crowd of couples who filled the interior and exterior grounds of Tea Totalers, my friend Genevieve Girard's tea-shop-turned-Parisian-nightclub, would filter down the sidewalk of Bonita Avenue and make their way toward the Waverly House for their annual stroll through the historic mansion's gardens.

The other reason midnight was important was that the coordinators of tonight's event had synced every clock in our small town of San Ladrón down to the second. They were set to chime, ring, buzz, and otherwise announce the arrival of twelve A.M. It was one thing to imagine the impact of that type of alarm coordination, but it might be quite another to experience it. If the several hundred guests who sipped champagne and nibbled at petit fours and hors d'oeuvres at Tea Totalers had followed suit of the city and set their cell phones to ring too, we could be looking at the kind of noise level that might launch missiles over Cuba.

Genevieve approached me with a flute of champagne. "Poly, things turned out better than I had hoped! We've gone through almost seventeen pounds of Brie, and the crusty French bread disappears as fast as it comes out of the oven. I've served almost as much of my special blend of tea as I have champagne. And people are asking if I'll cater their parties. People who have lived in San Ladrón their whole lives are telling me they wish they'd come here earlier. This idea was genius. It's really putting me on the map." She handed me a glass of champagne and clinked it with hers. "It's putting you on the map too," she added.

Genevieve had opened Tea Totalers a few years ago, with the help of her French husband. He was no longer in the picture, thanks to seedy business dealings with people who thought murder was an appropriate solution to a business dispute. Genevieve had been the number one suspect in her husband's murder, and I'd been instrumental in helping clear her name. In return, she'd been instrumental in helping me open Material Girl, the fabric shop I inherited from my great-uncle several months ago. Tonight we were both reaping the benefits of hard work and creative marketing.

Genevieve spun around her café's interior with her arms out. The champagne in her flute spilled from the glass, but she didn't seem to notice or care. "Can you believe it? It really does feel like we're in Paris at midnight."

I followed her gaze around the newly made-over café. I'd gotten the idea to use French fabrics from my shop to build on the theme Genevieve had wanted for the interior. Long toile curtains framed out sheer panels of voile that had almost gone into the Dumpster behind my fabric shop thanks to a wicked case of mildew, but an intensive treatment with vinegar and fresh air had cleared the fabric of its musty scent and brought it back to life. The chairs had been re-covered in gingham, provencal, linen, and even more toile, and napkins, place mats, and serving trays had been trimmed with the same fabrics. That was by day.

But tonight, for the Midnight in Paris party, I'd stepped things up a notch. Deep midnight-blue velvet covered the existing butter-yellow walls. I used a heat-set technique to create a fleur-de-lis pattern on the velvet that mirrored the pattern woven into the voile sheers, and I'd covered the chairs in luxurious velvet seat covers tied back with thick ivory grosgrain ribbon. Small tea light candles sat in clear glass votives on windowsills, tabletops, and counters inside the café.

The organizers of the city's part of the event—decorating the street between Tea Totalers and the Waverly House—had hung strands of tiny white twinkling lights around the exterior of the buildings and in an arch over the street, creating a blanket of stars under which people danced to the jazz quartet on the corner. The local high school had crafted a scale model of the Eiffel Tower that sat in the middle of the intersection of Bonita and San Ladrón Avenue. The roads had been closed for the night, so people could spill out into the street and enjoy the transformation of our small town.

"Are you heading over to the Waverly House when the bells chime? I bet Vaughn would love to see you in that dress," Genevieve asked.

I blushed. Since inheriting the fabric store and moving to San Ladrón, I'd spent enough time with Vaughn McMichael to get past the unfortunate first impression where I fell through a window and knocked him to the ground. We'd dined together, worked side by side, and even gone on a date. We'd also accused each other of having ulterior motives, resulting in alienation. And by *we*, I mean *me*, but I'd rather not get into that right now.

"I don't want to talk about Vaughn," I said.

"Didn't he have that dress made for you?" Genevieve asked pointedly.

"I don't want to talk about that, either," I said to her. Much like the interior of Genevieve's shop, I'd stepped up my own appearance for the night. I usually wore black all the time, but I'd traded it for a shimmering gold gown with a sweetheart neckline, embellished on the shoulders with spirals of matte gold and silver sequins. The gown was fitted around my waist and hips and cascaded to the floor in a pool of fabric.

"Poly, you had just as much to do with the garden stroll at the Waverly House as you did here at Tea Totalers," Genevieve said. "You have to go."

I didn't know how to explain to Genevieve that I was nervous about showing up at the Waverly House for more reasons than I could count.

The Waverly House was the most significant historical building in the town of San Ladrón. A Victorian mansion turned museum, it had become a certified landmark years back and now boasted a restaurant, a monthly murder mystery party, and the most exquisite gardens in the town. Adelaide Brooks, the most energetic and elegant seventy-year-old I'd ever met, managed the building and the day-to-day business.

The annual party had been the landmark's major fundraiser for years, and the money brought in from this singular party determined their operating budget for the following year. People flocked to San Ladrón for the night to consider the Waverly House for weddings and parties. All would have been fine, except that this year, the most powerful man in San Ladrón had raised questions about zoning and put a scare into the suppliers who donated food and drink. That halted any planning that could take place. It didn't help matters that the most powerful man in San Ladrón was Adelaide's ex-husband.

Or that he was Vaughn McMichael's father.

Only a few people knew that I'd been the one to come up with the idea of changing the location of the annual garden party to Genevieve's newly reopened shop. Food and drink distributors had been happy to make their regular donations, and Genevieve had been thrilled at the opportunity. After applying for her liquor license (ironic in a shop called Tea Totalers), she had been pleasantly surprised by the outpouring of support from suppliers who donated food and drink for the evening, and local restaurants who loaned out employees to help.

Ticket sales for the Midnight in Paris cocktail party still benefited the Waverly House, as did separate ticket sales to gain entrance to the exquisite gardens behind the Victorian manse at midnight. Adelaide had sidestepped the zoning regulations by leaving the restaurant and bar open for paying customers. Landscapers had been hard at work on the grounds surrounding the landmark, and whatever it was that they were planning to debut had been kept a well-guarded secret. All Adelaide would say was, "It's more magnificent than I ever could have expected." The perceived success of the night would be determined to be true or false tomorrow when she would tally the money pulled in by selling tickets and subtract out any unforeseen expenses. I didn't want credit for the idea. I wanted everyone to get what they wanted—or needed, in the case of the Waverly House—from the event.

Bong-Bong-Bong-Ding-Bong-Chime-Buzz-Clang-Ring-Bong

Midnight arrived, announced by a cacophony of sounds that originated from a distance of several miles. The chimes, bongs, dings, and dongs were slightly off from each other, resulting in a white noise that mixed with the various cell phone alarms that went off from the pockets of people around us. A couple of people put hands over their ears, and a few kissed like it was New Year's Eve. Conversation became impossible.

The drummer struck up a rhythm on the high hat, and the man playing the upright bass plucked out a note for each strike of the clock. Cheers erupted from the crowd.

When the noise died down, I heard a voice behind me. "Let me guess. That's your cue to turn into a pumpkin?" asked Charlie Brooks. Charlie was the resident tough girl and my closest friend in town. As a full-time mechanic with her own auto shop, Charlie favored work jeans, chambray shirts, and rock concert T-shirts, but tonight she wore a man's tuxedo over a white fitted T-shirt. The jacket was boxy, but the T-shirt hugged her fit body. The pants sat low on her hips and broke over red Chuck Taylors. "I heard you tell Frenchy you weren't going to the Waverly House. Good call. Wanna grab a beer at The Broadside?"

"The Broadside's closed. Duke and his bartenders are working for Genevieve tonight. Didn't you notice?"

"I just got here. This kind of thing isn't my scene."

"Which part don't you like? The free food or the free booze or the free ambiance?"

"The raising-money-for-rich-people part."

Rich people who gave her up for adoption, I thought to myself, but I didn't say out loud. Not many people knew Charlie was related to the wealthy McMichael family, and she wanted to keep it that way. I didn't judge her for her animosity toward Vic McMichael and Adelaide Brooks, but I wondered if there would be a day when she'd regret not forging a relationship with her birth parents.

This wasn't the first time I'd thwarted a plan of Mr. McMichael's. When I first inherited my family's fabric store, he tried to buy it out from under me. We'd gone toe-to-toe a couple of times since then. My ex-boyfriend, Carson Cole, was a financial analyst in Los Angeles and maintained a fantasy about becoming Mr. McMichael's protégé, even after our breakup. When the businessman had threatened Genevieve's tea shop, I'd called Carson to step in and save the day. Considering Vaughn was on his father's payroll, he'd been more than a little hurt that I hadn't asked him for help. Yet another reason I wanted to keep a low profile tonight.

"You're a liar," I said.

She raised her pierced eyebrow.

"Not a lot of people get away with calling me names."

"If you didn't care about this thing, you wouldn't have bothered to dress up."

"I'm meeting up with someone I haven't seen for a while. Thought I'd make an effort. Besides, you're one to talk," she said, scanning my ensemble from top to bottom.

Again with the dress.

"So I'm not wearing black for one night. It's not like it's a religion or anything."

She held her hands up and backed away. "It's a nice dress. You wouldn't be hoping to run into anybody while wearing it, would you?"

Before I could answer, Genevieve reappeared. "Hi, Charlie, are you coming to the Waverly House? I want to go and Poly won't come with me."

Charlie crossed the interior of Tea Totalers and looked out the front door. People filled the street, laughing and carrying on. A few policemen stood on the corners, trying to remain serious but failing miserably. One lady walked up to the town's sheriff, took his hand, and twirled like a ballerina. He let go of her hand and adjusted his hat. Charlie went inside and we followed her. A few minutes later, the front door opened and Sheriff Clark walked in.

"Is this a closed party or can anybody join?" he asked.

"Well, hello there, Sheriff Clark," sang Genevieve, who might have possibly had too much champagne. She must have been thinking the same thing, because she handed her glass to him. "Help yourself to champagne. I can't stand it anymore. I want to go see the gardens!" She hiked her dress up so the hem wouldn't drag and ran out the front door. "Poly, lock up when you leave?"

"Sure," I said.

Clark took the proffered glass and drank half. He lowered the glass and scanned me. "Nice dress," he said. "You going to waste it by staying here in hiding?"

"You heard Genevieve, she asked me to lock up."

"It takes about four seconds to lock a door." He looked at Charlie.

"Yo, Frenchy, wait up," Charlie called. She ran past Sheriff Clark without an acknowledgment and went outside.

I looked at Clark and shrugged. He shook his head and walked out front. I found Genevieve's keys and grabbed my beaded handbag from behind the counter. Sheriff Clark waited while I locked the doors, and together we trailed after Charlie and Genevieve.

Sheriff Clark and Charlie had had a secret romance that fizzled over a miscommunication. It was probably just as well that they steered clear of each other. When I pictured them being a couple, I was reminded of what happened to the gingham dog and the calico cat.

Genevieve, Charlie, and I were among the last of the people to reach the Waverly House. Volunteers from the historical society stood in front of a ten-foot-tall version of the Arc de Triomphe, fabricated for the evening by the employees of Get Hammered, the local hardware store, out of chicken wire. Green ivy and colorful flowers had been threaded through the wire. Couples walked under the arch to the luscious lawns behind the Waverly House, pointing at the gazebo, the white iron benches, and the brick pavers that had been carved with the names of each person who had made a donation when the building was in need of repair. They were trying on the location with their eyes, wondering how it would feel to celebrate a major event in the middle of all of this Victorian majesty.

"Excuse me," said a woman to my left. "Are you Polyester Monroe? Of the fabric shop on Bonita?"

"Yes, but I go by Poly."

"What's your shop called? Fabric Woman?"

"Material Girl."

"That's right." She held out her hand and I shook it. "I'm Nolene Kelly. I've heard people say you were responsible for the transformation of the tea shop for tonight. Who knew you could transform a place with fabric," she said.

"I hope people will be inspired to try it themselves," I said.

"It's a nice idea but it'll be a hard sell. People around here aren't used to making their own clothes or slipcovers or curtains."

"I had a lot of help," I said modestly.

"But it was all her idea. Wasn't it amazing?" Genevieve chimed in.

"It was very impressive. And the fabric—that was from your store?" Nolene asked. She tipped her head as she posed her question, and her dangly earrings set off a faint tinkling sound.

"Yes."

"Before you moved here, you worked in a dress shop in Los Angeles, didn't you?" It was odd to hear my recent history told to me by a stranger. "I'm afraid I've read up on your background. I'm the head judge of Miss Tangorli, San Ladrón's annual beauty pageant. Since you're new around here, you probably don't know much about it."

"You're right, I don't know much about the events of San Ladrón. This is my first time attending the Waverly

House's annual party." I glanced around me. Genevieve and Charlie had migrated in separate directions: Genevieve toward the gardens, and Charlie toward a strange man who stood alone a few feet from the tea and juice station outside. He had a white ponytail and wore a black leather blazer over a black T-shirt and black trousers.

"Rumor has it there wouldn't have been a party if it weren't for you," Nolene winked. "But I'm not here to spread rumors. I'm here to find judges. I've locked in two so far."

Immediately I felt awkward. "I don't think I'd be qualified to judge a beauty pageant."

"Don't worry about that. I have something else in mind for you."

FROM BESTSELLING AUTHOR

DIANE VALLERE

A DISGUISE TO DIE FOR

A COSTUME SHOP MYSTERY

No sooner does former magician's assistant Margo Tamblyn return home to Proper City, Nevada, to run Disguise DeLimit, her family's costume shop, than she gets her first big order. Wealthy nuisance Blitz Manners needs forty costumes for a detective-themed birthday bash. As for Blitz himself, his Sherlock Holmes is to die for—literally—when, in the middle of the festivities, Margo's friend and party planner Ebony Welles is caught brandishing a carving knife over a very dead Blitz.

For Margo, clearing Ebony's name is anything but elementary, especially after Ebony flees town. Now Margo is left to play real-life detective in a town full of masked motives, cloaked secrets, and veiled vendettas. But as she soon learns, even a killer disguise can't hide a murderer in plain sight for long.

INCLUDES RECIPES AND COSTUME IDEAS

dianevallere.com
facebook.com/DianeVallereAuthor
facebook.com/BerkleyPub
penguin.com

FROM BESTSELLING AUTHOR

DIANE VALLERE

Crushed Velvet

A MATERIAL WITNESS MYSTERY

With opening day of Material Girl approaching, Poly is stocking up on lush fabrics, colorful notions, and, best of all, a proprietary weave of velvet. But upon delivery, it's not quite the blend she expected, being ninety percent silk and ten percent corpse. Crushed under a dozen bolts of fabric is Phil Girard. His wife, Genevieve, local tea shop owner and close friend of Poly, is the prime suspect.

Granted, Phil may not have been the perfect husband, but surely Genevieve had no reason to kill him! There's just the small matter of Genevieve's own incriminating confession: *I'm afraid I killed my husband.* Now, as Material Girl's grand opening looms, Poly is torn between a friendship pulling apart at the seams—and finding a smooth killer with a velvet touch…

INCLUDES A CRAFT PROJECT

dianevallere.com
facebook.com/DianeVallereAuthor
facebook.com/BerkleyPub
penguin.com

Connect with Berkley Publishing Online!

For sneak peeks into the newest releases, news on all your favorite authors, book giveaways, and a central place to connect with fellow fans—

"Like" and follow Berkley Publishing!

facebook.com/BerkleyPub
twitter.com/BerkleyPub
instagram.com/BerkleyPub

Penguin
Random
House